TANIMA DAS

AF405363

THE SORCERY OF THE SENSES

ArtoonsInn
Room9 Publications
www.artoonsinn.com

First Edition 2022
ISBN: 9788194982432

Copyright © Tanima Das, 2023
Cover Design by Mithru Rachamalla

Published by ArtoonsInn Room9 Publications
Printed in India by ArtoonsInn

ArtoonsInn Room9 Publications
www.artoonsinn.com

Acknowledgements

I would like to express my deepest gratitude to the following people.

Mithru Rachamalla, my publisher, who stood rock solid behind my ideas and made this book happen. Right from designing the cover page to looking for endless ways to improve the book, he did it all.

Sarveswari Sai Krishna, my editor, for putting up with my endless questions and helping me to tidy up the manuscript.

Shankar Hosagoudar, my friend, for his incisive comments and inputs that helped me to polish my writing skills.

My friends from South Point, for the enthused reaction they have always given to my stories. Their kind words are directly responsible for this book getting written.

My friends at ArtoonsInn, who have nurtured and supported me during the dark moments of my writing journey.

My parents and elder sister, for loving me always.

My husband, Amit and son, Tavish, for making my life brighter.

To the four men in my life…
My father,
My husband, Amit,
My son, Tavish,
And fate, who has often been like the brother I never had.

Prologue

A weaver bird fluttered in and out of the nest he had just built. He hoped his mate would approve of the design. There was just one problem. It was pitch dark inside.

The bird flew away. Maybe he could bring back a firefly to light up the inky interior.

But now five orbs of white glow were materializing amidst the darkness, forming a tiny pentagon with glimmering corners.

The five senses.

They communicated through their thoughts.

Their enemies were growing powerful every minute.

They could not afford to be caught.

That was why they were meeting inside the nest.

To discuss him.

They needed to intercept his wayward life.

Make him aware of who he was. And what he needed to do.

Time was running out.

They needed to be quick.

The weaver bird came back. He had not found a single firefly. He peered into the nest and got the shock of his life. His cosy little space was lit up with pretty little lights.

The weaver bird flew away, chirruping loudly to inform his missus of the developments.

The five senses were in a fix.

They needed to leave.

Well, they could go one by one. Interact with him. Reason with him.

Maybe they would be able to pull it off.

Rather, he would be able to pull it off.

This time.

One of the four orbs extinguished. The rest four?

They stayed back.

They needed to light up the life of two birdies in love.

Part 1: Story of Dhruv

Chapter 1: The Crown in the Trunk

Dhruv is waiting at a four-point crossing. He glances at the map on his mobile phone and sees an Uber cab curve around a signal to crawl steadily towards him. One look at the tentative fare and his eyebrows do an involuntary dance.

Just a letter away from being Kuber, Dhruv smirks to himself.

He is headed to his parental home, at Raukipur. The one place in the world where he feels happy. At least, he used to. He suspects that now the place will either hurtle him forth towards clinical depression or revive his last bit of will to live. Dhruv does not know what will happen. He has been putting off visiting Raukipur for almost a year, but today he woke up feeling like going on this trip. And now he is making use of the moment before it fades away like most other ideas that bubble up his mind.

Dhruv's cab is still five minutes away and the severe Kolkata sun is enjoying a tête-à-tête with his best friend, humidity. With no rain around to nag them, this sky party can go on for hours. Dhruv sighs and uses his handkerchief to wipe off drops of perspiration from his face and arms. He observes that his fair skin has darkened by a couple of shades. They should market India as a free tanning booth to the tourists, he thinks idly.

There are few vehicles about. A heat wave can give an eerie look to the busiest cities of the world. Dhruv wonders if this is a stupid idea, and he should cancel the ride. At that very moment, the cab appears out of a side lane and halts with a small jerk in front of him.

An elated Dhruv steps into the healing coolness of the cab. He requests for the radio as he sinks into the comfy seat. The car gathers speed and Dhruv begins to observe the fleeting stretches of his favourite city doused in sparkling sunlight. It is so much easier to appreciate the sun when the air conditioner is dimming down its fury. The driver sifts through the radio stations and decides to halt at a particular channel where a cathartic love song by Tagore is playing. And without any warning, Dhruv finds his mind flooded with Juthika's thoughts.

What is Juthika doing now? Feeding Rudolf? Watching sitcoms? Is she busy? Or bored? Is she enjoying herself? Her career? Her new life? Dhruv's absence?

Who is winning the divorce? Her or him?

Questions cram his mind. Questions without answers. Dhruv starts to chew his lower lip. He wonders how long it will be until the unrest within his chest gives way to quietude. The divorce was supposed to give him peace. Is that not what we all seek from life? Some peace?

Juthika's memories continue to torment Dhruv. Memories of a time when things were simpler. And he could follow the blueprint of social norms to lay claim to his share of happiness. With that template gone, he struggles to deal with everyday life.

Dhruv requests the cab driver to change the radio station. The driver scans again and this time he settles at a station playing a peppy rap song, much to Dhruv's relief. The lyrics made simplistic observations about life and unlike that manipulative song by Tagore, it does not provoke him to descend into the bottomless pit of retrospection.

After an hour Dhruv arrives at his destination. He settles the bill with a tap on his phone and gets out of the cab, voicing a barely audible word of thanks to the driver. He can never say it loud enough even though he always wants to. He is afraid of being laughed at.

Dhruv cranes his neck around to take a good look at the neighbourhood and finally his eyes come to rest on the sweet shop in front of him. The shop has been right there since Dhruv's early childhood days, resisting all sorts of changes. It is still awash with a faintly pungent smell of cottage cheese. Inside, a sweaty man in brown knickers and grey sleeveless vest is shooing away the flies with a questionable rag. Dhruv spends a moment wondering if they use sweat to bind lumpy cottage-cheese into shapely sweets when he spots the shop-owner Kalipada reading a newspaper in front of the cash counter.

Dhruv lowers his head and starts to walk away quickly. If Kalipada looks up, Dhruv will have to buy a dozen sweets that he does not care for. Plus, he will be trapped into painful minutes of pointless conversation. Dhruv paces ahead and turns around a corner to go out of Kalipada's sight. He is now on a red-bricked lane, spotted with patches of green moss and continues along it for several long strides. At the end of the lane, he steps on a path of grey concrete that leads up to Dhruv's parental home. The house was built by his father and it still stands proudly, though the man of the house is no more. Dhruv stares at the lonely structure for a moment and then he opens the creaky iron gate to enter the compound.

As he walks, he notices the overgrown weeds on either side of the path. He can almost see his father crouching and working with the plants. The delicate blooms that he used to nurture have disappeared with him.

Dhruv is now at the threshold of his old home. No matter how luxurious his flat at Newtown is, it is Raukipur that still remains the home to his heart. He goes up the first few steps and carefully unlocks the three big locks holding together the gigantic collapsible gate. Once inside, he notices that the interiors look clean and well-maintained. He makes a mental note to thank Ramala mashi on his next visit. Maybe he can get her a nice sari and a box of sweets from Kalipada's shop. Ramala mashi has been keeping their home for the last twenty-seven years. She is everything that Dhruv wants a family member to be, trustworthy, silent, and uncomplaining.

The rooms are all dark due to the bolted windows. But it does not bother Dhruv. He meanders in confidently through the living room and dining hall to enter the master bedroom. His hand finds the electric switchboard and turns on a dim light. An olive-green bed sheet is stretched tightly over the huge, four-poster bed placed by the windows. He turns on the AC at full blast. Then he lets all five feet and ten inches of his slightly overweight body to fall on the bed. He closes his eyes and sighs heavily. He is home. It always feels safe here. And he rolls off into a soothing nap.

"Dhruv! When did you come?"

The lilting voice of his mother wakes him up. Dhruv stares with wonder at his mother entering the room. She has just showered and her scanty grey hair, knotted at the nape of her neck, is still dripping a drop or two. She is pleating an orange sari over a white petticoat.

"Why didn't you call me? I've cooked only a simple vegetarian lunch today," she laments as she tucks in the bunch of pleats into her petticoat and goes to face the mirror affixed to her wardrobe. She combs her hair and places a red bindi in between her eyebrows.

"It's alright, mum," Dhruv sits up. "Your meals always taste wonderful to me."

"Let me fry some potato fritters quickly," his mother says.

As she turns around, meaning to walk out, she trips and falls.

"Mum!" Dhruv yells and tries to jump out of the bed to help his mother.

Instead, he wakes up. He rubs his eyes and looks around. There is no one in the room. Of course not. His mother died a year ago.

Dhruv climbs down from the bed, savouring the aftertaste of his dream. He parts a curtain to look out from the glass square of the wooden window. The orange hue outside tells him that the day is preparing to hand over its duties to night. He must have been asleep for a couple of hours.

Dhruv walks into the kitchen hoping to chance upon a snack. There is nothing much in store. In her bid to keep the home sterile, Ramala mashi emptied out most of the jars and washed them clean. In the lowermost cabinet, Dhruv finds three unopened cups of instant noodles, kept perhaps for an emergency like this. He takes one out and begins to boil water in the tea maker. A minute later, Dhruv has poured hot water into the cup and is proceeding towards the staircase with it.

The stone-cold touch of the floor on his toes contrasts with the scalding heat at his fingertips as Dhruv goes up the stairs. He thinks about the yesteryears when he used to go up the same stairs every day, and the simple reflection gives him invigorating joy. Soon he reaches a spacious room on the mezzanine floor. His parents had turned it into a prayer room for their household. Dhruv slurps on the noodles sitting outside. His mother was deeply religious and never allowed anyone to eat inside the prayer room. His father, who had mostly been an atheist, used to unfailingly abide by the rule too. Dhruv used to find much joy in going against his mother's beliefs when she was alive. But with her not there to defend her views, Dhruv thinks it is better not to disturb the rules.

After finishing his noodles, Dhruv goes out onto the terrace and crumples the empty cup. Then he takes a careful aim and throws hard. The cup lands softly in the neighbour's backyard. Dhruv grins and washes his hands with water from the rusty terrace tap. He walks back to the prayer room feeling cleaner.

He steps in and switches on a light to fill the room with a soft white glow. There is a tiny temple stationed in the middle, complete with regal artwork engraved in sandalwood.

Dhruv sits down cross-legged in front of the temple and stares straight into the eyes of the deities, one by one. There was a time when he regularly subjected them to his barrage of fervent prayers. Older and wiser, he now knows that the gods never base their decisions on his prayers, or anyone's prayers, for that matter. Now, he just likes to look into their eyes sometimes.

After a while, he gets bored with the stare game and walks to the southeast corner of the room. An old, bulky trunk lies there, wrapped in a simple silk cloth. Dhruv unwraps it and gently rotates the circular lock in between his fingers to key in the secret code. The lock surrenders with an imperceptible click.

Dhruv lifts the heavy lid and observes carefully. The inside of the trunk is divided into a number of rectangular chambers. Each segment houses bracelets, armlets, chains, and necklaces, all made of inexpensive metal.

The ornaments belong to the deities and Dhruv's mother used to attach special value to them, even though they are of little monetary worth.

Dhruv's hands tremble a little as he explores the contents of the trunk. Most of the ornaments are studded with colourful stones and though oxidation has taken away their metallic sheen, they still effuse some sort of antique value.

Dhruv is looking for a small crown that had caught his fancy in his childhood. He lifts out each item one by one and puts them back in their respective places. The crown is nowhere to be found. As he puts the last bracelet back into its chamber, he finds it a little hard to make it fit. He takes it out and observes the circular imprint it had created on the velvet of the chamber with its weight. Dhruv places it exactly in that circle and presses down gently. As if by magic a second tray slides out from the lower portion of the trunk. The shiny golden crown that Dhruv was looking for, is resting safely on the tray. He lifts it out and smiles to himself.

The crown is probably made of real gold, and hence it enjoys extra protection. He looks around impulsively to check if the curtains are drawn well. It is now dark outside and the glow in this room must be making him super-visible to potential thieves or inquisitive neighbours. Thankfully, the thick and heavy curtains are stretching well beyond the seams of the lone window. Pleased, Dhruv focuses his attention back to the crown again.

The crown holds rather pale jewels in its crevices. They look more like pebbles than jewels. And at the centre of the crown, right where the biggest and the best jewel was supposed to nest, is a gaping hole, about the size of a cherry seed, with six extended hooks clutching sadly onto the nothingness within.

Dhruv wonders if he should leave the crown alone and go away. The haunting memory from decades back is still fresh in his mind. But even after a few long minutes, he is unable to pull himself away from the room. He is an adult now and should not be afraid, he tells himself as he brings the crown closer to his right eye. He pauses for a moment and then, closing his left eye, he peers into the darkness contained within the hole. It fits around his right eye, noiselessly but firmly.

Dhruv sees an infinite space of darkness in front of him. He can no longer feel the crown. He opens his left eye quickly to take a better look at the crown, but the same pitch darkness now stretches out everywhere. His heartbeat quickens, and he recollects memories from a long time ago.

Dhruv was a boy of eight when he had first found the crown in the trunk.

He remembers staring into the deep hole and then getting blinded momentarily by a witch from a popular fairy tale. Somehow, he had torn himself away from danger and his eyesight too had been restored. Dhruv cannot remember the details, but the darkness feels quite suffocating to him even now.

He is no longer a gullible child; Dhruv scolds himself and tries to calm down. He breathes in and out deeply and waits for his eyes to dilate in the darkness. Soon, a few things begin to appear in the sea of darkness. A bright dot here, a glittering spot there, and many more patches make themselves visible to Dhruv. As he watches the wondrous view, a faint sense of familiarity seeps into his mind, and he realises where he is. He is in the middle of the universe, staring at the glowing stars and planets scattered across cosmic space. Dhruv tries to locate the Milky Way, but his knowledge of astronomy is limited, and he fails to tell one galaxy from another.

Much closer to him, a soft glow of yellow and white begins to take form. As the light gets brighter, the shape of a woman becomes apparent. Dhruv startles as soon as he could make out her face, for he knows the woman. In fact, she works in the same organization as him but in a different department.

"Hi Dhruv," she smiles. "I've been waiting for you. Or, you have been waiting for me."

"You? Here?" Dhruv looks around. "Have you always lived here?"

"It is a rather difficult question," she answers. "I could say both yes and no."

"Do they know about this?" Dhruv asks, his eyes wide and eyebrows leaping.

"Who?"

"The folks at work. Are they aware of your magical powers?"

"I am not who you think I am."

Dhruv smirks.

"When will girls stop using that line? You are Meher, the beautiful HR girl."

"I am not Meher!"

"How come you look exactly like her?"

"That's because you want me to look like her."

Dhruv gulps and waits for the woman to explain further. But she too decides to be quiet.

"Am I in a dream?" Dhruv offers a possibility.

"This is not your first time," she smiles. "Why are you so surprised?"

"So, you know all about the blinding episode from my childhood? Do you know the witch? Is she still around?"

Dhruv scans the space around himself warily.

"You were never blinded and she was not a witch. The initial darkness scared you and then you ran away. You were only a child."

"Hmm," Dhruv nods. "But where am I now? Is this a world hidden within the crown hole?"

"You are looking at the Universe," she explains as she points at the stardust spread across the vast canvas of nothingness. "The crown hole is just a gateway; we are meeting at a nook of the Universe."

"I suspected so," Dhruv comments. "And you are?"

"I am vision. I don't have a name per se. But to you, I can be Dristi."

"You're a visionary?" Dhruv scratches his head, puzzled.

"Vision as in sight, I help all to see," Dristi explains further. "I am one of the five senses that you and everyone else need to perceive the universe."

Dhruv looks at her in stoned silence so Dristi speaks on.

"I don't have a form, at least not one that you would understand. You are seeing me as the person whose image is most persistent in your mind now."

Dhruv blushes and looks away. With his dreamy eyes and dimpled smile, he usually feels confident talking to women. But Meher is different. Dhruv has a crush on Meher. And now, Meher seems to be standing in front of him, reading his mind and spelling it out to him. But no, she said she is Dristi. That should give him some courage, but he still feels awkward.

"I am sorry, but I am very confused," Dhruv says after some time.

Dristi sighs audibly at this.

"You've always been confused," she regrets. "In every lifetime, we trusted you and you failed us due to your inner conflicts and confusions."

"We?" Dhruv startles. "Who are we? There are more people in your team? The witch is your teammate, isn't she?"

"The witch was the image that you had projected on one of us," Dristi says, looking incredulous. "We are the five senses, of course. Is that so hard to get? We are the gods who guard this realm of the universe. I am Dristi or vision. I rule sight. I help everyone to see things."

"You are a goddess?" Dhruv says, feeling quite sceptic. "Well, where are the other gods?"

"They are here too; because we are everywhere. They will show themselves when the time is right."

"And it is the right time for you and me?" Dhruv winks and stares into her eyes.

Dristi's eyes, however, remain cold and impassive.

"Yes, you will find out who you are," she says. "Perhaps then you will stop being a complete loser."

Dhruv feels a stab of pain at the insult. He laughs out hard to cover it.

"Let me out, crazy lady," he says defensively. "I don't wish to associate with you or your ramblings."

"You came here out of your own will; I didn't force you in."

"Yes, I was curious. But, I see that you do not make much sense. So, let me leave."

"You will go back, but first you must take a look at your past."

Dristi raises her hand in air and begins to conjure a spell. A bright point of yellow light starts to shine at the tip of her slender forefinger. As she begins to step ahead towards Dhruv, he suddenly feels very scared.

"What'll you do to me? Don't kill me!"

Dristi smiles.

"I do not kill," she claims as she gets uncomfortably close to Dhruv.

He gives out a frenzied shriek. Dristi stops abruptly.

"Don't you wish to know everything about yourself?"

Dhruv is able to nod feebly.

"It is difficult for me to explain it in your way. I can help you to see. I want you to allow me to let you see. I want you to see things that you have seen before. Seeing them again may give your suppressed memories a little jig. Are you ok with it?"

"That…that sounds alright," Dhruv replies, even though he is still as afraid as before.

He stands stiffly while Dristi comes and touches him on the forehead at the point between his eyes, where the third eye is supposed to be. Dhruv feels the blackness around him disintegrate in an instant and it takes him to a place so unknown yet so familiar. And he begins to observe the lives of people from another land, another time.

Part 2: Story of Ghriz

Chapter 1: Ghriz's Superpower

It was very early in the morning and the faint rays of the sun gave the forest an enchanted appearance. Herds of thirsty animals gathered to lap up the sapphire sweetness of the Nakesia river. Blooming flowers scented the air, and none of the animals could sense that they were being watched. It was not their fault. Usually, no human dared to come this deep into the forest to hunt. Especially not at this time of the year when the river was low and easy to ford. During summer, leopards and big bears who preferred the thicker forest on the left side of the Nakesia often crossed over to hunt from the right side where the smaller animals lived. The trees kept thinning out on this side of the river for a couple of miles before abruptly giving way to a small village where the human population had settled.

The villagers usually went to hunt in the tamer parts of the forest, looking for rabbits and wild boars. Only a handful of brave hunters dared to get closer to the river in the hope of shooting deer. One needed to look out constantly for ferocious animals and most of them thought it was not worth the risk.

But today it was different. There was no expert hunter watching the animals lazing by the Nakesia. It was a little girl, all five years of age, whose eyes were following their movements. Her name was Ghriz. She sat on the lowest branch of a huge *Rattel tree on the right side of the river, while her father Ghrexad, and uncle Khraex waited eagerly around the burgundy tree trunk for her to speak up.

*Rattel tree: A large tree with thick trunk and bushy leaves

Ghriz was blessed with super-vision and could spot even the smallest of the bees buzzing within a radius of five miles. So, while the grown-ups often failed to see the animals camouflaged by the thick foliage, Ghriz's vision was sharp enough to spot them from a distance.

"Is a *rikitisi deer in sight, Ghriz?" her uncle Khraex asked.

*rikitisi deer: a type of deer found in the forest.

He was looking up at her with hope, but Ghriz felt puzzled.

"How will she know what a rikitisi deer is?" Ghrexad snapped at his brother. "She is only sixty-two moons old!"

"Do you see any deer that is completely black with stubby horns on the head?" Khraex tried again.

He hunched over and held his bent-down fingers over his head to exhibit an example. Ghriz scanned the riverside one more time. Two dark deer could be seen, sitting face to face, and chewing in rhythm. They looked like a couple enjoying each other's company. Ghriz switched her eyes from her uncle to the deer duo for a few times and decided that they must be what Khraex was demonstrating as rikitisi deer. The deer were pitch black in colour with two bands of a sparkling hue close to their neck.

"I see two such deer munching on grass," Ghriz spoke out. "They have sparkling bands at their necks."

"What bands?" Khraex asked. "They are supposed to be black from head to toe."

Ghriz checked again. The unmistakable bands at their necks were now shining brightly in the sunlight.

"They are black, but a couple of bright bands run across their necks," Ghriz said as she traced her finger along her own neck.

Khraex was confused.

"Check carefully, Ghriz," he urged. "Rikitisi deer have no bands. It must be something else sticking to their fur."

Little Ghriz scanned again. At this point, Ghrexad got very annoyed and reached out for his daughter.

"Come down, dear," he lifted her off the branch. "This is not your age to come into the forest. You haven't even learned all the colours and your jupapella* wants to make a hunter out of you. Let's go back home. Your maella* will have cooked some hot potato stew."

*jupapella: uncle

*maella: mother

Ghrexad began to walk away carrying little Ghriz hoping that his brother would sense his displeasure and give up. But Khraex was not to be subdued so easily. He followed his big brother persistently.

"You can't ignore her gift, my jela*," he said.

*jela: brother

Ghrexad ignored his brother and kept walking in long and strong strides, holding Ghriz against his chest. Her small, round face bobbed up and down on her father's shoulder, smiling warmly at Khraex. Her uncle pulled her nose lightly and made a funny face, which made her chortle out in joy.

"Yesterday, Ghriz spotted lion footprints at the northern borders of our village from miles away," Khraex continued with his litany. "The young men going that way were saved due to your daughter's timely warning. I've never seen or heard of something like that. Neither have you. Why don't you see that your daughter is blessed with special powers?"

Ghrexad stopped and turned around. He set Ghriz down and placed his hands at his waist.

"Listen Khraex. You can't make a hunter out of her just because she can see very well. If her super-vision is a gift, then let her enjoy it. It's her age to play."

Ghriz moved closer to her father and started to tap together the beads that hung from Ghrexad's neck down to his navel. As she made a simple rhythm, Khraex looked down at her small frame and sighed. He caressed the curly bunch of hair knotted at the top of Ghriz's head.

"She's my blood too," Khraex mentioned. "And in about fifteen summers from now, when the tribe lead will select his successor, she can be a worthy nominee from our clan. I thought you being her papella* would like that."

*papella- father

For a moment there was a spot of shine in Ghrexad's eyes. No one from their family had ever been the tribe lead. His brother Khraex had gone really close but even he had not been able to clinch the title.

"Please let me train her," Khraex requested.

Ghrexad glared at him.

"Please, please, please," Khraex begged.

"Fine, but you must relent if she hates it," Ghrexad firmly said. "Don't push your dreams onto her."

"Drugadriga*, my jela," Khraex cried in joy, thanking his brother for his kindness.

*drugadriga- thank you

He bent down and touched the beads that hung around Ghrexad's neck with his head. It was their way of expressing respect.

Chapter 2: Zuzza

Little Ghriz's life changed dramatically once her father and uncle made the decision to train her to hunt. Till that point, her afternoons used to be spent with a bunch of kids at the village square. In summers, they would begin their days with outdoor games. But soon they would get tired of the searing heat and the children would escape into the cool comfort of the large play hut made of stone where the bigger kids took turn to tell stories.

One popular outdoor game was treasure in the trees. A child needed to pose as "treasure" and they would have to hide in the trees while the others looked for them. With her super-vision, Ghriz was always the first one to spot the treasure-child. The other kids got so tired of her dominance in the game that they insisted on Ghriz posing as "treasure" every time, to get a decent chance at winning.

"Since you are our eternal treasure," Bhmana, Ghriz's best friend, would say, "I think you can make a worthy tribe lead when we grow up."

Ghriz used to smile in joy. She did not fully understand the power or prestige that came with the position of tribe lead. Bhmana, being the son of the current tribe lead, was better informed about the role. He mentioned myriad details about the tribe lead and his duties as often as he could. It made him feel very important among the children.

Ghrexad and Khraex decided to spare Ghriz during the scorching summer and started her hunting lessons from early autumn. Most of the trees in the village looked bare now. So, the children spent their time making pottery instead of playing treasure in the trees.

One day, Bhmana was structuring the base of a clay castle while the smaller children crafted small dolls to populate the castle with. Ghriz sat by Bhmana, weaving a mesh for the castle gate with straws that some crows fetched for her. She had an unusual fondness for the crows, and they would reciprocate her love by bringing whatever gifts they could manage to find.

Bhmana raised the frame of the castle gate and asked Ghriz to fix the mesh into it when Khraex appeared at the scene. He cast a disapproving glance at Bhmana before calling out to his niece.

"Ghriz, jupapella is here to take you," Khraex said.

Ghriz sighed and handed over the thatched mesh to Bhmana.

"Won't you stay to build the rest of the castle?" Bhmana asked.

"No, Ghriz has some lessons to do with her papella and jupapella,"

Khraex answered and held Ghriz by her hand. "You kids continue with the game."

"I'll save the castle for you to see," Bhmana promised as he waved at Ghriz.

The other children crowded around him with the clay models and Bhmana got busy in examining those. Ghriz looked back longingly at them and Khraex had to drag her along.

"Now, you don't want to be like them," Khraex said. "Wasting time with mud and clay. Not a single skill they try to learn."

Ghriz's face was still forlorn.

"You can't look so sullen." Khraex was annoyed. "We're meeting your father under the big *Hriti tree. He will think I am forcing you to go."

*Hriti tree: Local tree of the forest

"You are!" Ghriz protested. "At home, maella is always busy with Jhluk. I was happy to play with Bhmana outside, but you had to put a stop to that too."

Jhluk was Ghriz's younger sister who had been born exactly twelve moons after her and ever since she seemed to be monopolising all of their maella's affection.

"Listen to me," Khraex said, holding Ghriz by the shoulders and turning her around. "Bhmana is the son of the tribe lead. He can't be the next tribe lead as per our laws. That's why he wastes away his time. But you have the potential to be the tribe lead. Don't let that idiot distract you from your path."

"Bhmana wants me to be the tribe lead so he wouldn't do anything bad for me," Ghriz defended her friend and resumed walking.

They were silent for the next few minutes.

"Someday you'll learn how much it takes to be the tribe lead," Khraex said. "And how painful it is to not be the lead, even after being the eligible one."

Ghriz made a face, but Khraex did not see that. They walked on and after a few more minutes Ghrexad appeared in sight. Waiting under the huge Hriti tree, he seemed to be tense. Ghrexad had brought all the hunting weapons and was looking straight in their direction. For a second, Ghriz thought of telling him that she would much rather play than learn to hunt, but then she remembered the wild nuts that Khraex always brought for her from the forest. It was a rare type of nut that only her jupapella could find and Ghriz absolutely loved their woody taste. Her gratitude for the wild nuts saved the day for Khraex.

Ghriz faked a smile at Ghrexad and said with a sudden dose of enthusiasm, "Let's go and hunt!"

Feeling reassured, Ghrexad handed out an iron spear to Khraex who took it and began to walk a little ahead to step onto a narrowing path lined by trees. The path meandered into the first part of the forest where the villagers generally hunted.

Ghrexad picked Ghriz up, placed her on his shoulders, and followed Khraex.

After a while, he asked Ghriz, "So, your maella tells me that you are jealous of Jhluk?"

Ghriz shook her head fervently and said, "No!"

"You'll always be your papella's favourite one, Ghriz," Ghrexad promised. "And your maella loves you too, even though she may seem to prefer Jhluk."

They walked through the forest which seemed to thicken fast. Khraex was now testing the trees with his spear before taking each step. Soon they reached a plot of clear space. There were some bright red and brown foliage to their left while a path continued straight ahead. Khraex asked Ghriz and Ghrexad to wait there while he vanished along the path. Ghrexad set his daughter down and pointed to the vibrant bushes to their left.

"Do you know what plant those are?" he asked.

Ghriz nodded her head. Everybody in the village knew that plant. It was the Death plant. The leaves exuded a fatal poison and anyone touching them was sure to die within minutes. One of the first lessons that mothers in the village would pass on to their children was about which leaves, roots, and fruits bore poison. So, Ghriz knew very well that she always had to maintain a safe distance from those plants.

"But do you know what secret lies beyond the rows of the Death plant?" Ghrexad questioned.

"Secret?" Ghriz was intrigued.

She stood up and took a good look at the bushes.

"If you go through the bushes and keep walking," Ghrexad continued. "A strange tall tree will appear at some point, one that bears big, woody nuts."

Ghrexad reached into the pouch that hung at his waist and took out a nut.

"Like this," he held the nut up to Ghriz, flashing all his teeth.

"Wow, a wild nut," Ghriz exclaimed, promptly putting it into her mouth. "Jupapella gets these for me."

"Right! I got this from him too," Ghrexad admitted. "He is the only one who can walk into those bushes and come out alive. In fact, I have never seen the nut tree. I've only heard about it from him."

Ghriz opened her mouth in bewilderment.

"Is that how he gets the nuts for me?" she asked. "Does he not even fall sick from the poisonous sap of the Death plants?"

"The Death plants are very powerful and they can gauge who the best people in the village are," Ghrexad explained. "Your jupapella is the best person alive in our generation, so he is exempt from the poisonous effect of those bushes. To be fair, he deserved to be our tribe lead."

"Why isn't he the tribe lead then?" Ghriz asked.

Suddenly there was a great rustling heard in the leaves. Khraex was coming back. Ghrexad changed the topic and began to tell Ghriz about the various songbirds that lived in the forest. Soon Khraex emerged out of the thick trees, dragging a dead rikitisi deer in tow.

"Ghriz, this is a rikitisi deer," Khraex broke into their conversation.

"Can't you wait for your turn?" Ghrexad snapped, creasing his eyebrows. "I was teaching her about the songbirds."

"Sorry my jela, I have to find out something. See Ghriz, doesn't this deer look completely black to you?"

Ghriz looked at the limp body of the dead rikitisi deer. The thick sparkling bands at the neck stood out in the otherwise black body.

"What about the bands?" Ghriz asked, pointing there.

"Which bands?" Ghrexad looked closely at the neck of the deer.

"Don't you see jupapella?" Ghriz turned to Khraex. "The shiny bands in the deer's neck? The colour we see in the crow's beak!"

The two men looked at each other.

"Crows are black, Ghriz; beaks and all," Ghrexad said, after a while.

"The beak is not black," Ghriz insisted. "It's a different colour. A sparkling sort of colour."

"She sees a new colour," Khraex gasped.

In the next few minutes, they made Ghriz list out all the things in which she had seen the special colour. She named a couple of random things.

All those things were plain black to Ghrexad and Khraex.

"Don't talk about your powers in the village," Khraex cautioned his niece after a moment of careful consideration. "You're destined to be the tribe lead one day. Till then you must stay very humble."

"Ghriz, you need to remain humble all your life, no matter who you become," Ghrexad interjected, glaring at his brother.

"Humility begets nothing," Khraex said tersely. "You and I may have been fools, but we will not raise her a fool as well. So, Ghriz, have you thought of a new name for this colour that you see?"

"Will you name them after crows?" Ghrexad joked.

"No, crows are my favourite," Ghriz said. "I will name my first child after them."

Khraex and Ghrexad burst out laughing. It annoyed Ghriz very much.

"I'll call the colour zuzza," Ghriz said. "It sparkles a lot like *zuzz."

*zuzz: mica

Ghrexad and Khraex felt that the name sounded too rich to fit a colour invisible to them. But they had already barred Ghriz from talking about it, so they let her name it as she pleased and it became zuzza to the three of them.

Chapter 3: Training Tales

The hunting lessons continued every day for Ghriz, cutting into her playtime with Bhmana and the other kids. She did not like to leave her friends to go into the dark and brooding forest and would have surely confessed to her father about it, had the Death plants not caught her fancy. Her father had mentioned that it does no harm to the best ones in the village. She began to wonder if she would be good enough to pass the test. Every day when they passed the thick red and brown leaves at the clearing, she would cast a furtive glance at the bushes.

On their next trip, Ghrexad, Khraex, and Ghriz went right up to the Rattel tree for the day's lessons. It was risky to go any deeper from there. The river was still some distance away and myriad dangers lurked ahead. Ghriz, however, could see everything perfectly and she began to broadcast a list of the animals that she saw by the Nakesia while Khraex laid out the weapons against the tree trunk.

"Wait, wait," Ghrexad interrupted his daughter. "First check if there are any leopards or lions about."

"None," Ghriz confirmed after another look. "Can we hunt now?"

"Not so fast, child," Khraex said. "Today we'll hunt only fruits."

He untied a bundle of arrows and divided them into two halves. Then he offered one half to Ghriz. Ghrexad sat himself down on a boulder to watch them.

"I can climb really fast and pluck out some fruits for you, jupapella," Ghriz said. "We don't have to hunt fruits."

"That's not the point," Khraex said. "You've to learn aiming. Your supervision is of no use if you can't aim well."

He took an arrow, set it against his crossbow, and took a careful aim at a bulbous, orange fruit hanging in the branch of a tree in front of them. He let it go after a moment's pause and the fruit fell on the ground with a dull thud. Khraex hopped three times and bowed to the tree to express his gratitude before turning around to Ghriz.

"Can you do the same?" he asked.

Khraex handed to her the small crossbow that he had crafted for Ghriz.

"Yes, it's very easy." Ghriz was confident.

She held the bow upwards and released an arrow. Then another, and another, and another. She fired away ten arrows in succession but could not dislodge a single fruit.

Finally, Ghrexad stood up and said, "Stop, your arrows might kill some ill-fated animal resting in the bushes behind."

Khraex was scratching his head uncomfortably.

"I told you she is too young to hunt," Ghrexad told him. "But you wouldn't listen."

Ghrexad marched away towards the tree to retrieve the arrows. Ghriz grinned at Khraex.

"You are doing this on purpose, aren't you?" Khraex whispered in a menacing voice, bending down to Ghriz's height. "You think jupapella will give up if your aim is lousy. And then you can go back to playing with that blunt-headed Bhmana."

"I really can't aim well," Ghriz replied quite truthfully but Khraex would not believe her.

"You will train for double time," Khraex declared. "Till you learn to aim properly."

"No, jupapella, please no," Ghriz begged.

But Khraex called out to his brother.

"My jela, Ghriz wants to put in double efforts," he yelled. "Did you hear that, my jela? Your girl is not a quitter."

Ghriz made a face and puffed out her cheeks. After a while, Ghrexad came back with the lost arrows. He looked very happy.

"Papella is proud of you," he told Ghriz. "Those who keep trying go on to win. I'm sure you'll learn to aim soon."

Khraex packed the weapons soon afterwards and the three started to walk back home. A crow that had been watching them all this time cawed loudly and flew away.

"Your friend, Ghriz?" Ghrexad joked.

"Yes," she replied casually.

The two brothers laughed as they made their way back to the village.

The next few days were incredibly hard for Ghriz. Even the little time that she had for herself had been taken away from her. It seemed like her life was a continuous blur of eating, sleeping, and shooting arrows. Sometimes Bhmana would knock at the window of their hut and pass on a clay doll or a piece of pottery to her. Whenever that happened, her mother Marizh would immediately come and tell Ghriz to share the gifts with her *seesul, Jhluk.

*seesul- sister

Jhluk always found Ghriz's possessions profoundly desirable but had no interest in playing with her elder sister. She would often use relentless crying to get hold of Ghriz's belongings and then go away without making any further demand on Ghriz's time or attention. This disappointed Ghriz, but she never spoke about it. She would diligently collect her crossbow and arrows and leave for the forest without so much as a shrug of the shoulders.

Ghriz worked hard to aim well. She wanted the punishing training hours to end. But even though she could see her targets clearer than anyone else, she still found it impossible to aim her arrows correctly. After one such gruelling shift in the forest, Ghriz was back at home. She washed herself quickly and went to the kitchen corner to get her lunch. Marizh had kept mashed vegetables and rhizomes in a pot for her. Ghriz wanted to eat with her maella. But she was feeding Jhluk in a corner of the hut. So, Ghriz grabbed her meal pot and crept out of the hut.

Ghriz sat with her legs thrown apart in the yard and ate hungrily. She was halfway through her lunch when she heard the gentle flapping of wings behind herself. Turning around, she saw a crow perching on the bamboo bar that encircled the courtyard in front of their hut. Ghriz clumped up some food within her palm and set it in front of the crow. The crow finished its portion fast and waited for Ghriz to be done with her lunch. As soon as Ghriz got up to go inside the hut, it cawed loudly and tugged at her hair. Ghriz was tired and wanted badly to take a nap, but the crow would not let go. It seemed determined to take her somewhere. Eventually, Ghriz set down the empty pot on the yard and walked with the crow. This seemed to please the crow very much. It gave out a celebratory call and flew up into the sky. The crow began to lead the way by flying at a low height while Ghriz followed it reluctantly.

As soon as they reached the village square, another flock of crows glided into the air from a tree and started to follow the first crow. Ghriz paused for a second and wondered what they were up to. She felt her heart going faster as she trailed the group.

The crows led Ghriz into the forest and kept flying till they reached the clearing by the Death bushes. Ghriz stared at the large, tinted bushes to her left while standing at a safe distance. The crows had settled on the ground and were flapping their wings busily, as if trying to get into a formation.

Then, without any warning, the first crow flew up and dived straight into the Death bushes. Ghriz was horrified at the sight and almost gave out a little scream. But the crow was flying in, its wings grazing the leaves of the poisonous Death plants. Ghriz wondered for a moment if she should turn back and run away from the strange scene. She badly wanted to bury herself in her maella's arms and hide her face till the vision of the crow flapping about the fatal leaves faded away. But she could not. Instead, she found herself running into the bushes right after the crow in an attempt to save her innocent little friend from imminent death.

The other crows cawed at this and one by one they began to fly in too. Ghriz was now running blindly through the dense bushes, pushing apart the big, glossy leaves to make way for herself. Some leaves were breaking open to leak their deadly juices into her hands and Ghriz began to cry. She could hear only a low rustle ahead and behind her, that told her that the crows were coming with her. It was the only thing that helped her to keep going.

She shut her eyes, and flaying her arms wildly, Ghriz continued to push ahead. All of a sudden, she felt her hands clutching on empty air. She opened her eyes and saw that she had crossed through the barricade of the plants and reached a circular span of land in the middle. She looked around in amazement. There were all kinds of strange plants which the Death bushes cordoned off from the outside world.

After walking around for a while, she spotted the wild nut tree and ran to it in joy. Just as she was about to break a nut from it, the first crow cawed and pulled her away. She saw that the other crows were arriving at the hidden span of land one after the other. They all made a single file on the ground and walked up to her.

Ghriz realised that perhaps she was not supposed to touch that wild nut tree and stepped back. She watched the crows who had stopped flying completely. At this point, Ghriz suddenly remembered that she had the juice of Death plant all over herself. Looking at her hands, she could see the distinct marks of hardening juice. She scratched at those spots. The drops came off easily. She smelled the spots, but there was no odour. Nor did she feel any itch or pain. But by now, she should have been in the throes of death. Yet, she felt fine. It could mean only one thing. Like her uncle Khraex, she too was immune to the poison of the Death plant.

Standing in the hidden span of land, surrounded by the Death plants, Ghriz blushed. Her jupapella was not one bit wrong in his ambition of making her the tribe lead. Taking a deep breath, Ghriz resolved to work hard and make his dream come true. A loud flapping sound broke her out of her reverie. The crows were getting impatient. As she began to follow the line of crows again, Ghriz figured that the birds lost their ability to fly in this secret place.

Soon they reached a rather stout tree that towered over its neighbours. The crows formed a circle around the tree and looked at Ghriz expectantly. As she stepped closer, the first crow pecked at the bark of the tree. Immediately, a bright stream of purplish zuzza sap began to ooze out. Ghriz bent forward and observed the sap in amazement. It looked lovely as it glistened down the mahogany bark of the tree.

A crow dipped its beak in the sap and walked over to a big, bushy shrub. It smeared a blob of the glistening sap at the centre of a leaf in the shrub. Then the crow took a few steps back and turned around. As soon as it turned its zuzza-coloured beak towards the marked leaf, it got torn off from the shrub and flew to stick to the crow's beak.

Ghriz was amazed by the strange demonstration. She dabbed a few drops of the zuzza sap on her finger and tried a similar trick. As soon as she went close to any crow, she felt a pull and her finger stuck to the crow's beak. After a few rounds she realised what the crows were trying to reveal to her. The zuzza sap was magical; it attracted anything else of the same colour. Ghriz stared back at the flock of crows. They were now taking a generous spraying of the zuzza sap all over their wings. The droplets stuck to their beaks like liquid magnet and they used it to preen their feathers carefully. It seemed like the crows were following some ritual of their own and Ghriz giggled loudly. The secret place made such humans out of the crows.

After a while the crows came back to Ghriz. The first one was carrying a pot-shaped leaf in its beak. Accepting the offering Ghriz saw that the leaf was filled to the brim with some zuzza sap. She wondered why. But there was no time for her to think. The crows were walking towards the section through which they had come in. Ghriz hurried towards them. On reaching the boundary, the crows regained their ability of flying. They rose to a low height one by one and began to dart out of the bushes. Ghriz started to push her way through the Death plants too, following the crows as she protected the leaf pot within her hands. It felt even stranger this time because she knew that the infamous Death plant juice will not harm her.

By the time they were out, Ghriz had figured out the purpose of the strange visit.

But there was no time to celebrate. The sky looked a faint shade of blue which meant that she had to get out of the forest fast. Nightfall happened rather suddenly inside the forest. Feeling worried, Ghriz began to run.

The crows paced their flight with Ghriz and stayed right above her head. After several rushed minutes, they found themselves at the edge of the forest. From here the trees were thinning out on both sides and the path in the middle widened to give way to the village lanes. Some distance away, the first rows of huts were visible. Ghriz paused for a moment to catch her breath. A crow snatched away the leaf pot from her hands and placed it behind a thick tree trunk. The rest of the crows added some pebbles around the pot and hid it from clear view.

Ghriz gaped at them and scratched her head. Things were starting to make sense to her but very slowly. The crows cawed in unison once and flew off to take shelter in the trees. The day was over for them. In the fading colours of twilight, Ghriz began to walk into the village slowly, thinking over the events of the past few hours. A plan was taking shape in her mind.

At this point, she spotted Bhmana running towards her in a rather distraught manner. He stopped abruptly the minute he saw Ghriz and let out a small shriek of joy.

"Ghriz, you are there," he said, resuming his run towards her. "You are not dead. You are there! Alive!"

He ran up to her and touched her on the head and shoulders. Then he flashed a huge smile at her.

"They are arranging a search team to look for you," he told Ghriz. "I thought you have died. So, I came to check for myself."

"I'm not dead," Ghriz said, smiling back.

"I will run back to the village and tell them that," Bhmana said, panting hard. "You follow me as fast as you can."

Ghriz nodded and off Bhmana went in the opposite direction, speeding into the village. Ghriz quickened her pace, too. She would now have to come up with a good excuse to explain her sudden disappearance.

When Ghriz reached the village square, Bhmana was already in an animated discussion with her folks. The search team had been just told to disperse. The torches would not have to be set alight to scan through the dark forest. The drums would not have to be beaten to keep the wild beasts away. So, the group of searchers got busy at a corner packing away all the sticks, oils, drums, and weapons neatly. A few caught sight of Ghriz and shook their heads disapprovingly.

She turned away hurriedly only to bump into Khraex. He looked down at her, his eyebrows curled in great anger. As he raised his right hand high, Ghriz braced for a slap. But someone else punched her on the head from behind.

"Bad girl," Marizh shouted, hitting her again. "Bad girl to run loose. I'll roast you for dinner tonight."

"Not if I harpoon her first," Khraex said, stopping his hand just short of Ghriz's cheeks.

"No, no, I will teach her a lesson tonight," Ghrexad said, separating himself from other village folks and marching towards his daughter. "I will pin her to a spot with my arrow so that she never runs loose again."

This went on for an hour and all the members of Ghriz's close family and even the neighbours took turns to come up with the most ingenious ways of torturing her. She stood in the middle of the circle, staring at the ground guiltily. Jhluk observed everything closely, but it was the sullen look on Ghriz's face that she found to be the funniest.

Finally, when everyone had run out of ideas on how to mutilate the errant child, people retreated to their own homes. Ghrexad went into his hut and his family followed him quickly. He set aside the weapons for the next day's hunt while Marizh served dinner to Ghriz and Khraex. Then, she took Jhluk on her lap and started to feed her.

Khraex always had dinner in his elder brother's hut before going back to his own hut across the front yard. His wife Shynex was a perpetually sick woman who lived on a diet of soupy lentils and stayed in bed for most of the time. After finishing his meal, Khraex thanked Marizh and gave Ghriz a final round of rebuke before leaving with Ghrexad. Ghrexad escorted his younger brother to his hut, even though it was only a few steps away. His actual fear was that someday Khraex might walk in to find his wife dead, and Ghrexad did not want his brother to be alone at such a delicate moment. That day, Shynex was very much alive and awake when Khraex walked in. Relieved, Ghrexad made his way back to his home while Khraex poured out a bowl of soup that he had cooked in the morning.

Shynex drank slowly from the bowl as her husband sat by her telling her about his day. Halfway through the story, Khraex thought he heard a snore. Turning to Shynex, he saw that she was fast asleep with the bowl precariously rested on her belly. He sighed as he moved the bowl away and put his wife's head properly on the pillow. Khraex put the leftover soup just outside the door of his hut as an offering to the spirit of the night. Then, bolting the door well, he ran to his bed. He quickly slipped in by his wife and within the count of five breaths, he fell asleep. The next day was going to be long. He had told Ghriz that she would have to start out early to make up for her bad behaviour.

The next morning, Ghriz appeared surprisingly upbeat. Ghrexad, however, grumbled a lot and cursed Khraex for his stupid plan. The three set out even before the rays of the sun had coloured all the corners of the sky. Unlike other days, Ghriz was walking a bit ahead of them. She went out of sight a couple of times, attracting more harpooning threats from Ghrexad and Khraex. Soon she recovered the leaf pot containing the zuzza sap and hid it in the small pouch tied at her waist. Thereafter she walked by her papella and jupapella like an obedient girl. They kept going without a pause until they had reached the Rattel tree.

"Do you see any danger ahead?" Ghrexad asked his daughter.

"No, I don't see any ferocious animals," Ghriz replied after taking a good look. "The Nakesia looks tame as well."

"Good, today we will go deeper," Khraex said. "And I'll show you how to hunt a rikitisi deer."

"I can see one," Ghriz answered as she pranced through the trees inhaling the sweet morning air.

They chose a spot close to the river where it was very easy to hide. This also made it risky for the hunters. Leopards often leapt out and bears pounced on humans without any kind of warning. But there was no such risk for the trio. Ghriz had double-checked the trees and bushes for all probable threats.

Ghrexad placed his hands at his hips and kept watch while Khraex took out the arrows.

"Let me show you-" Khraex was starting his demonstration, but Ghriz fired her first arrow without letting him complete his sentence. Both Ghrexad and Khraex failed to notice that she had dipped the tip of the arrow in zuzza sap prior to shooting it.

Ghrexad shook his head and went ahead towards the Nakesia to retrieve the arrow.

"That was too rash for a beginner," Khraex admonished Ghriz. "You need to position the crossbow and count out a dozen deep breaths to check if your hands are steady. Then you fit the arrow and count out another dozen breaths to test the position. Finally, when you are confident, you release the arrow with one long breath."

Ghrexad came back at this point. He stood there with a dead rikitisi in tow.

Khraex's mouth fell open. He dislodged the arrow from the deer and checked it carefully. It was indeed the one that Ghriz had shot.

"I learnt how to aim yesterday," Ghriz said, sitting down on the grass beside her uncle.

The deer was bleeding at the zuzza-coloured bands but of course, neither Ghrexad nor Khraex could make that out.

Khraex raised his hands, hopped, and clapped to express his joy.

"Future tribe lead our Ghriz is," he exclaimed. "Her powers are coming awake with age. Future tribe lead our Ghriz is!"

"Let's take this to Marizh for a grand lunch," Ghrexad remarked as he poked at the dead deer.

The three walked back with their haul to the end of the forest. Ghrexad and Khraex asked Ghriz to run off home to tell her maella about the short and successful hunt. Then the two brothers took the rikitisi to the shallow pit, where dead animals were skinned, gutted, and chopped into suitable chunks for roasting. Khraex ground some dry leaves between two stones and stuffed the bits into a clay pot. As he set it alight, a heavy smoke crept out of the vessel. Taking large swigs of smoke from the pot, the two brothers worked with the dead deer.

"You must be very proud, my jela, to have a daughter like Ghriz," Khraex spoke after a long while.

"She is more your daughter than mine," Ghrexad said.

Khraex smiled as he deftly separated a large sheet of meat from the ribs.

"I never thought I would not father a child of my own," he sighed. "I'm grateful that Marizh and you aren't too possessive about your children."

"Marizh doesn't appreciate these hunting lessons, though," Ghrexad said. "She thinks we're turning Ghriz into the deepest shade of black and no boy will want her when she's grown."

"Marizh has no good sense," Khraex commented reproachfully. "If only she knew how men choose their women."

Ghrexad did not like the way Khraex said the last sentence.

"Some men choose their women out of pity," Ghrexad sneered after a bit. "Marizh knows that well. She saw how you brought Shynex home."

"And does she not know that you wanted her because of her family money?" Khraex retorted.

"That's not true," Ghrexad asserted, looking down and working furiously with the deer.

The brothers spent an hour cutting up the rikitisi deer over regular banter. By the time they went home, Marizh had prepared the oven for a delicious roast. That day, they had sumptuous meals. Even Bhmana and a few other friends of Ghriz were invited to eat at Ghrexad's. It was, after all, their friend's first successful hunt.

After that day, Ghriz did not have to work double time to learn hunting. But she devoted every bit of her attention to picking up small tips and skills from her father and uncle. In the following thirteen years, Ghrizworked diligently and grew up to be the finest hunter of the tribe.

Chapter 4: Things Change

Ghriz sat in front of their hut, feeding grains to the crows. She was now eighteen summers old. After the children in the village had lived to see a hundred and twenty moons, their age was tracked by the number of summers they had seen. Everyone in the tribe now respected Ghriz. She was the brightest one among the younger lot and it looked like she would go on to be the next tribe lead. Most boys and girls of her age found it rather intimidating to talk to Ghriz and hence she was forced to spend a lot of time by herself.

On the other hand, Jhluk could always be found with a small group around her. Even as Ghriz fed the crows, her sister was sitting on the fence of a potato farm, flirting with the boys working inside. Ghriz observed Jhluk through the corner of her eyes and wondered how she found it so easy to gel with boys. Her coal-black curls swished against the air and the beads around her neck tinkled loudly each time she swayed in chatty giggles. Her deep brown skin had a soft glow and together with her big eyes and plump lips, Jhluk was now quite a beauty. Ghriz sighed as she glanced at her own skin, which appeared jaded in comparison. She scattered the rest of the grains on the yard for the crows. Then she moved to a corner and began to mix water with some red soil to prepare thick mud. Once done, she sat on the low bamboo bar that surrounded their hut and scrubbed her hands and face vigorously with the red paste. Marizh always insisted that red mud can erase blemishes of the skin and make it glow.

At this moment, Ghriz saw Bhmana appear in the horizon. Her best friend from childhood was now a tall and broad-shouldered young man with a head of short, thick curls. The mischief in his eyes paired well with his dimpled smile. Ghriz's heart started to beat wildly as Bhmana casually walked past the potato farm and came to sit on the bamboo bar with Ghriz. He, thankfully, had not grown distant over the years.

"Ghriz, what red muck are you rubbing on yourself?" he teased. "Just tell me once and I'll duck you whole in a big puddle. You'd come out glowing!"

"Shut up," Ghriz said as she stole another glance at Jhluk and quickly washed the red paste off herself.

Bhmana followed her eyes and saw Jhluk laughing wildly in a fit of self-approval.

"Ghriz, do you worry that Jhluk will break the barrier before you?" he asked frankly.

"Breaking the barrier" was a euphemism among the tribe for having sex.

"No." A feeble reply came from Ghriz.

"Don't worry, you'll get there first," Bhmana said.

"You think so?" Ghriz looked into Bhmana's eyes intently.

"Yes, I do," he replied firmly.

"Why?" Ghriz probed.

"Jhluk has too many options; she won't choose so early."

"And I?" Ghriz's voice was going dry.

"Everyone likes you, but they are a bit wary," Bhmana said as he gently traced the outline of her face with his right hand. "You are the future tribe lead."

"Have you chosen anyone, Bhmana?" Ghriz asked.

"What do you think?" Bhmana's lips looked wet and his eyes were shining.

Ghriz breathed in hard to savour the moment before Bhmana zoomed in to taste her lips.

"Ghriz, I've some serious planning to do with you," Khraex bellowed, appearing almost out of nowhere.

Ghriz and Bhmana withdrew from each other quickly. Khraex looked at Bhmana with disapproving eyes and sat down heavily between the two, pushing them apart.

"Bhmana, would you mind excusing us?" Khraex said. "You wouldn't want to jeopardize your best friend's future prospects, would you?"

"No," Bhmana replied, getting up. "I'll be off now. Good luck, Ghriz."

Bhmana jumped off the bamboo bar and pointed his fists in a gesture of good luck towards Ghriz before he started to walk away. As he passed the potato farm, he called out to Jhluk.

"Jhluk, your sister is preparing to be the tribe lead and you haven't even learnt to count," Bhmana joked.

"You smelly duckling," Jhluk hurled a common abuse at Bhmana.

Bhmana laughed and started to sprint away. Jhluk ran after him. The boys tending to the potatoes looked at her with open admiration as she jiggled away, leaving a faint trail of music and fragrance. But none of them noticed the stone that Jhluk was clutching in her fist. And when she grabbed and hurled a fistful of dust at Bhmana, nobody saw her rolling the stone in the dust first.

Jhluk and Bhmana faded away in the distance, but Ghriz kept staring with wistful eyes. Khraex cleared his voice audibly.

"Ghriz, don't get distracted by their frivolity," he coaxed. "Your sister hasn't got any talent. She has taken after Marizh. You, on the other hand, will be our pride… you are!"

Ghriz nodded and looked down. Khraex held her face up by the chin.

"Promise me that you won't break the barrier in the next two years. You have to learn all the tribe laws and there are almost four dozen of them. I can't coach you if you don't pour your heart into this."

"Promise jupapella," Ghriz replied.

Khraex smiled. His face was lined and his eyes looked weary, but his spirit was not broken. When Shynex died five years back, everybody thought that Khraex would take a new woman. But he did not. His only wish was to make Ghriz attain what had slipped away from him in his youth.

Ghriz and Khraex worked together for the next hour with the first four laws of their land. Khraex corrected her diction and posture as she tried to say the lines aloud. Just learning the laws by heart was not enough. Each law needed to be uttered in a prescribed rhythm while holding a particular pose. Only then a person was said to have perfect command over the ways of the land.

They were wrapping up the day's lessons when a loud celebratory gong was heard from the direction of the village square. A few people ran towards the sound to find out what it was all about.

A young couple was seated on a decorated log in the village square while an old lady was arranging a circle of fruits around them. She was chanting a sacred mantra meant to bind the couple together for eternity. The pair had got intimate for the first time or "broken the barrier" earlier that day. They had shared this bit with their parents, who in turn had reported the same to the tribe lead. Now, as per their laws, there was a ceremony to be held in the honour of their love and all the people in the village would make merry through the night.

The younger folks broke into spontaneous dancing in groups while the older people bundled together to plan for the communal dinner. Soon, Ghriz was sent for by the village elders.

"Ghriz, we've to go hunting," Ghrexad said. "The hunter boys can easily get us some boars and rabbits but with your help, we can hope to bring back a deer or two as well. That way our people will be able to throw a grand feast for all."

Ghriz ran back to their hut and went looking into her private den. Dens were private boxes that every villager was allowed to own once they completed fifteen summers in age. She took out her wooden crossbow, a bundle of zuzza-dipped arrows, and a thick tie-back rope before she set out to join the hunt-party.

As soon as the group reached the clearing by the Death plants, a group of boys broke off and veered into the part of the forest where smaller animals were found. Ghriz continued with Ghrexad, Khraex, and two more helper boys towards the Rattel tree.

Khraex and Ghrexad squinted trying to look out for the wild animals in the forest. But their eyesight was much weaker with age and they could not spot a thing. The two helper boys settled down on the ground and opened their sacks meaning to stuff the deer that Ghriz would kill.

"The banks of Nakesia seem empty today," Ghrexad said peering through the trees.

"Is there no rikitisi around?" Khraex asked.

Snike! Snike!

Ghriz released two arrows in succession without speaking a word.

"Did you get it?" Khraex asked, standing up in excitement.

"As always," Ghriz said with a smile.

Ghrexad hopped two times and turned round twice.

"Ghriz, I've frozen the good luck," he said enthusiastically. "See if you can get more."

The two boys were getting up to fetch the dead deer when Khraex stopped them.

"Wait a bit," he advised. "Let Ghriz scan the area once more for wild beasts. They could be hiding anywhere."

Ghriz held her head up and looked hard into the wilderness. As soon as the first deer was struck, the rest had dispersed off in different directions. There was no other beast around. But still she checked again.

To her amazement, Ghriz spotted a couple of humans concealed partially behind a thicket. The boy was taking the bosom rings off the girl one by one, following each removal with a deep kiss on the bare skin. The face of the writhing girl was completely hidden, and only the thick curls on the back of the boy's head could be seen. But it was enough for Ghriz to make out who it was. Bhmana. Ghriz craned her neck to catch a glimpse of the girl's face.

"Any leopard around?" the waiting boys asked anxiously.

Ghriz could not reply.

Bhmana was gently sucking the bared nipples while the girl crunched his hair, pulling him closer. It went on for about a minute before the girl sat up for a second and then lowered her face into Bhmana's loins, exploring his erection with her tongue. And in that moment, Ghriz had taken a good look at the girl's face; it belonged to her sister, Jhluk.

Ghriz found herself sitting down suddenly as her heart knotted itself into a tight ball. Ghrexad and Khraex rushed to her immediately.

"What is it?" Ghrexad asked, placing his hand on her head.

Ghriz felt so dazed that she could not give any reaction.

"Are you getting pains of the mother goddess?" Ghrexad asked again.

Ghriz shook her head. She needed a few long moments to steady herself. Eventually, she stood up and took in a deep breath. She scanned another part of the forest and released four arrows.

"Two more rikitisi deer are down," she announced and began to pack her weapons. "You can go and get the deer. There are no beasts around."

The boys clapped their hands and cheered for Ghriz. In response, she simply pointed to the directions in which the three dead deer were to be found. The boys ran off while Ghriz sat down to share a smoke with her father and uncle.

"You're unusually quiet today," Ghrexad mentioned as he released smoke rings into the air.

"She's growing up," Khraex said. "You don't expect her to chatter nonsense like your younger one, Jhluk."

Ghrexad smiled awkwardly. Ghriz's face was still blank.

The boys were back soon with the deer, much to Ghriz's relief. They walked back and met the other members of the hunt-party at the clearing. They had managed to catch two boars. It was a hugely successful hunt and they all went back to the village talking loudly about the festive night waiting ahead.

That evening, the village bustled with merriment. Torches were lit in the village square and people came with fruits to wish the couple seated at the centre. In the coming week, the tribe would build a hut for them to "light a fire together." It meant living formally as a conjugal couple.

At one side, some men and women kept busy with food preparation while another bunch was bringing out kegs of fermented juice and calabash pots to serve the drinks in. The night was still young and everyone celebrated with limitless gusto.

Ghriz sat leaning against the trunk of a tree, trying to be invisible. But she was the one who had brought food for the entire tribe and people kept looking for her. They came up to her with praises, blessings, and an occasional gift. She talked politely to all, but her eyes kept searching for Jhluk and Bhmana. They did not appear for a long time and then Bhmana finally broke into the picture. He went straight to the corner where the kegs were kept, grabbed a painted calabash pot, and poured out a large drink for himself. He drank fast and then he headed towards the area where the younger people took turns to dance. Bhmana cartwheeled into the field, attracting loud hooting from all. And then he went on to dance, exhibiting new moves, much to the delight of the crowd that had gathered.

Ghriz sat in the dark, watching and waiting for Bhmana to come looking for her. But he did not. At some point during the night, a deeply worried Marizh came to Ghriz.

"Jhluk is asleep," she reported to Ghriz. "She took her meal inside and went to sleep on a festive night! Can you believe it, Ghriz?"

Ghriz glared at her mother and turned her face away. Marizh shook her by the shoulders.

"Will you not come inside to take a look?" she urged. "Something is wrong with her."

"Stop it, maella," Ghriz said, pushing away her hands. "Nothing's wrong with her."

"You want Jhluk to die," Marizh said in despair. "Her own seesul wants her to die. Oh, poor Jhluk."

"Yes, I want her to die," Ghriz blurted out in fury. "But nothing happens according to my wish, does it?"

Marizh raised her hands to her lips in a fit of shock and ran back inside. Thankfully, the drumbeats were at their loudest and three girls were singing at the top of their voices so Ghriz was not heard by anyone else. The rest of the night passed in merriment. It was almost morning when people dawdled back to their huts. Ghriz left in the end with the elder ones of the tribe. She wondered when Bhmana would confess to her about his betrayal.

Chapter 5: Tribe Lead is Chosen

Nothing remained the same after Ghriz saw Bhmana breaking the barrier with Jhluk. On one hand, Ghriz's popularity with the village folk grew immensely and on the other hand, her friendship with Bhmana was on the wane. She kept waiting for him to start a conversation. But he never seemed to come close to their hut anymore and methodically stayed out of her way.

Ghriz wondered when Jhluk would talk about the bond she had entered with Bhmana. It was the law of the land to disclose such relations to the elders without any delay. She imagined the moment a hundred times in her head. And every time she pictured Ghrexad and Marizh going wild with joy as soon as Jhluk broke the news to them. It felt intolerable to her. She knew she would have to put up at least a charade of indifference, if not one of joy, and she did not know how she would pull it off. However, neither Jhluk nor Bhmana spoke out about their relationship even as the days rolled on.

Khraex noted that Ghriz was taking her tribe law lessons more seriously than ever. It made him very happy. He thought that attention and respect from the villagers have enthused the girl and he taught her with doubled vigour.

As time went by Ghriz began to doubt her own eyes. Was it really Jhluk and Bhmana that she had seen? She had not spotted Bhmana and Jhluk getting together after that day. So, one afternoon she made up her mind to seek out Bhmana and confront him. Someone needed to clear the air and set things straight. She went out of their hut and walked up to the huge praying stone in the backyard. Sitting on it she prayed to the setting sun and sought his blessings. Ghriz felt a whole lot calmer and was about to step out of the bamboo fence that surrounded their courtyard when she heard a terrible commotion from inside.

She retraced her steps fast and got inside, only to see Ghrexad kneeling on the floor, holding his head between the hands. And Marizh was shouting wildly while beating Jhluk with a broom as she crouched in a corner, sobbing furiously.

"You stupid girl," Marizh yelled. "Bringing shame to the clan."

Ghriz savoured the scene for a few moments before her conscience kicked in. She ran to restrain her mother.

"Bhmana put life in her belly," Marizh screamed in a fit of tearful rage. "And she didn't even tell us!"

Marizh threw away the broom, sat down, and started to howl, beating her chest. Ghriz could not bear to stay there for any longer. Perhaps Ghrexad was expecting some wise words of comfort from her. Perhaps Marizh thought her elder daughter would find out ways to tweak the tribe laws to protect Jhluk. But Ghriz could not bring herself to do any of those things. The minute she heard about Bhmana's baby growing in her sister's womb, she went straight out of the hut and paced all the way to the village square. The place looked bright and busy, being a market day. Ghriz sat down under a tree and watched the multitude of people bustle along. Many saw her sitting there. Nobody ventured a question. They assumed that their future tribe lead liked to keep watch. Some bowed their heads, some nodded and smiled at her, but no one could muster up the courage to talk. Ghriz was glad. She had no wish to engage in conversation.

Ghriz closed her eyes for a second, meaning to focus on her thoughts, but someone shook her by the shoulder immediately.

"Ghriz, are you napping here?" Khraex asked, bending down and looking at her nervously. "Get up quickly. We need to go to the tribe lead now."

Ghriz stood up instantly, ready to follow her uncle. But then it occurred to her why Khraex wanted to go see the tribe lead.

"I'm not going to plead to the tribe lead on behalf of Jhluk," she said, stomping on the ground with vehemence.

"What?" Khraex turned back and scratched his head.

"Don't you know about Jhluk and Bhmana?" Ghriz asked.

"I found out," he nodded. "I had long known Jhluk to be a no-good girl. She got your mother's blood. No, you and I are going to see the tribe lead for a different reason. He sent for us."

"What reason?"

"I don't know, and I'm a little tense," Khraex snapped. "Shall we stand here trying to guess, or shall we walk to his house?"

Ghriz walked without further delay as Khraex led the way. When they reached the residence of the tribe lead, they found Ghrexad waiting outside.

"You came to talk about Jhluk, I presume?" Khraex asked while Ghriz looked away.

Ghrexad nodded.

"Well, you've to let us go inside first," Khraex argued. "Don't ruin the tribe lead's mood."

The housekeeper of the tribe lead came out at this point and ushered the trio inside. Khraex whispered irately into Ghrexad's ears that he was not to pour out his troubles to the tribe lead.

The interior of the tribe lead's house was prettier than the rest of the huts in the village. Due to ventilation holes and stone walls, it was considerably cooler, too. Ghriz looked around in admiration and wondered if this would ever become her own home.

The trio was asked to sit on the floor on a circular, woven mat with a large, round hole in the middle. Then the housekeeper placed a large tray on the hole for the guests to eat from. There was roasted duck flesh, lemon halves, and small heaps of black salt along with three calabash pots filled with sweet concoction.

The tribe lead Ogella entered from the opposite door and sat on the floor facing the guests.

"Please have a small bite before we talk," Ogella requested making a ritualistic circle in air with the little finger of the left hand.

The guests began to eat without any further talk while Ogella kept staring at Ghriz. Once done with eating, they squeezed the lemon halves into their palms and washed their hands in a small pot of water that the housekeeper brought. As they were drying their hands in the jute wad served, the tribe lead spoke up.

"I had imagined you as the one who will light the fire with my Bhmana," Ogella said in a small voice.

Ghriz looked up, startled.

"You and Bhmana would have made a wonderful pair, I always thought," Ogella continued. "But unfortunately, Bhmana could not be worthy of you. Anyway, after what Bhmana and Jhluk have done, I do not have the wish to remain the tribe lead anymore. Tomorrow I will give up my position and you will be christened the new tribe lead. Your dream, your family's dream, will be fulfilled."

Khraex's small eyes shone with joy as he landed a happy thump on Ghrexad's back. Ghrexad could only manage a weak smile. If only Jhluk had not ruined this moment for him.

"Tribe lead, to replace you was never my dream," Ghriz blabbered. "If you command me to light a fire with Bhmana, so I will. He does not have to be with Jhluk."

At this Khraex coughed loudly in an attempt to block out Ghriz's words.

"It's ok Khraex," the tribe lead assured. "I've made my decision. Ghriz's thoughts will not revert that. Tonight, I will take off my armlet of authority and Ghriz will be the one to wear it tomorrow. We have been discussing her eligibility for many weeks now. Everybody respects her and her early ascendance to power will be beneficial to our tribe."

Khraex got up and gave the tribe lead a spontaneous hug.

"Drugadriga, tribe lead," he said with moist eyes.

"It feels good to get your friendship back, Khraex," he replied hugging Khraex back. "From tomorrow, you'll call me Ogella again, like old times."

Ghriz stood up and made long bows to the tribe lead as well as to her father and uncle as a mark of respect.

"I was a bit tense while coming here," Khraex confessed. "Drugadriga, Ogella, if I may call you so from tonight, you've made me very happy."

As he proceeded towards the exit, Ghrexad began to mumble something.

"Tribe lead, about Jhluk," he began as he stood, rubbing his palms together.

"What about her, Ghrexad?" Ogella asked, his voice turning icy cold.

"Can we let Bhmana and Jhluk have a small ceremony of lighting the fire?" he asked. "They have to raise a life soon."

Ogella sighed audibly.

"You know the rules, Ghrexad," he said after a short pause. "The price of secrecy is seclusion. They will be given a plot of land far from the village square and close to the forest line. They can build their own hut and raise the new life there. No communal ceremony for them; it is against the tribe law. You must realise that this pains me as much as it pains you."

Ghrexad nodded his head and joined Khraex and Ghriz, who were waiting at the threshold of the tribe lead's house.

"Pack your belongings tonight, Ghriz," Khraex said as they walked. "You will move into the hut allocated for the tribe lead tomorrow."

"I'm nervous, jupapella," Ghriz replied.

"I will help you in every step," he promised. "To be fair, even I don't think you are ready to be the tribe lead. Ogella gave up his role in a hurry because of the shame Bhmana has brought to him. But you mustn't get complacent. There are so many things to learn."

They almost forgot about Jhluk while walking back home. But on entering the hut, they saw Bhmana crouching by the door with a sorry-looking bundle and Marizh seated by him. Ghriz ignored them and proceeded to her den to pack her belongings.

Ghrexad cleared his voice and began a dramatic speech as Khraex looked on.

"Tomorrow, both my daughters will leave," he boomed. "And think how! One will shine in the hearts of all. And the other will rot in the collective disgust of our tribe. One has brought us pride, the other has brought us shame."

Marizh began to wail. Khraex grimaced. Her cries always made him think of the noise one made while scraping the bottom of an empty meal pot.

Meanwhile, Jhluk sat in her den, insulated from the worries of her family. She was done packing and now she was sitting cross-legged, holding a small stone in her palm.

Ghriz was not the only one with special powers, thought Jhluk. If Ghriz could see far, so could she. If Ghriz saw an extra colour before violet, Jhluk saw one beyond red.

Jhluk knew that the only real advantage Ghriz had over her was the fact that she was born twelve moons earlier. Jhluk had never told anyone about the powers she wielded. There was no glory in being second.

And then one day during her stay at Marizh's parents, Jhluk had come upon a small, inconspicuous stone. Nobody had presented it to her. Nor did she dig it out of anywhere. She had simply woken up one morning with the stone nestled within her fist.

Jhluk remembered the mix of fear and excitement she had felt when she had gripped it properly for the first time. The stone connected her to other beings, five powerful beings, who promised her power over the universe if she could get them what they wanted.

And Jhluk had understood over time that what they were looking for would come into Ghriz's possession, some day, some way.

The small, magical stone bestowed Jhluk with more powers. She would sometimes roll the stone in dust and sprinkle that dust on unsuspecting boys. And each time, they would fall for her.

Jhluk went on to charm Bhmana for a very simple reason. Ghriz loved him madly. And Bhmana loved the convenience of it. If he could not be the tribe lead, he could at least be the tribe lead's man. The powers and comforts were practically the same. To reach Ghriz, Jhluk had to get to

Bhmana first.

The first part of her plan had gone well. Bhmana and Jhluk would now light the fire and raise a new life. But something else happened that she was not ready for. Ever since Jhluk felt another life within her body, she was also struck with another realization. Most of her powers were fading away. She could not see afar, nor distinguish the band in the rainbow beyond red, nor charm a boy using bewitched dust.

For a few days, Jhluk felt like her life no longer had a meaning or purpose. Losing all the powers just for the sake of getting Bhmana was in no way a fair bargain. Then she found out that the small stone was still connecting her to the five power beings. And through that connection they gave her the resolve to work towards her destiny.

"Jhluk, come," Marizh called out, entering the den. Her appearance broke Jhluk out of the trance. Marizh helped her seemingly numb daughter to her feet.

Ghriz would be just the tribe lead, thought Jhluk. But one day, when the time was right, Jhluk would take what she needed from her sister. And then she would be the one to rule the universe. Jhluk stood up and sighed.

Outside the hut, Bhmana was being lectured by Khraex when Jhluk appeared with her mother.

"Bhmana, take her and go to your father.," Khraex ordered. "Ogella will tell you which plot has been allotted to you two. You must go there to begin your new life."

"Good that you two will be gone tonight," Ghrexad remarked. "Tomorrow is an auspicious day. We don't wish to see your faces in the morning. It'd bring us ill luck."

Bhmana and Jhluk started to walk away. A distressed Marizh shouted words of comfort to her daughter in between her sobs. She begged Bhmana to take care of the life growing within Jhluk. Ghriz came out, declared that it was dinner time, and went back in. Marizh wiped off her eyes at the cue and followed her inside.

Khraex began to tell his favourite niece a few stories of valour as Marizh served them dinner. Jhluk and Bhmana's fall from grace did not affect him one bit. In fact, he would have been surprised if they had somehow not got into trouble and managed to lead decent lives.

As Jhluk and Bhmana traced the path to Ogella's house, they heard the crier announce the timing of the ceremony scheduled for the next day. On the same day, they would have to convert a bare stretch of land into a liveable home on their own. Jhluk began to sob at the thought while

Bhmana quickened his pace and dragged her along to Ogella's. The tribe lead received them with a grumpy face and sent them off with perfunctory blessings. He said he was busy with preparations for the tribe lead selection ceremony.

The next day started late for everyone in the village. The ceremony was to begin from sunset and nobody wanted to be worn out by then.

Ghriz took her bath in the afternoon with water warmed in the heat of the sun. As the water touched her skin, she felt like she was receiving the blessings of the sun god. She put on a flouncy jute skirt and wore polished bosom rings made of shells on her chest. A woman had been sent by Ogella who tied Ghriz's hair in a neat bun and painted intricate patterns on her face with red and white sandalwood paste. The lady finished off Ghriz's look by adorning her with ornaments taken out of the chest of the tribe lead. From now on, every possession kept in the name of the tribe lead would belong to Ghriz till she passed the power on to the next chosen one.

About an hour before sunset, some men and women came to escort Ghriz and her family to the tribe lead's house for the ceremony. Ogella welcomed Khraex with a big hug as soon as he saw him enter the compound. He had vacated the place and moved back to his own hut in the previous night, right after sending Bhmana and Jhluk off. He always thought giving up the role of the tribe lead would be very difficult. But standing by his old friend Khraex, waiting for Ghriz to ascend to power, Ogella felt a lot lighter in the heart.

Ghriz was guided by a group of elders to sit on the warm stone slab in the tribe lead's front yard. The dying rays of the sun cast an orange glow on her face and made her look a demigod. As Ogella walked up to her, throngs of villagers witnessing the event, began to cheer for the prosperity of their tribe. He placed both his palms on Ghriz's head and began to chant mantras to pass on the knowledge and wisdom that he had amassed during his stint as the tribe lead. The drummers beat their drums in a low hum and people nodded their heads in rhythm. After a long time when Ogella had finished the ritual, he opened his eyes, took off the heavy armlet of authority, and tied it around Ghriz's left arm. Rows of glass beads shone from the armlet, splitting the last rays of the sun into delightful colours.

The villagers threw up their arms and hooted to celebrate the holy moment. A group of crows glided over Ghriz's head twice and cawed once before retiring towards their nests. And then the sun set.

The evening that followed saw the greatest of all celebrations in the village. There was a grand feast of vegetables, roots, and fruits. Being an auspicious day for the tribe, animal slaughter was forbidden and people gorged on a vegetarian spread. The villagers drank from the kegs, sang songs of glory, told tales of valour and danced in mirth throughout the long, warm night. It would be a new era under the new tribe lead and everyone was hopeful of positive changes.

Far away from the village square, Bhmana and Jhluk sat on a pile of hay sharing a piece of dry bread that Marizh had baked for them. As the sounds of the ceremonies reached their ears, they quietly stretched their bodies and tried to sleep under the open sky. They had absolutely nothing to say to each other on that day.

Chapter 6: The Story of Khraex

Ghriz was too young and inexperienced to be the tribe lead, so it was Khraex who actually made all the key decisions on behalf of her. Additionally, there was a council of village elders consisting of five wise men and five wise women who helped Ghriz to run things.

Khraex regularly reminded Ghriz that the most important job of the tribe lead was to keep people safe from ferocious animals of the forest. She now enjoyed going on hunting trips, bringing down deer and boars that no one else could see. Her troops marvelled at the powers of the tribe lead as they collected the booty. Even five years after Ghriz assumed power, her uncle continued to accompany the hunting party into the forest. And on some days, he would go for a walk with Ghriz alone. On such days, he would tell her a lot about the unwritten rules and ways of their land. Ghriz had curiosity as well as talent and the way she conducted herself showed promises of her being a revolutionary tribe lead in the future.

One day Ghriz and her uncle Khraex were sitting in the clearing inside the forest, just by the Death plant bushes. They shared a smoke and discussed the problems of the swelling waters of Nakesia that seemed to be causing graver floods every year. Then came a point when both fell silent and focused on the high that flooded their senses. Ghriz's thoughts veered to Bhmana. She had seen him a few times with his family. His and Jhluk's child was now a four-year-old boy. Ghriz found herself wondering if he still made love to Jhluk. Did he ever think of Ghriz while losing himself in the warmth of Jhluk's arms?

"Want to know what I am thinking of?" Khraex asked suddenly, breaking the silence.

Ghriz coughed uncomfortably to cover the inappropriateness of her own thoughts.

"In my youth, they all thought that I would go on to be the tribe lead," Khraex said, without waiting for his niece's reply. "You may think of me as your crazy jupapella who talks too much but, in those days, I was very handsome, very sharp and surprisingly reticent."

"I don't think you are crazy," Ghriz quickly clarified.

Khraex smiled, baring all his teeth.

"I know," he said. "But in those days, everybody in the village agreed that

I would make the most capable tribe lead. Even the ones who hated me, hated me because of my abilities.

"Ogella was a great friend of mine back then. He always used to tell me how much he wanted to be like me. I never really understood that deep down he wanted to be the tribe lead. Now, Ogella was not a bad guy. Not like his son Bhmana. Ogella had ambitions. He was a fighter. A little dull in the head, but all in all, he was a decent guy.

"But I didn't really think he was better than me. And I never felt the need to be over-modest. So, whenever he told me that I was the best, I accepted his words happily and simply thanked him. Ogella probably expected me to compliment him back which I never did. This inequality gnawed at his heart and he began to cherish the idea of overtaking me some day.

"Now, you must not imagine your jupapella as a proud man. There is a specific reason for which I knew that I deserved to be the tribe lead. But I will come to that later on. So, when the time to select a new tribe lead came, everybody was expecting me to be the next tribe lead, including Nikkel, who was the tribe lead back then. But to my utter surprise Ogella submitted his nomination too. And then he started a rumour about me intending to light the fire with childhood buddy Shynex. That changed everything.

"In those days there was a tribe law in place that decreed the tribe lead to birth at least one child with a man or woman of their choice. In the past many past tribe leads had been removed from their posts after they failed to be a parent. The law was really stupid according to me as many capable leads had given up their position to lesser men or women just because they had not birthed a child. I used to be very vocal about this unfair practice and promised the villagers to amend the law once I ascended to power.

"Ogella used my words against me and convinced everyone that I wanted to change the law as I knew that Shynex will not be able to give me any children in the future.

"The rumour caught the fancy of the tribe and before I knew, there were scores of people confronting me, asking me about my intentions with Shynex. Poor Shynex was smothered by strange diseases right from her early youth. She was so weak that she could not even walk properly. The rumour affected her badly and she stopped going out of her home altogether. Her parents insisted on her behalf that she and I had not broken the barrier furtively.

"I asserted before the tribe that we did not intend to light a fire. And then Ogella put another twist to the story. He told everyone that I was abandoning the woman I loved because I loved power more. He claimed that no one was going to light the fire with Shynex now that her name was deep in muck. I still stuck to the truth and refused to make her my woman under pressure.

"But I was having sleepless nights. All I had to do was to ignore Ogella's taunts. But then I knew that Shynex's difficult life had been made much harder in the past few weeks. She was now doomed to a lifetime of suffering alone. Nowadays, you see kids like Jhluk breaking the barrier casually. But in those days, we had to be very careful. If one's name got meddled up with someone anyhow, they found it quite impossible to find another partner to light a fire with.

"So, on the day before the scheduled tribe selection, I walked up to Nikkel and withdrew my nomination. And on the very next day I lit the fire with Shynex even though I had not broken the barrier with her. And Ogella went on to be the tribe lead instead of me.

"There were twin ceremonies in the village that night but many were disappointed to see Ogella ascend to power. I was devastated with what had happened. But I tried not to complain. I guess Ogella too felt guilty about what he had done to me because even though I ignored him completely after the incident, he made persistent efforts to keep our friendship alive. Also, the first reform that Ogella did after becoming the tribe lead was to abolish the law mandating the tribe lead to have a child. The law didn't make sense anyway for the children of the tribe lead are barred from getting elected as the next tribe lead.

"Now, you know why I was so desperate to see you as the tribe lead. What had slid right through my fingertips had to be brought back to our clan."

Ghriz listened to the story with wide eyes and when Khraex was done, she inhaled deeply a couple of times, like she had been holding her breath all this time.

"Is that why you detested Bhmana too?" Ghriz asked, after thinking a bit.

"What? No!" Khraex was surprised. "I didn't detest him. I was worried that he might try to light the fire with you. Ogella too wanted you two to be together. But the boy was as greedy as his father. Talentless too. Now that Bhmana is with Jhluk, I no longer have anything against him."

Ghriz opened her mouth twice, meaning to confess her feelings for Bhmana. But she could only manage a few awkward gulps. After a while, she decided to tell Khraex a different secret, an easier one.

"Jupapella, do you like the Death plants?" she began.

"Why would I like them?" Khraex laughed.

"Well, because they don't kill you," Ghriz replied, shrugging her shoulders nonchalantly.

"You know?" Khraex looked around and brought his index finger to his lips. "Well, I guess now you are big enough to know."

"I've known the secret for a long time now," Ghriz said as she began to grind some dried grass for the next round of smoke. "Papella told me."

Khraex eyebrows rose in surprise and stayed like that for a minute.

"I've one favour to ask of you," Khraex said when he could speak again.

"Tell," Ghriz said, while stuffing the crumbled mix into the smoking pot.

"If you ever find someone else in our village who has the holy pardon of the Death plant, do tell me," Khraex said.

"Why do you want to look for another person?" Ghriz asked. "Won't it mean that they should have been the tribe lead? And like Ogella, I have become the tribe lead out of turn?"

"Well, maybe so." Khraex scratched his ears. "But, you are gifted. Not worthless like Ogella. I ask because I have a duty to do. I don't doubt your abilities as the tribe lead."

"It's me," Ghriz said curtly and took a long puff out of the pot.

"No, it's no joke, and there's no hurry," Khraex assured. "Tell me when you find out."

Ghriz got up and walked over to the Death plants. She parted the bushes and took two steps inside. Then, turning back, she gestured at Khraex to follow her.

"Ghriz, no, you've nothing to prove to me," he got up and dashed towards the bushes.

But Ghriz was now running into the bushes, towards the protected span of land deep inside. Khraex followed her fast and soon both of them had reached the circular patch in the middle. Ghriz went to the zuzza tree calmly and refilled a pouch at her waist with some zuzza sap. Khraex looked on, panting at a distance.

"So, it's true," he said when he managed to catch his breath. "You're indeed the one chosen by the Death plants. Why did Ghrexad and you keep this from me for so long?"

Ghriz turned to Khraex sharply.

"Papella knows nothing about it," she said. "I come here alone and collect zuzza sap from this tree."

"Like I collect wild nuts for you," Khraex said, walking up to the wild nut tree.

"This one is my guardian tree. My protector. The zuzza tree must be yours. Every person chosen by the Death plants gets a special tree."

"What's the gift of your tree?" Ghriz asked.

"It helps me to make the best decisions," Khraex said. "And yours?"

Khraex went closer to the zuzza tree to take a better look at it. He kept some distance from it, as if he was afraid to touch.

"It helps me to hunt," Ghriz said in short.

"I see," Khraex said sitting down on the grass. "Well, this makes it easier for me. The Death plants have the tradition of choosing the best one in every generation. This person may or may not be the tribe lead but they will certainly get one responsibility."

He removed a chain from around his neck. A single stone pendant was hanging from it which he held out for Ghriz to see. Khraex, like most other people of his clan, wore an awful lot of beads, jewels, and shells around his neck, so Ghriz had never really taken note of this particular one.

"What is it?" she asked.

'It's a rather precious jewel," Khraex said. "This stone has been passed down from and to the best ones of all generations. Nikkel had called me before his death to present it to me. And now I present it to you. Remember, this stone must not fall into enemy hands. Wear it casually, too casually, so that its presence is overshadowed by other jewels of yours."

Ghriz accepted the chain and observed the chunky pendant carefully. It seemed ordinary.

"It has immense powers," Khraex reiterated, as if reading her thoughts. "If you ever feel that someone is after it, do everything that you can to prevent them from laying their hands on it."

"What kind of powers?" Ghriz asked.

"To be very honest, the powers have not revealed themselves to me," Khraex admitted. "But Nikkel told me that the one who will unlock the true powers of this pendant will go on to preside over the universe."

Ghriz was exploring the texture of the pendant and Khraex used this time to collect some wild nuts from his guardian tree. Then he kneeled in front of the tree, preparing to pray.

"Don't you pray to your guardian tree?" he asked Ghriz who was still busy with the special stone.

"No, I never have," Ghriz replied, shrugging her shoulders.

"Well, you should start now," Khraex said. "How did you find out about the guardian tree anyway?"

"You won't believe me," Ghriz said, proceeding towards the Death plants, meaning to leave the area.

"Try telling me," Khraex said.

"Crows," Ghriz said softly as she went into the bushes.

"Crows taught you to do this?" Khraex yelled, following her.

"Yes," Ghriz shouted back, walking ahead through the leaves.

Khraex wanted to lecture his niece a bit about how it is rude to joke with elders but walking through the Death plant bushes made it difficult to talk. Plus, he had been able to present the powerful stone rightfully to one of his own blood, Ghriz. It made him so content that he found it impossible to get into a bad mood. Neither he nor Ghriz realised how close the enemy was. It was this pendant that Jhluk needed to unlock greater powers.

Chapter 7: New Relations

When Ghriz moved into the hut assigned for the tribe lead, Khraex had moved homes too. There was a row of huts just beyond the tribe lead's home where the ten counsellors lived with their families. Khraex lived in one such hut even though he was not an official counsellor. Nobody objected to this. They knew that Ghriz had a lot to learn from her wise uncle.

One day, Ghriz was resting in the inner room of her hut when the housekeeper announced that Khraex had arrived and was waiting in the outer room to see her. She quickly went out to the external section to meet her jupapella.

"Ghriz," Khraex began as soon as she appeared. "Ghrexad and Marizh have come to see you. They are waiting outside your home."

Ghriz was puzzled by the formal tone.

"Tell the housekeeper to arrange a protocol meal," Khraex continued. "And then you must present yourself for a talk with them."

"Protocol meal with my parents?" Ghriz was sceptical. "Why?"

"They have come with a formal proposal," Khraex explained.

Ghriz grunted and called out to the housekeeper. She told him to fetch the meal while she went out to welcome her parents. Food was served after some time and Ghriz requested her parents to eat. Khraex sat down beside Ghriz while Ghrexad and Marizh ate.

Ghriz watched uncomfortably. This was their traditional way of receiving village folks when they came with an official purpose. She wondered why her parents were taking that route.

At length, when Ghrexad and Marizh were done eating, they smacked their lips audibly to express their appreciation and washed their hands. The housekeeper came in quietly and removed the trays.

"It is our great desire to see you light the fire with a good man," Ghrexad started.

And then he turned to Marizh as if to pass on the baton.

"Break the barrier with Iphizhna." Marizh came to the point straight away.

Then she went on to present an elaborate description of this man named Iphizhna. She took about a third of an hour to list out all the qualities that the man supposedly had and rounded up her speech with the sentence she had begun with, "Break the barrier with Iphizhna."

Ever since Bhmana had betrayed her, Ghriz had never been able to fall in love again. She was now shocked to see her parents selecting a potential partner for her. Ghriz looked helplessly at her uncle.

"You are not like others," Khraex explained, reading her mind. "You can't go out and choose just any boy to light the fire with. You are the tribe lead; you need to light the fire with someone who looks proper beside you. So, your papella and maella have chosen Iphizhna for you."

"I don't even know who Iphizhna is," Ghriz said with a gulp.

"Your maella just told you everything that there is to know about him," Ghrexad retorted with a frown.

"Look Ghriz," Khraex continued in his calm, convincing tone. "This boy is good-looking, polite and he worships you. He is a little younger than you, which is why I think he will obey your commands readily. You don't want a defiant, ambitious man. A strong yet meek guy will suit you the best."

A cloud came over Ghriz. Despite being the tribe lead, she felt like she was the most powerless person in the room.

"Iphizhna will come to see you tomorrow, at daybreak," Khraex stated.

"Were you a part of this, too?" Ghriz asked, her voice sounding like a whimper.

"It is our duty to help you find the right man," Khraex replied, dodging the actual question. "If you don't like Iphizhna, you can try to convince me in the afternoon regarding why he is not a good fit for you."

Ghriz gave a small nod of her head. Nobody in the village has ever successfully convinced Khraex about anything; he always managed to assert his point.

Ghrexad and Marizh got up. Khraex joined them and walked out, discussing random things.

Ghriz sat alone mulling over how to behave with this person, Iphizhna who would present himself in the hope of breaking the barrier with her. Suddenly the whole episode seemed to be very comical to Ghriz, and she laughed. It began as a small giggle, but soon she was laughing uncontrollably. Then, without so much as a warning, Bhmana's face flashed in her mind and she stopped laughing. The images of him making love to Jhluk in the wilderness played in her mind and a long, deep sigh heaved out of Ghriz's broken heart. The housekeeper appeared again and announced that Bhmana was waiting at the tribe lead's door, hoping for a word.

Ghriz stared at her housekeeper, wondering if he was an apparition and then asked him to repeat what he just said. And he dutifully repeated that Bhmana had come to see the tribe lead. Ghriz could not believe the coincidence. Her mind refused to work.

"Bring him in," she said eventually. "And ask our cook to prepare one more meal."

The housekeeper acknowledged the order and went out to show Bhmana in.

"Regards to the tribe lead," Bhmana said with a bow and held out a bunch of bananas towards her.

Ghriz stiffly received the bananas and mumbled a word of thanks. She gestured with her right hand for Bhmana to take a seat. He sat down.

"I don't know where to begin," Bhmana said after a long pause.

"Begin with how your family is doing," Ghriz replied flatly. "That's a good starting point."

"I'm doing ok, Jhluk is good too," he said, scratching his head. "Little Pygix will soon complete sixty moons of age."

"Good to know," Ghriz said.

It felt strange talking to him after almost six years. Ghriz wondered why he appeared at the very moment when she was thinking of him. Bhmana began to speak again.

"Tribe lead, I owe you an explanation," he said. "What happened between Jhluk and me was not something I had full control over. You knew I loved you. You knew it, right?"

Ghriz looked at Bhmana. His eyes were earnest. But her heart sank the moment he said he "loved" her. She knew very well that everything that had happened or could have happened between Bhmana and her was completely in the past. But hearing him actually say it made it even more painful.

"I always thought we'd break the barrier, you and I," Bhmana continued. "But Jhluk tricked me. She is not what she looks like. There is more to her. She just–"

Ghriz cleared her voice making Bhmana stop.

"I don't want to listen to why you chose Jhluk over me," she said simply.

"It's not that," Bhmana began again. "Please let me finish, tribe lead. It took me so many years to gather the courage to come to speak with you."

Ghriz gnashed her teeth and followed it with a huff. Bhmana carried on.

"Jhluk cast a spell on me," Bhmana claimed. "And forced me to break the barrier with her."

"Forced you?" Ghriz said, her lips bent in a half-smile. "And you couldn't resist? Oh, you poor weak boy!"

"Please don't mock me," Bhmana begged.

He got up and came closer to her. He hesitated for a moment and then sat down beside her. Taking Ghriz's hands in his own, he insisted that Jhluk had used sorcery on him.

Ghriz wanted to pull away her hands and say she did not believe him. Instead, streams of hot tears rolled down her cheeks. Bhmana drew her closer and hugged her.

"I'm so sorry," Bhmana apologized. "I truly loved you."

Ghriz cried into Bhmana's chest for several minutes before she found the strength to withdraw herself. Then, she sat apart again and wiped her eyes dry.

"Is this why you came to see me?" she asked in a throaty voice.

"I came to warn you about something else," Bhmana replied. "I heard that you are going to light the fire with Iphizhna."

"Shouldn't I?" Ghriz asked.

"Iphizhna is a decent boy," Bhmana said.

"Then?" Ghriz asked. "Do you want me to stall this whole thing under some pretext? I'm in no hurry to break the barrier. If you ask me to-"

"No, you should break the barrier with Iphizhna," Bhmana said firmly. "I wanted to warn you about something else."

"About what?" Ghriz was puzzled.

"Iphizhna may try to be the tribe lead himself," he whispered.

"How?" Ghriz asked.

"Don't let him put a life in you," warned Bhmana. "Then you'll be busy with the children, making it easier for him to displace you as the tribe lead."

Ghriz's head began to spin as the full weight of Bhmana's words sunk in. She did not know who Iphizhna was. But if she were ever to light the fire with a man, she knew that she would want children.

"Are you sure about this?" Ghriz asked.

"No," Bhmana said as he turned away. "I just had an odd feeling and thought I'd tell you."

"I'm glad that you came," Ghriz said, wrapping her arms around his shoulders from behind.

"Ghriz, I've one more thing to ask for," Bhmana said.

"Ask and it will be yours," Ghriz said, her voice soft and buttery.

"It's difficult for us to live on the village outskirts," Bhmana explained. "Can you allot another plot of land closer to the village square? Pygix is growing up fast and Jhluk now has another life growing within her."

Ghriz jerked away her arms.

"Another life?" she asked.

"Yes," Bhmana replied. "We'll be four soon. We badly need a new home, a proper home."

"You put another life in Jhluk?" Ghriz was outraged. "So, she is still casting spells on you?"

The scenes from the past began to play out in Ghriz's mind. She realised painfully that Jhluk and Bhmana still made love as often as they could.

"Of course, you did," Ghriz rambled on. "You lit the fire with her, you are madly in love with her."

"It's not like that," Bhmana protested.

"Go home, Bhmana," Ghriz almost yelled. "Your land will be allotted."

She called for the housekeeper, who brought a meal for Bhmana. He ate in silence. After he was done, Bhmana lingered for a minute and tried to make further conversation with Ghriz. But she sat with a blank and rigid face. He realised that there was nothing that he could say or do to ease the hurt he had caused.

"Drugadriga, tribe lead," he said and left quickly.

Ghriz filled up the rest of her day with work and kept her thoughts away from everything that her parents, uncle or Bhmana had said. At night when she fell asleep, she had a strange dream about a faceless man calling out to her from the deep waters of Nakesia.

Chapter 8: Iphizhna

When Ghriz woke up the next morning, she decided that she would light the fire with this new boy, Iphizhna, whoever he might be. She sent for the housekeeper and asked him to bring to her some of the jewels from the chest of the tribe lead. The housekeeper served breakfast and vanished for what seemed like a long time. When he was back, he had brought a woman.

"Perhaps the jewels would look too stark in the glaze of morning light," the housekeeper remarked and signalled towards the woman to talk.

"Yes, I'd do something else to bring out your subtle essence," she said in a smooth voice as she set up her workstation at a corner of the hut.

The woman began by rubbing one half of a raw potato all over Ghriz's face. Leaving the starch to work on the skin, she started braiding the tribe lead's dense hair into an exquisite pattern. Once she was done with the hairdo, the woman held an oiled banana leaf over an open flame to collect some soot. She then wiped the starch off Ghriz's face and outlined her eyes with the blackness she had prepared. Dabbing a bit of betel juice, she gave the tribe lead's full lips a lovely hint of red. Finally, she painted intricate motifs on her chin and cheekbones to finish the look.

"You look like the sun, tribe lead," the housekeeper said, with an appreciative smile.

Ghriz smiled shyly.

"Eat with us," she requested the woman who was proceeding to leave after Ghriz paid her time's worth.

"I will eat during the ceremony," she said as she bowed out of the hut.

It was now time for Ghriz to wait for Iphizhna to come. He arrived soon. Since everyone had stressed on his youth, Ghriz had imagined him to be a thin boy of smaller proportions. So, when Iphizhna, with all six feet of height and a wide frame walked in to see Ghriz, she kept gawking for a few moments. He held out a basket of fruits.

"For you, tribe lead," he said in a gruff voice.

Ghriz liked the sound of it very much. Their hands touched briefly when she accepted the basket and the warmth of Iphizhna's hairy hands made something tremble within Ghriz. She looked up at him and he smiled spontaneously. It made Ghriz blush and she broke off the eye contact hastily.

Iphizhna did not sit down. He was looking around as if trying to locate something.

"Is something amiss?" Ghriz asked.

"I'm wondering where we will break the barrier," Iphizhna explained. "Is there no bed?"

Ghriz laughed out at his frankness and walked a few steps closer to Iphizhna.

"Should I have brought a bed?" he asked, alarmed.

Ghriz caught him by the wrist and led him to the inner room. The bed of the tribe lead was placed in the middle of the room. Iphizhna climbed on to it promptly and began to take off the layers of chains and beads hanging around his waist. Ghriz raised her eyebrows in shock and thought she should stop him, but by then he had already yanked off his loincloth. Displaying his huge manhood proudly, he looked at Ghriz, waiting for her to join him.

He looked so innocent and eager that Ghriz felt compelled to step ahead. She sat facing Iphizhna. He was indeed a very handsome man, Ghriz thought to herself as Iphizhna inched ahead, propping himself on his knees. She wondered why she could not make herself want him. Iphizhna cupped her face and breathed heavily. A tiny thread of panic was beginning to take shape within Ghriz, growing every second. She did not know if she would be able to go through this. And then, all of a sudden, she saw Bhmana in front of her, taking her gently in his strong arms, loving every bit of her body with his full, moist lips. The blinding panic turned into passion at the last minute and Ghriz was saved from a scene. The barrier was broken.

That afternoon, the crier announced to the entire village that the tribe lead would light the fire with Iphizhna. The ceremony was scheduled for the very next day. In the early morning of her special day, Ghriz went to the forest with her beau to hunt for the entire tribe. By midday, they were back to the village square with dead deer, rabbits and boars. Iphizhna asked Ghriz to rest in the hut while he offered to help people to prepare food for the celebrations.

"It is my very lucky day to get the tribe lead as my own woman," he declared. "I wish to feed everyone with my own hands."

Ghriz smiled. It felt good to be appreciated by a man. But she somehow could not make herself reciprocate the feeling.

At twilight, Ghriz and Iphizhna sat together on a painted log placed at the village square. An old man came and chanted sacred mantras to send prayers on their behalf to the sun god. Then he sought permission from nature for Ghriz and Iphizhna to light the fire. They bowed to the setting sun and then to the old man who signalled to the villagers that the tribe lead was now officially joined with the man of her choice. It was time for every member of the tribe to come and greet the new couple.

Jhluk was the first person to walk up to them.

"Wish the tribe lead and his man, a life of love and mirth," she said, leaning ahead. "Drugadriga tribe lead, for taking us back into the village."

She held out a wooden box filled with buns that she had baked. Ghriz looked at her sister closely as she took the buns. She had not seen much of her in the last few years. Jhluk looked thinner than ever and her eyes were sunken. Her beauty, once magnificent had faded away with motherhood and seclusion. Her belly was swollen, and Ghriz thought it looked odd against Jhluk's reed-thin body.

Iphizhna thanked Jhluk heartily which helped Ghriz to find her tongue. She smiled and said, "May you have a blessed baby."

It looked like Jhluk had more to say but the impatient villagers were jostling to meet the new couple and so, she had to vacate the place. Everyone brought something for the couple and wished them a wonderful future. Iphizhna was most courteous with everyone and whenever Ghriz found herself at a loss for words, he filled in well for her. Late in the evening Iphizhna walked up to the drinks corner to fetch some refreshment for his woman and himself.

Bhmana had been waiting for this moment all evening. He immediately walked up to Ghriz. He held out a bag containing sugarcane and flowers.

"So, you did break the barrier with him," Bhmana whispered.

Ghriz was about to accept the gift graciously but Bhmana's choice of words surprised her. Her smile vanished and she froze with her fingers placed around the bag. Ghriz looked at Bhmana, trying to figure out his intentions.

"Was Iphizhna any good?" Bhmana asked, unabashed curiosity shining through his eyes.

Ghriz's thoughts were racing in her head, looking for an appropriate reply.

At length she said, "Yes, he was. That's why I am lighting the fire with him."

Bhmana sighed audibly and said, "Have a good life."

Iphizhna was walking back fast, but Bhmana left in a huff and avoided meeting him.

"I'm sorry, I couldn't thank him," Iphizhna said, handing out the food and drinks to Ghriz.

"Don't be sorry," Ghriz murmured absently as she took a sip of the drink.

When everyone had eaten their meal, Ghriz and Iphizhna's families came to bless them. The four parents showered their love on the couple. Khraex congratulated them with all his heart but left for home quickly. He said he was coming down with something. When Ghriz finally went back to her hut with her man later that night, they were both exhausted. Ghriz felt grateful when Iphizhna suggested that they skip sex and go directly to sleep.

Chapter 9: The Rains Come and Khraex Leaves

The new couple woke up the next morning to the sound of heavy rains. The room felt much cooler and the air had a fresh scent in it. Ghriz sat up in bed and stretched her arms lazily. She noticed Iphizhna standing by the window, staring outside. He turned as soon as Ghriz's eyes fell on him.

"Tribe lead," he said earnestly. "Come and look outside. We must do something fast."

There was something in his voice that scared Ghriz. She told Iphizhna to address her by the name as she rushed to look out of the window. The rain-god seemed to have diverted all seven heavenly rivers towards their village. Ghriz rubbed her eyes in the hope of erasing the sight. But of course, that changed nothing. She stared in a mixture of fright and dismay at the sorry village huts that seemed to be floating on a rippled, brown lake.

"The rain god is angry," Iphizhna said as he assessed the overcast sky. "If this continues, the huts on the eastern fringes will collapse. I'll go out and see if I can help those people."

He pulled out his rain-hat made of fan-shaped palm leaves and tied it firmly to his head.

"Wait, I'll go too," Ghriz said.

"No, we need you here," Iphizhna reminded. "You have to think of a way to save the village."

Ghriz gulped and nodded in assent. As soon as Iphizhna left, she ran to the outer room and called out for the housekeeper, who was in an adjoining section of the same hut. He appeared after a while.

"The cooking lady has not come," he said, holding out a big breakfast platter. "I took the liberty of cooking for the tribe lead and his man."

"I will eat my half," Ghriz said. "Please preserve the rest for Iphizhna. He had to leave for urgent work.

"Very well," the housekeeper agreed, placing the tray on the floor.

"Can you also ask jupapella to come have a talk with me?" Ghriz asked.

"I will," the housekeeper promised before going out.

Usually, Ghriz had her morning meeting with the ten counsellors of the village right after breakfast. However, she wanted to talk to Khraex personally once. Not everything was to be shared with everyone.

After eating Ghriz did her hair and washed her face. Then she peeked out of the window once more and stared at the thick downpour for a while. The rains seemed to cloud her senses, too. She began to indulge in idles fantasies about Bhmana instead of working on a plan to avert the impending danger.

It was the sound of Khraex's cough that brought Ghriz back to her senses. She turned sharply to see him hunched up at her threshold.

"Jupapella!" she said, getting up to fetch him. "Did you slip on the mud? I'm sorry I didn't hear you coming in."

"Stop, don't come forward," Khraex said in a raspy voice, raising his left hand, before breaking into a fit of coughs.

He had two blankets wrapped around himself and even though he had worn his oversized rain-hat, the blankets looked quite soaked.

"Talk to me from there," Khraex croaked.

He paused to gasp in a few breaths.

"You're sick, jupapella," Ghriz said, taking a step towards him. "And wet! Allow me to bring you inside to rest."

"No!" Khraex was firm. "That won't be safe. I think I'm suffering from a rare fever. It could be infectious; ask your housekeeper to clean my traces after I leave."

"I'll not let you leave," Ghriz insisted and called out to her housekeeper. He came out promptly.

Khraex glared at them both with bloodshot eyes as another coughing bout seized him hard. There was something in his gaze that scared them both. Ghriz and her housekeeper stood still, waiting for the fit to subside.

"Look for a new village to live in," Khraex said after he could catch his breath. "This one is sinking. If you move north, I believe you will come across a beautiful land where crops will flourish and the Nakesia is tamer. It takes three days and two nights to reach there, so it is not impossible to shift."

He paused and panted for breath.

"What are you saying?" Ghriz exclaimed. "You know the rains give us trouble every year; some years are harder. But that's no reason to leave this village."

The housekeeper kept his head lowered; it did not feel right to be standing there, yet he could not walk away until commanded.

"Ghriz, I just know that this village will drown," Khraex stated. "Find out a way to move the people. I have to leave now, discuss with the counsellors, and make a good plan."

"What about your health, jupapella?" Ghriz asked.

"I can handle it myself," Khraex said with a dimissory wave of his hand.

"What to do about the floods?" Ghriz called out as Khraex got up and turned to leave. "Some people might lose their homes."

"You figure that out, tribe lead," Khraex said, alternating coughs with words. "Certain things you have to manage on your own."

He re-wrapped the blankets tightly around himself, pulled down the rain-hat and stepped out into the water which now reached up to his ankles. Then, he melted into the torrential rains murmuring inscrutable phrases. Although Khraex lived close to Ghriz's hut, as she stared at him walking away, she felt like he was going away on a long journey.

The housekeeper brought his big broom and began to clean away the threshold of the hut where Khraex had been sitting. Ghriz sighed and went into the inner room. The counsellors would come soon and she needed to be ready to receive them.

There was not much to debate over. Everyone unanimously agreed that people living in the weak and old homes of the village had to be moved to guard them against the possibility of getting washed away. Ghriz said that she was thinking of using the stone play hut as a temporary shelter and her suggestion received immediate approval from the counsellors. She thought once about discussing what Khraex had forecasted but decided against it. She could not say something so preposterous without any evidence.

Iphizhna came back home late in the afternoon. The sky was still gloomy and the rains showed no sign of relenting. Iphizhna was completely drenched and looked weary. He had helped ten families and two old men to move to the stone play hut with their beds and belongings. Their houses seemed to be the most vulnerable ones to him.

Ghriz was furious when she heard about it.

"Explain your actions," she commanded her man.

Iphizhna looked into Ghriz's eyes for a while, trying to figure out what it was that made her so angry. But finding no tangible reason, he decided to state a fact instead.

"I'm very hungry," he said.

"Don't change the topic," Ghriz barked. "Did I command you to move anyone?"

"Their roofs were caving in." Iphizhna explained. "The weak mud walls could have given away any moment."

"I had the plan to evacuate those people before disaster struck," she said. "Now you've ruined everything."

She huffed off inside, leaving Iphizhna alone in the outer section. He went to the food tray in the corner and started to eat from it. As he chewed his food, he wondered why Ghriz was so mad at him.

The rains finally subsided at night. Ghriz looked outside. The sky looked starless and dark. She prayed for the sun to come out in the morning as she prepared to sleep. She got into bed with some hope and Iphizhna wordlessly curled in beside her. Though Ghriz was still angry with him, she could not quite snap at him. She just pretended to be asleep. And before she knew, she had fallen asleep. Ghriz dreamt of sunny days and drying grounds and the night passed well.

The tribe lead's dream had no resemblance with reality for in the dead of the night the rain god changed her mind and let her rivers loose again. The row of huts in the eastern fringes of the village could not take it any longer. Half a dozen huts blended into the roaring waters of the Nakesia that night.

A village counsellor came to see Ghriz early in the morning with the news. He said that Iphizhna's foresight had saved many lives. The sky was still dark and he urged Ghriz to make quick plans of shifting more people away from the weaker homes. Ghriz peeped into the inner room; Iphizhna was still asleep. For a brief while she felt guilty about her conduct. As the village counsellor rose to leave, Ghriz promised him that she would have some ideas chalked out before their morning meeting. He nodded briefly, put on his rain hat and waded away towards his place.

Ghriz stared at the grey canopy of falling rains as the departing counsellor seemed to merge into it, but in a while, someone else broke through the rains, coming towards her hut in a frantic manner. It was Khraex's neighbour, Quela.

"Tribe lead," he shouted in desperation. "Your jupapella needs your help. Please come quickly, tribe lead. He might be dying."

For a second, Ghriz felt like her heart would stop. But she steadied herself and went in to grab her rain-hat. Then wrapping a deer hide around her shoulders, she ran out to join Quela. Together, they proceeded as fast as they could towards his hut.

As soon as they appeared at his threshold, Khraex called out in his strictest voice.

"Stop, Ghriz," Khraex said. "Wait outside and ask Quela to leave. I have important things to tell you."

"I'll be in my hut, tribe lead," Quela assured Ghriz. Then, after casting one painful look at Khraex, he walked away to his home.

Ghriz stepped ahead and peered in through Khraex's door.

"The rains are not the real problem," Khraex croaked to Ghriz. "Save your people, and soon the sun will save you."

He sipped some water from a water bag to suppress a rising cough.

"Then you must move all your people to the new land," he said. "I have drawn a map in the corner of my hut for you."

Khraex pointed to the northern corner of his room.

"I don't have much time, so you must come inside only after I'm gone," Khraex said. "Bad times are coming. Awfully bad times. You must protect the pendant I had handed down to you. Someone in the village is after the powers. Do not let them succeed. Protect it if you wish to protect our tribe. That's your first duty as the tribe lead."

"You're going nowhere," Ghriz said as she sobbed. "You will recover soon."

"I'm going away soon," Khraex asserted before breaking into a spell of cough.

"Don't say that jupapella," Ghriz cried. "I can save you."

"Stop behaving like a weakling," Khraex scolded. "It's your time to step up as the tribe lead. I've one last favour to ask from you."

"How can you be so sure?" Ghriz asked, wiping away her tears. "People fall ill all the time; doesn't mean they are going to die."

"Ghriz dear, you and I are not like other people," Khraex said. "When death is close, we can sense it. Our powers are heightened and we can clearly see the misfortunes that are about to come. I now know that we would lose this village. The rains would subside this season but let this deluge serve as a warning. Some sort of calamity would strike our tribe for sure; perhaps it would be the rains that would sink the village in the future. I do not know for sure, but people need to move if they want to live. This much I am sure of. And since I am getting such vivid premonitions, it only means that death is remarkably close, waiting to strike upon me."

Ghriz sat there with her mouth open.

"Close your mouth, tribe lead," Khraex ordered. "I don't want to die with that silly expression of yours stuck in my mind. Now go and fetch an ox from Quela. The strongest one he has."

"The strongest ox?" Ghriz thought Khraex's mind was muddled due to his fever. "What for?"

"I'll get on its back and you will guide it to the Death plants," Khraex said. "I had taught you about this ritual. Don't you recall?"

He sipped some more water and breathed heavily for a couple of times.

"I have to go inside the Death bushes to wait for my time," Khraex explained after getting a grip on himself. "That is the way we, the special ones must go. Now get the ox."

Ghriz felt numb as she trudged over to Quela's hut. She did not have to say anything. One look at her ashen face and Quela brought out his best ox, handing over the reins to the tribe lead. As Ghriz guided the ox to her uncle's hut, she saw that the sky was clearing up and the flood water was creeping away surreptitiously into the deep folds of the earth.

Khraex was already sitting at the threshold of his hut when Ghriz brought the ox. With her help, he mounted the animal. But he felt too weak to sit steady, so he laid himself face down on the ox, held on to it with both his arms and signalled Ghriz to lead the animal. She held it by the left horn and guided it through the muddy waters. People watched their tribe lead take her uncle towards the forest on ox back. The elder ones were not surprised, for they knew about the custom. When the younger people asked about it, they were told that a great man was passing away.

Ghriz and the ox were exhausted by the time they reached the clearing by the Death bushes. Khraex got off the ox and stood straight.

"I'll go inside now," he stated with seeming resurgence. "When you visit the span of land guarded by the Death plants later, I will be gone and a new plant will have taken my place. No matter how much you miss me, don't go inside until the next moon. If you do, it will sully my death."

Khraex began to hobble towards the Death plants with a determined look on his face.

"Don't leave me, jupapella," Ghriz suddenly burst into tears.

Khraex did not look back. Ghriz fell to the ground and began to howl. But her uncle parted the thick bushes and deftly disappeared into them.

Chapter 10: Decisions to Make

After a long time, Ghriz found the strength to go back into the village. She returned the ox to Quela and was walking home from the village square when a loud commotion caught her ears. It was coming from Jhluk and Bhmana's hut. Ghriz quickened her pace and walked towards their place.

The door of the hut was ajar and a crowd of people were shouting angrily in their yard. Jhluk sat at the threshold, hugging her son Pygix and crying.

"Pygix is cursed," Bhmana explained as soon as he saw Ghriz.

He pried open his son's mouth to display his lower jaw. There were two rows of teeth sticking out monstrously from the child's innocent mouth.

"The child is a demon," some villagers opined.

"He has caused the relentless rains," an aged man explained to the tribe lead. "The rain god took the sacrifice of a great man to diminish in severity. The minute I saw our tribe lead taking Khraex to his death, I knew there was foul play involved."

The crowd resumed their demands and ordered Jhluk to give up her demon child.

"Ghriz…tribe lead," Bhmana sobbed. "Let Pygix live. Break an arm or a leg as punishment. But let him live."

The crowd urged Ghriz to not be weak and to order fast execution of the boy. Ghriz looked at Pygix. He looked so scared, clutching hard at his mother. Could he be a demon? She was confused. On one hand, she did not wish to take the life of a small child, but on the other hand she could not allow a demon to feast on the souls of her people. She sighed, wishing her jupapella was there to guide her, and the minute she thought of him, she remembered that Khraex had mentioned nothing about the threat of a demonic child. She looked up, feeling braver.

"I'll adopt the boy myself," Ghriz declared.

"Tribe lead, please don't risk your life," urged an old man. "We already lost your uncle. Don't take in this monster."

This was met with murmurs of support from the crowd.

"I have the powers to neuter the evil in him," Ghriz boomed in a raised voice. "I will turn Pygix into a regular boy."

Everyone fell quiet and Ghriz grabbed Pygix by the hand.

"You can come to see him whenever you want to," Ghriz told Jhluk.

She did not respond. She was looking away, her eyes clouded with dark gloom.

Pygix was too scared to respond to the events.

When Ghriz came home, it was early evening and Iphizhna was lighting the lamps.

"Pygix will stay with us from now on," she stated.

"Jhluk and Bhmana's son?" Iphizhna asked.

"From now on, he is our son," Ghriz answered.

Iphizhna got up and came closer to the boy. Ghriz parted Pygix's mouth to show the double rows of teeth. Iphizhna took a step back. It was the sign of evil, he thought.

"They think he's a demon," Ghriz said.

He stood there scratching his head.

"What are you thinking?" Ghriz asked.

Iphizhna did not wish to defy Ghriz.

"I think we should eat now," Iphizhna said with a shrug of his shoulders.

Ghriz looked closely at Iphizhna but could not read his face. She thought hard as the housekeeper set out a large meal for all three of them.

After dinner Pygix got a bed of his own in the outer room while Ghriz and Iphizhna went inside.

"Tribe lead," Iphizhna began. "I'm sorry that I didn't wait for your orders."

Ghriz smiled and said, "You did the right thing by saving lives."

She thought for a moment and sat Iphizhna down.

"I have important things to say to you," she began.

Ghriz narrated everything that Khraex had told her before disappearing into the Death plants. As she spoke she felt like she would break into tears. But she held herself back, for she did not feel ready to show her weakness to Iphizhna yet.

"I'd help you to move our people to the new land," Iphizhna promised as soon as Ghriz finished her tale.

###

The next village meeting took place at Khraex's hut.

"I know this place," remarked a counsellor after they studied the map Khraex had scratched out.

"What do you think?" Ghriz asked. "Is it feasible?"

"It'd be tough but possible, I think," answered the counsellor.

"Well, we don't have much time," said another counsellor. "It's autumn already."

"Tribe lead, we must pick the strongest men on this mission," advised the first counsellor. "It will be hard work to convert that place into a liveable village."

Over the coming weeks, Ghriz selected twenty men from the village for the new mission. Iphizhna was appointed as the leader of these men and the counsellors trained them for three days. After that, on a bright and sunny morning, Iphizhna left in search of the new lands along with the chosen twenty men. The entire village cheered for them. With the cloud of uncertainty looming large, this expedition seemed like a much-needed silver lining.

Ghriz knew that she had to move the villagers before the next monsoon. Khraex had not told her how their homeland will meet its end, but she had a strong feeling that real disaster would strike the next time when the rain god unleashed her fury.

Around this time Jhluk gave birth to a girl. So, it was only Bhmana who went to the tribe lead's hut to see Pygix. One night, it was rather late and Bhmana was still hanging around in Ghriz's hut. Pygix was fast asleep, yet he did not show any signs of leaving. Oddly, it delighted Ghriz.

"You miss Khraex, a lot, don't you, Ghriz?" Bhmana asked suddenly.

Ghriz could only sigh in response. Her parents were alive, but there was not a day when she did not miss her jupapella.

"He could solve all the problems in a snap," Bhmana said, clicking his fingers.

"Indeed," Ghriz smiled. "I thought you hated him, though."

"I did not hate him; he hated me," Bhmana corrected her and they both laughed.

"He loved you a lot and wanted you to be with a worthy man," Bhmana carried on. "Perhaps he was right in hating me. He knew all along that I wasn't fit for your love."

Ghriz looked away to avoid his eyes. Tears began to well up and she fought hard to not let them fall from her eyes. Bhmana crept forward and patted her back.

"I'm really sorry for everything," he whispered. "You don't know how much it kills me to see you with Iphizhna. But I bear the pain. I've lit the fire. You needed to light the fire, too."

"I feel so alone, Bhmana," Ghriz said as she began to weep.

"I am always with you," Bhmana said.

She sniffled and tried to steady herself.

"You are the bravest one in the village, everyone knows that," Bhmana continued. "Iphizhna is trying to be clever. He is using you to win over the people. The minute you have a child, he would try to assume power."

"But he promised to not get me pregnant," Ghriz protested.

"He will try," Bhmana said. "He is young and full of vigour. Did he ask you even once to go with him in search of the new lands? No! He will make use of this time and try to turn those men against you. Once he gets the support of the strongest ones, convincing the rest will become easier."

Ghriz sat still, shocked at what Bhmana just told her. She wanted to dismiss it as an impossible theory but then she remembered how Iphizhna always insisted on being at the forefront whenever it came to any kind of community work. And it was true that he had not shown even the faintest of inclination to have Ghriz's company when he left in search of new lands.

"What will I do?" she asked Bhmana. Her voice came out as a feeble moan.

"We'll find out a way to defeat him," Bhmana promised, embracing Ghriz.

She breathed in hard, relishing the warmth of Bhmana's arms around her. He pulled up her face and kissed her mouth.

After Bhmana left, Ghriz found herself praying to the sun god for his allegations to be true. She now wanted Iphizhna to be a treacherous man. She knew she would not be able to give herself to him anymore. And she did not wish to cheat on an honest man.

On some nights, Ghriz would stay up late wondering if it would ever be possible for her and Bhmana to renounce Iphizhna and Jhluk. Would their folks allow it? Would Jhluk accept it? How would Iphizhna react? On other nights, she would sleep soundly, dreaming of a happier future with Bhmana. She had not hunted ever since Khraex died. And now slowly she started to neglect most of her duties as a tribe lead. The intoxication of Bhmana's love waylaid her just as her jupapella had once feared.

Iphizhna and the twenty men came back with good news. The new lands appeared to be fertile with the promise of good times. It would require a few years of hard work from the villagers, but they felt that the move will be totally worth it. When Iphizhna did not show any overt signs of rebellion, Ghriz made quick plans to send him away again. She asked him to lay the basic foundation of a few huts and prepare the village for the first lot of migrants. This time she ordered Iphizhna and the twenty men to stay in the new lands until the end of winter.

With Iphizhna gone, Ghriz hoped to spend more time with Bhmana. But Jhluk started to visit sometimes, now that she had recovered from childbirth. Sometimes both Bhmana and Jhluk would come over with the baby. The situation frustrated Ghriz, but Bhmana told her to have patience.

"We'll be together in the new village," he promised. "But not like this. If someone finds out, we'll be ostracized. And I can tell you from experience, it is hell to live like that."

Iphizhna came back with his men at the end of winter. The council decided that the migration would begin as soon as the first colours of spring hit the trees in the village.

Iphizhna told Ghriz that he was thinking of moving people in small batches of twenty instead of moving everyone at once. He said it would be easier to manage things that way.

"So, now you are the tribe lead?" Ghriz asked, her voice icy-cold.

Iphizhna was taken aback.

"Who's the tribe lead?" Ghriz asked sharply.

"You are the tribe lead," Iphiznna said, with a small bow.

"Then, why are you making decisions on how to run the village?" Ghriz demanded.

"I… I thought you… you trusted me with this," Iphizhna fumbled with his words.

"And I shouldn't have," Ghriz said.

"What do you mean?" Iphizhna looked hurt.

"You are trying to turn people against me," Ghriz accused. "You spent months in the new lands trying to form your own band of followers."

"How can you say that?" Iphizhna looked bewildered. "The months were so hard. My body ached all night from the work I did during the day. You think… you think-"

He could not finish his sentence. Iphizhna sat down and looked away. He felt angry. He thought his woman should come ahead and take back her words. But Ghriz sat quietly for a few moments and then retreated into the inner room.

Later that day, Ghriz sat down with the ten advisors to make plans for migration. Ghriz suggested that they should start to lead people to the new lands in small batches. But she did not tell them that it was originally Iphizhna's idea. Everybody loved the plan and things were finalized. Deep down, it angered Ghriz to see how readily the counsellors approved Iphizhna's ideas.

After a week, Iphizhna and the twenty men guided the first batch of people from their village to the new lands. It would be a long and arduous journey. Prior to it, Ghriz and the other village counsellors had tried their best to prepare them to deal with the changes.

Chapter 11: Migration and More

Jhluk was sitting in her hut, trying to rock her baby girl, Rhmin to sleep. When the baby finally fell asleep, Jhluk placed her gently on the mattress and sighed. She looked around cautiously. Bhmana had gone to see Pygix. Ghrexad and Marizh were in their hut. They would come only after Marizh had finished cooking lunch. Jhluk had complete privacy for some time. She rushed to her den and dug out a shabby, wooden box from underneath her collection of colourful beads. Jhluk opened it and took out the small stone.

She sat for long, holding the guiding stone in her palms. As always, she felt the connection with the five power beings getting established. She realised that Ghriz now had in her possession what they were looking for. And Jhluk needed to be very careful in taking it from her, for it could not be taken by force. Ghriz had to give it up wilfully for the ownership to transfer.

The door of the hut was opened at this point. Bhmana came in with his in-laws, all of them talking busily. Jhluk broke the connection with the five beings and quickly hid her stone. Then she rushed out to join her family.

Ghrexad was staring at his sleeping grandchild while Marizh served food.

"Reminds you of baby Jhluk, isn't it?" Marizh asked.

"Nah, Marizh," Bhmana commented as he sat down to eat. "Your grandchildren take after their handsome papella."

"This is why Khraex never liked you," Ghrexad remarked as he sat by his son-in-law. "You never say things we want to hear. In fact, Khraex made sure that Ghriz didn't come to like you!"

Bhmana raised his eyebrows and placed a meatball in his mouth.

"That's a pity," he said.

"Ghriz badly wanted to break the barrier with Bhmana," Jhluk spoke up. "Their friendship was strained since he chose me. It has got nothing to do with jupapella."

"Shut it, Jhluk," Marizh reprimanded.

"Why should I shut up?" Jhluk cried. "Ghriz never really thought about my happiness!"

"Forgive Ghriz," Bhmana urged. "She did give us this hut to live in."

"Listen to your man, Jhluk," Ghrexad advised. "Bhmana is right. It shows that deep down he is a decent fellow."

"Your brother was a good man too," Bhmana responded. "He was ambitious about Ghriz. Guess who I am reminded of as we speak of ambition?"

"Ogella?" Ghrexad guessed.

"No," Bhmana narrowed his eyes and brought his voice down to a hush. "It is Iphizhna."

Ghrexad stopped munching and Marizh bent forward with her eyebrows creased. Bhmana chewed his food confidently as he explained how Iphizhna was a clever man who was turning everyone in his favour and how his eventual aim was to overthrow Ghriz and be the tribe lead himself.

"I say you two move to the new settlement as early as you can," Bhmana said. "We need someone to keep an eye on him."

"What am I going to do?" Jhluk sounded miffed at the suggestion of her parents moving away.

"You'll be here with Rhmin and me," Bhmana told her firmly.

"You are away for long spells," Jhluk accused. "I can't manage the household on my own with Rhmin so small. Don't send maella and papella away."

"I won't go to see Pygix anymore," Bhmana replied. "Don't stop your parents. We need to make sure that someone watches Iphizhna."

"I think we'd better go soon," Ghrexad said, after thinking a bit. "This is for our good only. One wrong man can wipe out an entire tribe; we have to be cautious."

"Then I'll go too," Jhluk declared firmly.

"First the senior generation leaves as per the laws," Bhmana reminded. "You can't go. I told you I'll stay here with you."

"Pygix needs to see at least one of us regularly," Jhluk screamed. "You think we should trust Ghriz fully with him?"

"Ask your seesul," Marizh moaned in her weepy voice. "Beg her, plead with her. She won't refuse; she can grant the special permission for you to come with us. That'd solve it."

The rest of the meal was eaten in silence. Everyone chased their own line of thought as they ate.

###

Iphizhna was gone with the first lot of families. Soon afterwards, Bhmana began to spend most of his evenings at Ghriz's place, sharing dinner with Pygix and Ghriz. One such evening, Ghriz's housekeeper was away and Pygix happened to fall asleep early. Bhmana and Ghriz retired to the inner room and sat down facing each other.

"Feels like old times," Bhmana said.

Ghriz smiled.

She knew she had to say something but could not think of anything. Bhmana went quiet too and looked into Ghriz's eyes. With each passing moment of silence, the air between them grew heavier with tension. Suddenly they fell upon each other, ripping off the clothes and beads that stood in their way. Before they knew, they were making love with untamed ferocity. After waiting out long parched summers, Ghriz finally felt satiated in Bhmana's arms. When they fell asleep curled in each other's arms, she realised that she had never been happier.

Bhmana went home in the wee hours of the morning. He would make up a good excuse to convince Jhluk, he assured Ghriz.

But once the sun was up, Jhluk went to see Ghriz at her residence. Her very sight made Ghriz go stiff with guilt. How was she going to answer her accusations?

"Tribe lead, my dear seesul," Jhluk began. "I hope you are well."

Ghriz swallowed twice and then managed to mumble, "What do you want?"

"Papella and maella want to move to the new settlement," Jhluk said. "They've made up their minds. They'll come soon and inform you of the same."

"I see no problem in that," Ghriz said, slowly regaining composure, for Jhluk seemed to have no clue about what Bhmana had done.

"I want to go with them," Jhluk pleaded. "Please let me go too."

"What?" Ghriz was confused. "If Bhmana and you go now, then you won't be able to see your son till he goes with me in the last batch."

"Bhmana will stay," Jhluk clarified. "I need to leave with our parents. It's so hard to raise an infant alone…"

She covered her face with her hands and started to sniffle. But Ghriz was not listening. Jhluk had just offered to leave without taking Bhmana along. She could not believe her luck.

"I've to think about it," Ghriz said brusquely, so that she did not seem too eager.

"Please, Ghriz," Jhluk begged.

Ghriz pretended to think hard for some time.

"I'll try my best," she said at length. "But I can't guarantee anything. People might think that I am favouring my own blood. So, I need to consult the other counsellors before I decide anything."

Jhluk looked straight into Ghriz's eyes and for a second Ghriz was afraid that her sister would accuse her of stealing her man. But the moment passed and Jhluk smiled.

"You are a wonderful tribe lead," she said. "And a great seesul."

"Go home and start packing," Ghriz replied with a forced smile. "Take a small load; it's a tiresome journey. I'll tell Iphizhna to take good care of you and your baby."

Jhluk caressed the curls on her sleeping son's head a couple of times and then she stood up to leave. Ghriz led her sister to the door and waved her goodbye.

Jhluk walked home, her mind filled with a thousand thoughts. Once home, she began to pack. She took out her guiding stone and hid it in a small pouch that contained Rhmin's toys. Then she put the pouch among her clothes. She felt sure that she was close to victory now.

###

Iphizhna came back on the next day with fifteen men. Five of his men had stayed back to help in building and guarding the new lands. Ghriz and the counsellors met them and discussed everything. It was decided that the men would start off with another batch of families after resting for a couple of days in the village.

Very soon it was time for Ghrexad, Marizh, Jhluk and Rhmin to leave for the new settlement. Ogella too was leaving in the same batch with the family of his youngest son. Ghriz, Bhmana and Pygix came to wave them goodbye.

"Take good care of my seesul," Ghriz instructed Iphizhna. "And even better care of the baby."

Iphizhna promised to do his best. The team of people began to walk steadily towards the village boundaries. Soon they would be out of their home territories, treading over unknown terrains, making way to a completely new place. Some of them flicked away hot tears from their eyes. Others let them stream down steadily and blend into perspiration. Most people in the tribe did not like to make a display of their emotions.

Ghriz and Bhmana began to walk together after the last of the people had disappeared beyond the horizon. Perked on his father's shoulders, Pygix was humming a playful tone.

"Good times," Bhmana said with a wink.

Ghriz stared at his twinkling smile and her heart started to dance. She wondered how she managed to fall in love with Bhmana so many times over. She smiled shyly and broke away eye contact.

Jhluk realised that Iphizhna was the kindest man she had ever seen. He carried Rhmin for most of the journey and made sure that Jhluk and her parents had no trouble in the way. At some point, she even toyed with the idea of charming him for herself. But her powers were lost, so she had to abandon the plan.

By night, they had reached an open field where the men set up a few tents. People rested there for an hour and then they got busy in preparing simple meals over an open flame. After dinner, everyone slept on the camping ground. Only Iphizhna and one other guy stayed up. They were supposed to keep watch for wild animals and dangers till the moon had risen. Then two more men would take over.

Suddenly, Iphizhna heard a muffled voice. Alerted, he began to circle the sleeping people, trying to locate the source of the sound. It was coming from Jhluk's tent. Rhmin was choking on something. Iphizhna picked her up and patted her back. She coughed out a small stone into Iphizhna's hands. He brought it close to his eyes to get a good look. Perhaps it was the sinister darkness of the night or perhaps it was his wild imagination, but the stone seemed to him like alive and evil. He flung it away with all his might and the stone went rolling into thick bushes at a distance.

Iphizhna then helped Rhmin to have some water and then he thumped her back to sleep. Just as he was placing the sleeping child next to her mother, Jhluk turned in her sleep and reached out for Rhmin. The tender touch of her daughter's skin reassured her and she fell back into deep sleep without even opening her eyes.

Two and a half days later the troops reached the new settlement. The homes were half-built and things were chaotic. Jhluk, Ghrexad, and Marizh had to share one hut with two other families. The minute Jhluk could get out of the hut, she dug a deep hole and buried the pouch containing her daughter's toys. She decided to take it out after settling down properly. Jhluk felt clever about using the toys as a cover. Even if anyone found the pouch, they would not want it. And in her complacency, she did not check for the stone.

Iphizhna entered their hut minutes after Jhluk came back. He dropped off some provisions and explained how to make do with less things in the new village. Everyone looked around and sighed. It would take years to convert this place into home.

Back in the village, Ghriz was living the best days of her life. People revered her more than ever for the way she was leading them out of danger. And though Bhmana took care to never spend the night at Ghriz's hut again, he was practically all hers.

For Iphizhna, things were not so rosy. He was constantly flitting between the old village and the new lands, helping the young and the old to shift. He moved his aged parents into the same hut as Ghrexad and Marizh as they had promised to look after them.

There were about three weeks left for the monsoons to come when Iphizhna had migrated all but the last batch of villagers. At this point, Bhmana had to leave for the new settlement too. He loaded all the luggage from his hut into an ox-cart and prepared for his journey. Ghriz looked sullen as she stood watching him.

"I will be back in a week," Bhmana promised taking Ghriz's hands in his own. "To take you with me."

"And what would we do once we are there?" Ghriz asked.

"We'll tell everyone the truth," Bhmana said. "We've hidden our feelings for too long."

"Come back soon," Ghriz cried, almost sounding helpless, as Bhmana began to drive away his cart.

He looked back with a reassuring smile.

Two days after Bhmana had left, Ghriz decided to take Pygix into the forest. There were less than ten people left in the village, and the empty huts looked shrouded in sorrow. Ghriz thought that a rikitisi deer for lunch would help to bring some joy.

Pygix danced along the winding paths as he accompanied his aunt, enjoying his first trip to the forest very much. Ghriz told him little secrets of the wild and they gave much amusement to the boy. She showed him the Death plants and told him how the leaves did not harm Ghriz. Pygix was visibly impressed.

"Now, show me how to hunt, sumaella," Pygix urged.

Ghriz smiled and walked him up to the Rattel tree. She placed him on the branch where Ghrexad used to put her as a child. And then she began to prepare her weapons.

"They say you hunt deer like this," Pygix snapped his fingers.

"Yes, usually I can," Ghriz said, as she placed an arrow against her bow.

Then she looked into the thick forest, trying to locate a rikitisi deer. The view appeared a bit blurred, so Ghriz set down her weapons and rubbed her eyes. She looked into the forest again, but to her surprise, she could not see too far. She blinked hard and splashed water onto them from her water-bag, trying to clear her vision. But no, for some reason she was unable to penetrate deep into the forest. It had never happened before.

Ghriz thought of the wild animals that could be crouching behind the thick foliage, preparing to pounce at any moment. The thought frightened her for the first time, and she quickly grabbed Pygix and set him down.

"Will you not hunt?" he asked.

Ghriz said nothing. She stuffed the weapons back into the sack and took the boy by his hand. And then she began to walk back briskly towards the Death bushes.

"Are we not hunting?" Pygix asked again.

"I remembered something else," Ghriz murmured.

"But I want deer meat for lunch," Pygix complained.

Ghriz turned around and gave him a light smack on the head.

"Be quiet and keep walking," she told him sharply.

Pygix began to wail as Ghriz dragged him along.

"A forest houses many terrors," Ghriz said. "It is no place to cry your lungs out."

Her eyes were scanning the sky for a crow. When she finally saw one, her heart sank. The beak appeared a dull black instead of the usual sparkling zuzza. None of her powers were working. Panic began to shimmy up her guts. Ghriz started to run fast towards the Death plants. She needed to check if they were still forgiving to her. Pygix complained that he could not keep up with the speed, but Ghriz did not pay any attention to him and kept rushing. She panted for a while when they finally reached the clearing at the outer border of the Death plants.

Asking Pygix to sit on a tree root, she stepped ahead. Ghriz broke a leaf of the Death plant and dripped the juice on herself. She held her breath and waited. Will a crippling pain grab her and lead her to the doors of death? A few moments passed in tense excitement. But nothing happened to Ghriz. The Death plants, for some reason, were still as kind to her as before. Ghriz pursed her lips for a few seconds, trying to figure out the reasons behind such strange happenings. And then, without a warning, she dived into the bushes and start to make her way in.

"Sumaella," Pygix screamed. "Don't leave me here alone, sumaella! I'm scared."

But Ghriz was going in fast. Soon she found herself in the hidden span of land. Ghriz stood still and looked around as if searching for someone. She had not been to the place after Khraex had vanished inside to embrace his end. Ghriz walked around for some time, half expecting her jupapella to appear from somewhere. She explored the spaces between the scattered trees, looking carefully into each nook, hoping to see something connected with Khraex. The trees and the shrubs looked unchanged; they stood still, appearing only a little dazed in the summer heat. Then, just when she was about to leave, she stumbled upon a new plant among the trees. It was only as tall as herself and she was sure to have not seen it before.

Ghriz observed carefully, circling the plant in slow steps. Then, she touched a leaf hesitantly. Two silent tear drops rolled out of her eyes as she realised that the plant had grown out of her jupapella's remains. Ghriz crouched on the ground and sobbed. She would never see him ever again. She looked around at all the plants. They were all live tombs of great men and women from her tribe. She felt very small and went on crying.

After a long time, Ghriz thought she felt a light touch. Startled, she looked up. There was a gentle wind blowing and a low branch was brushing softly against her head. A lone leaf fell from the branch and wafted down to rest on her belly. Ghriz picked it up. The leaf looked very strange, almost like a curled-up infant. She recoiled and threw it away. She stood up quickly, meaning to leave, but felt very dizzy. As Ghriz was forced to sit down again, she realised what was wrong with her. Bhmana had put life within her womb.

Horrified, she wrapped her arms around herself trying to steady her shivering body. After a long time, she could get a grip on herself and then she slowly stepped out of the Death bushes. Pygix was seated at the same spot, cupping his head with his small hands. He had stopped crying.

"I was scared, sumaella," he simply said.

"Let's go back," Ghriz said, pulling him up.

"What about the hunt?" he asked.

Ghriz said nothing. Pygix kept asking her questions, one after another, as they walked out of the forest, along the village lanes and made way to the tribe lead's hut. Even as they lunched together on roasted potatoes and nuts served by the housekeeper, Pygix kept questioning her.

But Ghriz ate in stony silence and went inside after instructing the housekeeper to keep Pygix entertained. She stayed in her room for the rest of the day, unable to think properly. When night came, she fell on her bed and thought of Bhmana. Thankfully, sleep came to her fast and paused the train of her unruly thoughts.

Ghriz woke up screaming at daybreak. She found herself soaked in sweat. She rushed to the window and looked out. It was a peaceful sunny morning, nothing like the burning village she was trapped in, a few moments earlier. She drank some water from the jug and wiped her forehead. She could clearly remember every detail that she had seen in her dream. The village was up in flames. But the lanes were empty and the fire was razing down the desolate huts. Ghriz inferred that most of the villagers will be safe by the time the fire breaks out. Everyone but her. As per her dream.

Ghriz reached for the pendant hanging around her neck and grabbed it tight. It felt alive to her. Closing her eyes, she prayed to it. Again, the same scenes from her dreams flashed in front of her eyes. Scared, Ghriz opened her eyes and went to the outer room. Pygix was asleep on his bed. She called out for the housekeeper. He came in quickly and got a shock to see Ghriz's disoriented appearance.

"Tribe lead, is your health all right?" he asked.

"Your family must have left for the new settlement?" Ghriz ignored his question.

"Yes, they have," he answered.

"Good, you will leave today," Ghriz ordered. "As soon as you can."

"Today?" the housekeeper was surprised. "I thought we were leaving after two more weeks. I haven't packed-"

"Stop ranting!" Ghriz raised her voice. "Just run as fast as you can."

Shocked by the sudden outburst, the housekeeper stood still, staring with an open mouth at Ghriz.

"Listen to me very carefully," Ghriz spoke again, her voice softer. "It is not the rains but a fire that will end this village. I saw everything clearly."

The housekeeper still could not say anything.

"Jupapella had warned me that it will all end," she said aloud though she was speaking mostly to herself. "But he couldn't clearly see the end. But I could see it all. It is coming."

The housekeeper scratched his head and wondered if he should make a comment.

"You should go," Ghriz repeated. "I'm saying it for your own good."

"Tribe lead," the housekeeper said. "About ten people are left in the village. I think we should inform everyone and start together."

Ghriz looked at him absently.

"Do whatever you feel is right," she said. "You are a good man, I trust you."

The housekeeper thought for a moment and said, "I will tell others and form a group. Then we'll come here and leave together."

"No, I'll send Pygix to join you," Ghriz said. "Don't wait for me. I have things to do. It is an order."

The housekeeper bowed and left. Ghriz did not even see him leaving. She was lost in her thoughts. Khraex had told her that he could see the future when his end was close. That was the way it happened with them, the gifted ones in the tribe. So, it could mean only one thing. Ghriz's time was up too. A solid block of sorrow seemed to weigh down on her chest, and she found it hard to process her thoughts.

"Sumaella," Pygix called out.

He was standing at the door, peeping in with a puzzled face. Usually, the housekeeper woke him up and helped him with his bath. Then, he was given his breakfast. Today, none of that had happened. So when he woke up on his own, he went to check on his aunt.

Ghriz sighed and got up. She gave Pygix a hasty bath and some bananas to eat. Then, Ghriz packed a bag of victuals while the boy observed her quietly. He had many questions, but he kept silent.

"You've to leave today," Ghriz said, handing him the bag.

Pygix nodded and accepted the bag. He was about to say something when Ghriz pulled him closer and made him sit down. She looked around cautiously before starting to speak.

"Listen to me carefully," she whispered as she took off a chain and placed it around Pygix's neck. "Keep this safe."

"Is it something powerful?" Pygix asked, probing the stone pendant with his fingers.

"I'll explain when you get bigger," she said. "Give it to your papella and say I told him to keep it safe. Now, run off to the village square and join others."

Ghriz had thought it would be hard to make Pygix leave her, but he ran out of the door without any comment or question and went towards the village centre. Ghriz closed her eyes and took a deep breath. She wondered how it would end for her.

At length, she got up and walked to the door to make sure that Pygix was with the rest of the villagers. But she saw that Pygix had stopped under a shady tree on the way and seemed to be talking to someone. Ghriz peered carefully and despite her weakened eyesight, she could make out that it was Bhmana kneeling down by his son. He got up after a while and led his boy into the stone play hut, located to their right.

Immediately, Ghriz felt a surge of strength. She began to run towards them. Perhaps Bhmana would be able to help. On reaching the stone play hut, she paused for a moment to catch her breath. She could hear Bhmana clearly now.

"Are you sure this pendant is the powerful thing we wanted?" Bhmana asked.

"Sumaella said so," Pygix replied.

"She gave it to you just like that?" Bhmana asked.

"Yes," Pygix said. "Are we powerful now?"

"We are," Bhmana confirmed. "You will soon see your papella as the tribe lead."

"Bhmana!" Ghriz burst in.

Bhmana did not waste any time in trying to explain himself. He simply grabbed Pygix and slipped out of the hut.

"Bhmana, wait," Ghriz cried out desperately. "You have put life in me. Come back, please."

Bhmana turned around, his face blank.

"Don't leave me," Ghriz begged. "Please."

She sat down and began to sob. Pygix started to step towards her, but his father restrained him. Bhmana walked in and crouched by Ghriz. He took in a long breath and then, in one swift motion, he jabbed a poisoned thorn into her throat.

"Sorry, Ghriz," Bhmana whispered. "You keep getting in my way. Putting another life in you was Jhluk's idea. She thought you'd never hand over something truly precious to Pygix, who isn't born of you. She was clearly wrong. Now we don't have to wait any longer. Jhluk can resurrect her magical powers with this pendant. And then I will be the tribe lead, like it was supposed to be."

He got up and pulled his son away, who was now screaming at the sight of his sumaella in pain.

"Shut up," Bhmana ordered Pygix. "We have to join the others at the village square."

Ghriz felt extreme pain in her throat and it seemed like her eyes would pop out any second. The thorn had paralyzed her vocal cords and no sound came out of her mouth. She stretched her lips and tried to call for help. Only a faint squeak could be heard. But it was enough to alert the crows sitting on a nearby tree. They flapped towards her and hovered close to the door of the stone play hut for a few seconds. Then, they began to fly towards the village square.

Bhmana and Pygix had almost reached the group assembled at the village square when a crow swooped down and snatched the pendant away from Pygix's neck. The other crows cawed aloud and the entire flock flew away towards the forest.

Bhmana broke into a run and began to follow the crows madly. The villagers called out frantically.

"Stop, a fire has started in the forest," Ghriz's housekeeper shouted. "Tribe lead has cautioned me. We need to leave right away."

A few men sprinted up to Bhmana and brought him back.

"Forget that chain," the housekeeper counselled him. "If you are alive, you can buy ten more."

Bhmana looked back helplessly as the group led him away. Indeed, he could already hear a faint crackling of fire coming from the direction of the forest.

"Where's the tribe lead?" a villager asked.

"She's not at her hut," the housekeeper replied. "I have checked her home. I think the tribe lead is using her special powers in an attempt to curb the fire. Let's start to walk. She wanted me to guide everyone to safety."

So, the last of the villagers started to walk away fast, leaving the village at the mercy of the approaching forest fire.

Ghriz lay alive on the floor of the stone hut. Her blood had dried and clogged the puncture so she was not losing blood anymore. But she felt terrible pain ravaging through her neck and chest. She closed her eyes and thought of her jupapella. He had always been right about Bhmana.

"Ghriz!" She heard a familiar voice.

Opening her eyes, she saw the blurred outline of Iphizhna.

Ghriz pointed feebly to the thorn in her neck. Iphizhna sat down and dislodged the thorn. Ghriz coughed and thick blood began to ooze out of her mouth and the wound.

"I'm dying," she said haltingly.

"Who did this to you?" Iphizhna was outraged. "Tell me…"

The sounds of fire were getting louder.

"Go away, Iphizhna," Ghriz managed to say. "The people need you."

Iphizhna looked towards the forest. The flames were now visible and soon the inferno would engulf everything in its wake. He could already hear the terrible cries of running animals trying to escape the inevitable. Iphizhna cradled Ghriz in his arms and stood up.

"You can't… you can't save me," Ghriz whispered. "Leave me here."

Iphizhna knew he needed to run, but with the numb weight of Ghriz in his arms, he could only manage to trudge ahead slowly. It was getting hotter every minute, and every step he took was harder than the previous one. The flames were racing while Iphizhna slowed down.

After a while, he fell to his knees, dazed in the heat. Ghriz parted her lips, meaning to apologize to Iphizhna, but no sound came out. She locked eyes with him and then she died.

Part 1: Dhruv's story continues

Chapter 2: Dristi bids Goodbye

Dhruv finds himself back in the nook of the universe where he had met Dristi. He blinks hard, expecting everything to melt away like a weird bit of hallucination. But nothing changes and in a moment Dristi takes entry into his field of vision.

"You're still here," Dhruv exclaims, feeling oddly relieved.

"Just as you are," Dristi smiles. "How was it?"

"How was what?" Dhruv asks.

"Do you remember?" Dristi asks, raising one brow just like Meher.

Dhruv ogles at her for a moment and then blushes. She claims to be a goddess, he reminds himself. A literal goddess, not the type he is allowed to drool at.

"What am I supposed to remember?" Dhruv pitches forth his doubt in a fairly stiff voice.

"Your life as Ghriz," she says. "I just let you glimpse over your lifetime as Ghriz, the girl with super-vision."

"That was I?" Dhruv screams in a mini shock. "How can I be a woman?"

Dristi circles him once and shakes her head.

"You are dull in this lifetime," she judges. "I'll explain again. You have been born on this planet several times, and in some of those births you had been blessed with explicit super powers. We, the five senses had entrusted you with certain duties. Sometimes you were a man, sometimes a woman, and sometimes a person of the third gender. The lifetime you just saw was your time as a powerful woman named Ghriz. You had super vision. Basically, we wanted you to protect the holy stone and bring it to us."

"The stone that Bhmana tried to steal?" Dhruv asks in a sudden bout of excitement.

"Yes," Dristi replies. "The crows managed to save it from ill use. But you ended that life in a rather miserable way, failing everyone in some way."

"What happened after Ghriz's death?" Dhruv asks. "Why didn't you show me that?"

Dristi looks bewildered.

"How can you expect to see anything after you die?" she says after a pause. "You died when Ghriz died. Why is this so hard for you to grasp?"

"Oh, I see," Dhruv says quickly. "But at least tell me what happens after she dies."

"You mean what happened after *you* died in that lifetime," Dristi corrects him with a condescending nod of her head.

Dhruv feels like making a face at her but resists. He decides that he would definitely find a way to talk to Meher when he goes to his office next. But first he has to get out of this mess.

"Ok, tell me what happens after *I* die in that life," Dhruv rephrases his demand.

"Iphizhna died soon after Ghriz, engulfed by the forest fires," Dristi says. "In the new settlement, Bhmana rose to power and assumed the title of the new tribe lead. Thankfully he could never lay his hands on the holy stone. And he found out soon that even Jhluk's magic stone was lost. Though they lived rich and powerful, they could never be what they had aspired for.

On the other hand, the spell protecting the tribe was broken since you, as Ghriz, had failed to make it into the area cordoned by the Death plants to give up your life. No more magical people were born into the tribe after your death. The tribe lived on for a few generations, surviving the odds and ills in quite an ordinary manner till the unstoppable onslaught of time wiped them and their memories off from the annals of recorded history."

"What happened to the holy stone eventually?" Dhruv asks.

"It is an ongoing fight between us and them," Dristi says. "We need the stone before they can get it."

"Who are they?"

"They are five in number too," Dristi informs. "The malevolent counterparts of us, the evil ones. If they gain access to the holy stone, they can unleash doom. The sanctity of the Universe will be lost forever and they will wreak havoc everywhere. Nothing will remain the same again."

Dhruv nods along, though he is still pretty confused with everything.

"You fight for us every time," Dristi says. "But you have a propensity to lose so we gift you with generous powers. But you still do not lose the propensity to lose. This has been going on for many lifetimes. And not once did you succeed in your quest."

Dristi looks so gloomy that Dhruv almost begins to hate himself for his inabilities.

"It is time for us to part ways," Dristi speaks again. "Come back here soon. The next sense will be waiting to take you through another lifetime."

With this, the glorious form of Dristi begins to crumble away into white and golden dust. Dhruv has many more questions to ask, but there is no one in front of him anymore. He suddenly feels a metallic touch on his face and notices that his left eye is closed. He is back in the prayer room, holding his right eye against the gaping hole of the gold crown. Dhruv pulls away the crown from his eyes and looks around. Everything seems to be completely normal. However, a glance at his watch shows that several hours have passed. He puts away the crown carefully into the secret chamber of the trunk and locks the prayer room.

As Dhruv comes down the stairs, he feels strange and unsettled. He quickly goes out of the house and locks the gate. There is no way he can spend the night in his parental home now. He books a cab and heads back to the safety of his flat at Cinnamon Residency, the luxury housing complex at Newtown. But Dhruv promises himself that he will be coming back soon.

Chapter 3: A Peep into the Past

Dhruv had married Juthika about six years back. He did it because that seemed to be the fashion back then. His friends were racing to locate and garland the best possible girl or boy. It was like school sports day all over again. Dhruv felt a crippling fear of coming last and knew he had to find a bride soon. He had no proper girlfriend whom he could propose marriage to. So, he went up to his parents and handed to them the most honourable duty of finding him a trophy bride. They were quite elated and managed to scour out a suitable girl from a matrimonial site within a record time of two months. Their find, Juthika, was a conventionally pretty girl with a svelte frame, two large eyes, a small nose and a gorgeous smile. Dhruv was very happy with his parents' efforts. He could have never ensnared the affections of such a girl by himself.

Dhruv realised while holding Juthika's hands during the marriage ceremony that he did not feel any connection with the woman sitting opposite to him. But it was too late to have wedding jitters. He still did look around nervously. Friends and relatives were mirroring back overt smiles of envy. That calmed Dhruv down, and he continued with the ceremony.

His first days with his new wife were not that difficult. It was impossible to not feel lusty for a woman like Juthika. Dhruv tried his best to give her what he considered "excellent performance", but to his utter horror, Juthika giggled in bed while he climaxed. For many days he could not make out if she was laughing at him or with him. And he was too afraid to ask. But Dhruv knew one thing for sure. She was not having orgasms. No woman breaks into laughter while having her moment in bed.

After spending a few more months with Juthika, Dhruv concluded that his wife was a narcissist who issued her laughs like prizes to anyone who tried to please her in any way. Though the realization made him uncomfortable, he was much relieved to find that she had not intended to ridicule him in bed.

Dhruv spent about four years with Juthika. Everyone around him seemed to be gushing about his perfect marriage. Sometimes even Dhruv felt convinced about his own happiness when he looked at the evidence of his perfect life splattered all over social media. But honestly, he felt imprisoned in a marriage that did not quite suit him.

Then, one fine day Dhruv's boss called him to his cabin and asked if he was ok to fly to the US on a business trip. The offer almost made Dhruv's heart jump out of his mouth. Three months of freedom from his domesticated, Indian existence.

That night, when he reached home, he found Juthika rearranging the lamps in their flat. A life coach had given her tips to rejig the energy vibrations at home. She was very dedicated to it. The very idea made Dhruv's guts rile.

"Hey Jui," Dhruv started with a smile. "I got a wonderful opportunity today."

"Hmmm." Juthika seemed to be unmindful.

It made Dhruv lose his confidence a bit.

"I'd be flying to the US soon," he continued. "For three months."

"Oh, my goodness!" Juthika exclaimed, spinning around too fast and dropping the lamps in the process.

None were lit and they fell on the carpet, so there was no damage. She got to her knees and began to collect the lamps. But her face was turned towards Dhruv. The sparkle in her eyes frightened Dhruv.

"I can ask my parents to come and keep you company here," he said quickly. "Or you can ask your parents to come over."

Juthika's eyes went round for a while and then they were normal again. She placed the lamps back on the shelf and stormed out of the room. Dhruv began to think fast. Juthika never started a fight directly. She had a pattern. It started with stormy silence, which had to be stoked by desperate begging to unleash its full fury. And then there would be no way for Dhruv to tame it other than by accepting her terms.

This time, Dhruv decided to not cajole Juthika out of her silence. He wanted to go on this business trip alone, and alone he would go. He went straight into the washroom and took a hot bath to ease away the knots of fatigue that stiffened his body. Then, he wafted into the living room and turned on ESPN. Watching a bunch of sweaty men chase a big ball made him feel so invigorated. That's what all men wanted, bigger balls.

Dhruv poured out a large peg of single malt scotch for himself and tore open a packet of chips. Dimming the lights, he sank into the sofa and took a sip. He felt like a winner already.

Juthika remained silent and sullen through the week, and in the next week her resolve began to weaken. She tried to make eye contact with Dhruv, but he was wary enough to skirt her efforts. On the night before Dhruv was to leave, Juthika spoke out finally. But she had withdrawn her feelings for too long, so the words came out too harsh.

"I hope you never come back," she said to Dhruv.

He looked up, startled and a little hurt. He was immediately structuring a nice reply to pacify his wife, but his old buddy Varun called him just then. Dhruv had to take the call. Varun was the one who would be receiving him in the US. Dhruv talked to him for nearly twenty minutes. Varun sounded excited and his voice rubbed off some of the enthusiasm on Dhruv, too. By the time he disconnected the call, he had forgotten all the kind words that he had thought of saying to his wife.

"Well, if it suits me," he told Juthika cheekily, as he pocketed his phone. "I might as well settle down there."

And he left the room immediately. He was not going to let Juthika storm out every time.

The next day Dhruv flew off to Michigan for his work assignment and within a week Juthika locked their flat and went to Pune to stay with her parents. In the next three months, Dhruv and Juthika spoke only twice. And none made any effort to dislodge the fragments of amassing resentment.

The three months refreshed Dhruv in many ways and when it was time for him to be back home, he was armed with a huge diamond ring to melt his wife's heart. It was time to rejuvenate the marriage, thought Dhruv, as he ensconced himself in the window seat of the aeroplane that would take him home.

Chapter 4 : Going downhill

Dhruv landed in Kolkata, feeling very happy about everything. The air was cool and his heart was full of zest for life. He booked a ride home from the airport and the car sped towards Cinnamon Residency. As soon as they entered through the gates, Dhruv directed the driver to take the right lane and drive up to the fourth tower. He got off when the car stopped, gazed up, and smiled. His home was on the twelfth floor. Juthika must be sitting inside, still upset with Dhruv. He stepped into the elevator, revising his plans of winning over his wife. However, on reaching his flat, he found it to be locked from the outside. There were two big padlocks securing the front door. Dhruv took out his phone and placed a call to Juthika. She had not received his last few calls, but he hoped it would be different this time. It was not. The call got disconnected after a minute of persistent ringing.

Dhruv left his luggage at the doorstep of his home and went down the elevator to the manned kiosk at the bottom. Salim saluted him and gave him a smile.

"Did you return home today, sir?" he asked.

"Yes, just now," Dhruv replied. "Where's Juthika? Did she go out?"

"Juthika madam isn't with you?" Salim said with a put-on expression of shock.

It made Dhruv's blood boil. So, people have been gossiping about his marital strains.

"Where's Juthika?" Dhruv asked again, his voice sterner than he had intended it to be.

It helped a bit to curb Salim's enthusiasm.

"Juthika madam went to Pune about two or two and a half months back," he replied. "That's what she told me. I will fetch the keys to your flat from the vault."

Salim went into the strong room while Dhruv stood there wondering what he should do next. In the handful of phone calls that they had exchanged, Juthika did not mention anything about her going away to Pune. When Salim came back with the bunch of keys, Dhruv almost snatched them from his hands. Then he said a perfunctory thank-you and rushed to his flat.

Entering his empty home after his trip from the US, seemed so eerie to him. Dhruv pictured Juthika at her parents' place, sitting between his in-laws and complaining to them about him. He was already feeling tired and defeated. It was going to be so hard to make up with his wife while she remained in Pune. He knew he had to bring her back. He kept calling Juthika a couple of times every hour, hoping that she would eventually pick up the phone. But no, she ignored him with resolve.

At last, in the evening, Dhruv mustered up the courage to call up his mother-in-law, Smita. She was a little dramatic, but way less scary than his father-in-law, Pramod. Unlike Juthika her mother received the call promptly.

"Dhruv beta," she started in a congenial tone that made him feel hopeful. "Why do you not call more often? We have been so worried."

"Yes mamma," Dhruv mumbled. "Work just ate away all my time. How are you? How is papa?"

He felt guilty to ask about his wife straightaway.

"We're very sad," she got to the point without the need of prodding. "Jui and you are not even trying to fix your marriage. This isn't what we wanted for her."

"Mamma, can I talk to her?" Dhruv requested.

"Yes," Smita asserted and immediately carried the phone to another part of the house where her daughter was.

Dhruv heard her swish through the rooms, her gold bangles jangling, as she called out for Juthika. Then, in a voice that she considered to be hushed enough, Smita urged her daughter to speak to Dhruv. But Juthika made it very clear that she had no wish to waste her time or fine mood by getting into a conversation with someone as worthless as her husband. The more her mother tried to convince her, the harsher grew the expletives that flew out of Juthika's lips. Eventually, Smita gave up and spoke into the phone.

"She's a little tired," Smita lied. "I will tell her to call you later."

Dhruv sighed as he disconnected the call. He knew he would have to go to Pune to bring his wife back. He purchased the flight tickets quickly for the next evening. A round-trip ticket for himself and a one-way ticket for Juthika. It would be a small trip of four days. Feeling good about his benevolence, Dhruv went to bed that night. He would have to visit his own parents at Raukipur early in the morning before he flew to Pune to fix his marriage.

Dhruv's parents were not at all happy when they heard about Juthika's abrupt vanishing act.

"This is unacceptable behaviour," his mother opined. "Your wife behaves like a chameleon. Do you know that she has not called us even for once in the last few months? With you out of the country one would think that the daughter-in-law will try to step up and do her duties."

"Well, to be fair, I didn't call her parents either," Dhruv said, shrugging his shoulders.

"It's not the same," she insisted. "Their daughter has gone to take care of them."

"Leave it, Suprava," Dhruv's father Mrinmoy spoke up. "Our boy doesn't like to hear ill of his in-laws. Don't put him into further discomfiture."

Suprava grumbled and went into the kitchen to get tea while Mrinmoy took off his glasses and rubbed his eyes.

"Baba," Dhruv enquired. "How are you?"

"Worried," he replied. "Your mother and I are worried all the time. Can't believe that we chose that stubborn girl for you."

The rest of the day passed in grim silence. At lunch Dhruv and his parents tried very hard to be cheerful and to talk about the wonderful time he had spent in the US but Juthika's absence at the table loomed large and prevented them from having a truly relaxed disposition. When Dhruv left early for the airport, his parents hugged him and offered their blessings to salvage his marriage.

It was pretty late when Dhruv reached the home of his in-laws in Pune that night. Juthika's father, Pramod, answered the door.

"Why are you here?" he asked with palpable hostility in his voice.

Dhruv always cherished the thought of talking back to his father-in-law, but stage fright got to him every time when such an opportunity presented itself.

"I... I thought I will come down to take Jui home," Dhruv managed to say.

"You want to take her away from us," Pramod observed. "Because we are villains who are keeping her away from her 'real home.' Right?"

"No papa," Dhruv said, looking down and sounding as unconvincing as Johnny, the sugar-stealer.

Dhruv hoped that Pramod would at least budge from the door and let him inside while he chided him with more of his thoughtless remarks. But no, he blocked the entrance with his rather stout frame and placed his hands firmly at the frames on either side, leaving absolutely no room for Dhruv to slip in. Pramod lectured him on how he had failed in his duties while Dhruv stood outside wondering when his mother-in-law will come out to rescue him.

Almost ten minutes passed like this and then, Juthika came out to resolve the matter.

"Papa, don't let him create a scene outside," she told her father. "Ask him to come inside and talk."

Dhruv opened his mouth to say something but closed it on second thoughts. He walked in and sat down on the sofa.

"Why didn't you tell us that you'd be coming?" Juthika questioned him.

"I'm sorry that I hurt you," Dhruv said, without replying to her question. "But you can't stay away from me forever."

"So, you admit that you hurt my daughter," Pramod remarked, sitting down heavily.

"Please papa," Dhruv requested in a meek voice. "Can I talk to her for a minute, alone?"

"Why? So that you can ruin her health? Her happiness?" he blared.

"I didn't ruin anything," Dhruv yelled back. "I went to the US on a business trip. That's all I did. It's neither illegal nor unethical for a man to keep his job."

"You did that to teach me a lesson," Juthika spoke up. "I saw it in your demeanour. You enjoyed it when I suffered."

"Oh, I see, now I understand why you ran away," Dhruv said in a mockery-laced tone. "You had to teach me back my lesson!"

Pramod stood up and huffed. He would have probably thrown his son-in-law out, had Smita not appeared at that very moment.

"Dhruv beta, come in please," she said kindly. "Don't get carried away by the sentimental rant. Malati has served tea and puri for you. Please eat, beta."

She almost yanked Dhruv into the dining hall and made him sit down to a huge meal. Then she ran back to give father and daughter a big scolding. She reminded them that Juthika and Dhruv should work together to find their happiness. Then, she retreated into the dining hall to flatter her son-in-law.

When it was time for the household to retire for the night, Smita took charge again and led Dhruv into her daughter's room. She wished them goodnight and almost locked the door on her way out.

Dhruv smiled to himself and turned. He found Juthika staring at him suspiciously.

"What are you laughing at?" she demanded. "Is my mother funny?"

"Relax," Dhruv said, climbing on the bed and pulling Juthika towards himself. "I was just thinking how much mamma trusts me now. She badly wants me to spend the night with her reluctant daughter!"

Juthika did not reply. But it gave Dhruv some courage. So far, she had been giving bitter retorts only. Silence was an improvement.

He wrapped his arms around Juthika and started to plant soft kisses on her face. She seemed hesitant at first but gave in soon. They undressed each other and went on to have surprisingly good sex that night.

Dhruv noted that his wife did not laugh in bed for the first time. He took it as a good sign and reached for the right pocket of his trousers which were now hanging on the lamp by the bed. Then he slid the ring that he had purchased in the US into Juthika's finger. She had been looking blankly at the wall and the sudden gesture startled her. She sat up and examined the ring for a few seconds and then looked at Dhruv.

"But Dhruv, I have a job here now," she said. "I appreciate your efforts, but I can't go back to Kolkata. I just can't."

She shook her head vehemently, and it seemed to Dhruv that she even shuddered a bit. He thought for a while and wondered what else he could say or do to change her mind.

"I've already purchased the tickets for you and me to fly back," he said after a pause. "My money will be wasted if you don't come."

Juthika glared at him and promptly took off the ring to hand it back.

"Use it to compensate for your monetary loss," she said.

Then she fell back on the bed and retreated into a blanket. Turning to the wall, away from Dhruv, she shut her eyes.

Dhruv wanted to tell her that both the ring and the ticket were bought with his money and hence one cannot pay for the other. But he desisted in the end. He sighed as he lay down and after a few minutes, he was snoring away peacefully, unlike Juthika who feigned indifference for two long hours before finally falling asleep.

After four days, Dhruv went back to Kolkata, alone. He and Juthika decided to try out long distance marriage for a while. With a great deal of intervention from Smita, they promised to work hard on their relationship and parted with smiles.

Dhruv carried on with his life in Kolkata and flew to his wife every alternate month. A few months later, Juthika asked her husband to consider moving to Pune. He told her that with his job and flat in Kolkata, it would be impossible for him to do that. A week after this, Mrinmoy's health began to fail badly. Dhruv promptly shared the news with Juthika, hoping to strengthen his case. He told her that he would love to have his wife by his side, now that his parents needed some help. Juthika declined politely and Dhruv realised that he was quite glad to know that she was not coming back to Kolkata. He had begun to enjoy the company of other girls and there were times when he had almost asked out a girl or two whom he had met at house parties. But he never did eventually; there was always some good friend around to remind him that he was married before he crossed any line.

One night after coming home from a raucous party, Dhruv was lying in his bed, relishing the aftertaste of the evening. Juthika called him at some point and they had an insipid conversation for about five minutes. He had just hung up and was about to sleep when his mother called. Suprava's voice was shaky, and she seemed to be in complete distress. Mrinmoy had suffered a cerebral attack.

Dhruv rushed to the hospital in Raukipur immediately, but Mrinmoy had passed away by the time his son reached. During the sombre moments of the funeral that followed, Dhruv could feel absolutely nothing.

In the following days, Suprava's anguish at her husband's sudden demise troubled Dhruv more than his father's death. He stayed back at Raukipur to offer some support to his mother. When Juthika found out about Mrinmoy's demise, she called her mother-in-law and promised to come down.

"There's no point in coming now," Suprava told her coldly. "He is gone."

Shortly after the call, Dhruv told his wife that he would have to skip his visits to Pune till things seemed to get better at home. Juthika did not press on.

Dhruv went to work from Raukipur for a month, but his workplace was more than two hours away and the irksome commute left him worn out. Suprava noted the change and told her son that she would take diligent care of herself and that Dhruv should move back to his flat in Newtown, which was very close to his office. Dhruv felt relieved to hear his mother's words. He left for Cinnamon Residency the very next day after promising his mother to call her multiple times a day.

Once back in his flat, Dhruv knew what he had to do next. He had to plan his trip to Pune. The very thought made him grimace. Somewhere in the last twelve months of flitting between two cities, he had lost the last shred of affection that he had in his heart for Juthika. Now the marriage had reduced to a rule that he was too afraid to break.

For one week, Dhruv did nothing but retrospect on his marriage. By the end of seven days he had made his decision. He booked his tickets to Pune and informed Juthika that he was coming.

Dhruv waited to be alone in Juthika's room before he said anything.

"I want a divorce, Jui," he said the minute they had some privacy. "I don't see any good future for this marriage. You have been trying, I have been trying, but somehow-"

"I agree," Juthika cut in. "A divorce through mutual consent will be the best thing to do at this juncture."

Dhruv looked at Juthika, a little shocked. Was that sarcasm? Or a deep-seated hurt? But no, Juthika looked stable. There was only peace in her countenance. Dhruv had expected drama and he had come prepared with arguments and retorts. He even felt a little regretful that his rigorous homework will now go down the drain.

"Thank you, Juthika," he said aloud. "I appreciate your understanding."

She nodded.

"I will be leaving tonight," he said. "Please explain to mamma and papa in a way they understand, but please do it after I leave."

"I will," Juthika assured.

She seemed to have something else on her mind.

"Do you wish to tell me something?" Dhruv asked. "If you wish to yell at me, please do so. If you wish to call me names, please do so. I owe you this much."

"No, I don't hold any grudge against you," Juthika confirmed. "Not anymore. It's just that I am pregnant. I didn't want to tell you. But then I thought if you found out from someone else then it could upset you."

"Pregnant? You are having a baby?" Dhruv exclaimed.

"Yes, I am having a baby," Juthika repeated. "This doesn't change anything. We *are* divorcing."

"This changes *everything!*"

Dhruv stood up defiantly.

"Look, I wouldn't anyway want to raise my child around you," Juthika explained, her voice calm as ice. "Please take your freedom and go."

"What do you mean by that?" Dhruv was yelling now. "That you wouldn't want your child to grow up near me?"

"Oh, how I hoped we could skip this bit," Juthika muttered. "You aren't quite an ideal husband and you certainly can't be a good role model to an impressionable mind."

Dhruv kept shouting for a while, but Juthika ignored him. She looked at her phone while he said all kinds of things.

"Look at me when I am talking to you," Dhruv commanded.

"Give me a minute." Juthika was patient.

She scrolled furiously and after a few seconds, she held up the phone for Dhruv to see. There were multiple pictures of him at a strip club in the US. Juthika scrolled past the bunch to show more pictures of him and a couple of other men hanging out at a bar with a few white girls.

"I found out why you were so desperate to fly to the US, alone," Juthika smirked. "Now leave."

"Wait, I did nothing with those girls," Dhruv explained, his suddenly voice calmer. "It was Varun's idea. I swear I did nothing."

Juthika only smirked in response.

"You can't take away my child from me," Dhruv protested. "I didn't break any marital rule, I didn't sleep with anyone."

"I did," Juthika said, caressing her womb. "It's not your baby."

"That's impossible," Dhruv yelled, banging his fist against the wall and instantly regretting it.

"Let's divorce and part ways, peacefully," Juthika stated. "Please…"

She was rubbing her temples now.

"You are saying all these things to hurt me," Dhruv said. "I know. You and I had sex every time I came to Pune. You couldn't have been sleeping with someone else."

"I did it when you were not here," Juthika said, shrugging her shoulders. "Is that so hard to figure out?"

"Is that who you have become, Jui?" Dhruv asked, his voice caustic. "A slut? Is that your new job?"

"Wow! And you still wonder why I don't want you around my baby?" Juthika said with a laugh. "I found someone else whom I can love."

"Basically, you cheated on me," Dhruv said.

"Call it whatever you want to," Juthika replied.

The conversation went back and forth, and Dhruv fluctuated between spells of anger and begging. But nothing could change Juthika's stance. That night, when Dhruv flew back to his flat, he was more confused than he ever had been in life. He only knew that his life would never be the same again.

It was not. In fact, a lot of things changed for Dhruv in the next year. Just before his divorce was finalized, his mother died. Her sudden death was eerily similar to that of his father's and it shook Dhruv from the bottom of his heart. The only consolation for him was that neither of his parents found out about the dissolution of his marriage before they passed away.

Soon afterwards, Juthika gave birth to a beautiful boy. Dhruv still felt that the child was his own and his wife was just making up a boyfriend to get even with him. But there was no point in trying to convince her. Eventually, they went ahead with the divorce and it formally severed Dhruv from Juthika and her son, whom she had named Rudolf.

After this, began Dhruv's life of utter solitude. He felt like some unseen force had cut him free from all the bindings of a normal, mortal life just to make him look for a deeper purpose. But in reality, he struggled to find a strong connection with anything and lived aimlessly for many months. And then, one day, he decided to travel to his parental home at Raukipur where he went on to meet Dristi.

Chapter 5: Back to present times

Dhruv is back to Cinnamon Residency after the strange meeting with Dristi at Raukipur. Salim, the man at the kiosk, is no longer curious and there is no gossip doing rounds about his divorce anymore. Everybody lets go after a point, even the local paparazzi. Dhruv presses the button in the elevator and yawns as it goes up to the twelfth floor. He breathes out wearily as he unlocks the door to get into his home. The huge living room stares back at him. He ignores the random mess lying around and turns the television on. It feels good to hear someone talking. He walks over to the fridge and examines its contents. Luckily, there is leftover chicken curry and good beer. Dhruv sips from the bottle as he reheats the curry. Then he takes out the three rotis that he has bought on his way back home and they remind him of his mother. Suprava never served three portions of anything. She used to make Dhruv eat either two or four portions, as three would supposedly bring ill luck. Little details about his parents, annoying things that bothered him so much when they were alive, have lost their edge. Those very things now give him a pleasant sense of reminiscence. He eats his dinner, pondering over the myriad memories of his mother.

Dhruv tries to sleep right after dinner, but no, his mind stays up and dissects Juthika instead. He imagines her cuddling the baby to sleep and insane jealousy fills his mind. There is no way the boy is not his. She is doing it just to punish him. Dhruv gnashes his teeth as he thinks of the one way left to prove it to her. Paternity test. But he does not wish to walk down that road. It would embitter things too much and seal all doors forever.

Actually, Dhruv is very afraid to take the test. What if Rudolf is proved to be somebody else's child? Such a truth will be truly unbearable.

Dhruv takes out his phone and stalks Juthika's social media handle. They have neither blocked nor unfriended each other. So, Dhruv pries as much as he wants to. There is no evidence of a boyfriend on her profile. It pleases Dhruv. He sets the alarm for early next morning and closes his eyes. He reminds himself that he has to get into a relationship before Juthika. Clinging on to that lone motivation in life, he finally goes to sleep.

The next day, Dhruv is at his workplace before most other people. He walks into the sprawling cafeteria and buys a cup of steaming tea and a slice of warmed cake. Dhruv sits down with his food and stares out of the thick glass sheet that serves as one wall of the cafeteria. The view is excellent from the tenth floor and the bucolic charm of the green acres outside fascinates him. Beyond the office building, there is hardly any sign of city life. Only a group of ugly, concrete towers can be seen huddling together towards the right where a foresighted builder is erecting homes for future buyers. Dhruv wonders idly how much time it would take for city life to encroach the unspoilt lands and throttle the peace out. Suddenly, a faint rustle catches Dhruv's ears and he turns his head around. It is Meher, the HR girl, walking towards him, holding a cup in her left hand and staring at the phone in her right hand. She sits down on the chair opposite to Dhruv and pays a few more moments of attention to the phone, before putting it away. Meher gives out a small sigh, sips from her cup, and finally looks up.

"Oops," she remarks, a little startled to see Dhruv. "Is this your seat? I'm sorry I didn't see."

Dhruv observes that Meher does not immediately get up, but waits for his reply. He likes it.

"My seat? Do we get a seat of our own in the cafeteria now?" he asks in feigned ignorance. "I must have missed your policy update mail."

The joke is lame beyond wits, but Meher still giggles. Dhruv feels very confident. He adores people who are quick to giggle. He smiles back but keeps quiet. He knows that there will be a few moments of silence now, and then it will get really awkward, and that is when Meher will be forced to start a topic.

"You stay late at office often," Meher says after a while, taking the bait. "Is the work pressure too high?"

"So, you have noticed," Dhruv comments as he takes a sip of tea.

Meher's cheeks turn red and she stares, having no words to defend herself.

"Honestly, the pressure isn't that high," Dhruv whispers, leaning ahead. "If I stay back till late, the bosses seem to think that I'm earning my salary's worth. My wife complains a lot about it, though."

"I thought you were divorced," Meher remarks.

She regrets her words as soon as they leave her mouth. She tries to observe Dhruv's reaction, but his countenance is inscrutable.

"I'm glad that you keep track of my life," he says in a diplomatic tone. "Tell me Meher, does everyone gossip about it?"

"It's not like that," she replies quickly. "I'm sorry, really sorry. I shouldn't have said that."

"It's alright," Dhruv smiles. "Actually, I feel good to know that you cared enough to find out about me."

"If it makes you feel a little better, I'd tell you about myself," Meher says, still feeling apologetic.

She puts out her hands on the table in a conciliatory manner. Dhruv wonders if he is supposed to take them in his own as Meher speaks on.

"I just came out of a bitter break-up," Meher states. "So, I understand how troubled you feel."

"Is that so?" Dhruv quips in. "But your Facebook profile claims that you are single for years."

Meher looks stumped.

"Don't be surprised, I obviously stalk you," Dhruv confesses casually. "But most of your information is locked out of reach. So unfair!"

He throws up his arms in mock anguish and Meher laughs.

"I was in a relationship for five years," she elaborates. "We never spoke about it on social media as our families were opposed to it. Last year, he dumped me and married someone else."

Dhruv nods as he crumples the cup in his hands. So, the last year has been hellish for both of them.

"Listen, is it ok if I ask you out?" he says abruptly. "Will you go out with me? Also, are you allowed to go out with me?"

"If you are asking about the HR policy, then there isn't a problem," Meher rattles away in a matter-of-factly tone, though her cheeks look flushed. "Our company only forbids people in a manager-reportee structure from dating."

"Great, then how about going to a movie with me in the coming weekend?" Dhruv looks straight into Meher's eyes.

"That'd be nice," Meher replies with a smile.

Then she glances at her mobile and gives out a little shriek.

"I'm late for the morning meeting. Please take down my number. We'll connect soon."

"You run along," Dhruv tells her. "I'll pull out your number from the company database."

Meher throws away her teacup into the dustbin and hastens out of the cafeteria with one last smile at Dhruv. He feels a strange feeling in his heart after a long time. Someone just sacrificed a few minutes of a scheduled meeting to talk to him; he feels so redeemed.

In the following days of the week, Meher and Dhruv run into each other a couple of times at their workplace. They pick Sunday for their date because there is an office picnic scheduled on Saturday. Though Dhruv knows that he will be skipping the picnic on some pretext, he cannot trust Meher with that information yet.

Soon it is Friday, the end of the workweek. Dhruv decides in the evening that he will not go back to his flat. So, he boards a bus to Raukipur instead. He plans to get into the prayer room and see if he can invoke one of the senses to visit him again. Even as he thinks of the last encounter, it seems like a ludicrous vision, but still he cannot help feeling a little excited. Also, being stationed at Raukipur would make it easier for him to cook up excuses to avoid the office picnic. Thinking of such random things, he drifts off into a nap.

As soon as the bus reaches Dhruv's stoppage, the conductor wakes him up. He deboards clumsily and heads off to his childhood home. Stepping into the house, Dhruv feels that there is some kind of sorcery in the air, like something special is about to happen. He is locking the doors when the lights go off. Dhruv looks around carefully. Perhaps the senses are emboldened by the previous experience and will materialize right into the room. Oddly enough, Dhruv does not feel scared at all. When he used to live in the same house with his parents, any duration of power cut at night would convince him of the presence of supernatural beings all around. He would need the comforting presence of his parents to keep the deadly beings from clawing at him.

But tonight Dhruv feels nothing. With his parents in the other world, he has a strong sense of confidence that they will not allow an unwarranted attack on their dear son. However, neither electricity nor the senses make an appearance even after many minutes have passed. So, Dhruv gets up reluctantly and goes into the small room in the corner where a pair of emergency lights are kept. He hates going into that room.

In the past, a college-going Dhruv had walked into that room while his father was helping his mother to get out of her brassiere. Suprava was facing the door, her sari clumped over her bosom with one hand, while Mrinmoy was unhooking the bra from behind. The scene burnt hard into his mind and Dhruv could never quite block the memory. What hurt him even more was the blatant refusal of his parents to show some overt embarrassment at being caught. Dhruv had retracted his steps, vowing to never enter that sinful room. It was actually arthritic pain that made Suprava take Mrinmoy's help to undress sometimes. This lust-free explanation could have given much peace of mind to Dhruv but then nobody thought it necessary to clarify the matter and he had to live forever with the awkward memory.

Dhruv grunts as he bumps his way into the small room and turns on the switch of the emergency light. It flickers twice and then gives out a steady glow. He sighs and walks out with the light when his phone rings.

It is Verma, his boss from office.

"Can you get three bottles of beer?" he asks as soon as Dhruv takes the call.

"Now?"

"Not now, silly!" Verma snorts. "Tomorrow."

"But I'm away," Dhruv says, scratching his head.

"Away as in? Away from your desk?"

Away from your clutches, Dhruv thinks angrily, but he cannot say that aloud.

"I came to my parental home at Raukipur for the weekend," he says flatly.

"But your parents are de-" Verma checks himself at the last moment.

"Yes, my parents are dead," Dhruv confirms. "But I am still allowed to come here."

"Yeah, of course," Verma coughs to brush away his uneasiness. "So, you are coming to the picnic tomorrow from Raukipur. Won't that be rather inconvenient?"

"You don't understand," Dhruv talks back tersely. "I'm not coming."

"What do you mean by you are not coming?" Verma raises his voice. "It is the mandatory annual picnic. Top management will be monitoring this. You can't just choose to not come."

Dhruv grits his teeth to restrain the expletives that try to fly out.

"Come a little late," Verma softens his tone after a pause. "But do come and bring those beers."

"I'll try," he says.

"Fine, goodnight," Verma says.

"Goodnight," Dhruv replies, and allows Verma the pleasure of ending the call.

And then he curses aloud. The lights come back. It cheers Dhruv up a bit. He decides to go up to the prayer room. As he climbs up the stairs, the prospect of adventure freshens his mind.

Dhruv opens the door of the prayer room and looks around once. Nothing has changed since his last visit. He takes the crown out from the trunk and holds it carefully for a few seconds. Dhruv brings it close to his face and latches his right eye to the gaping hole in the middle. Nothing happens. He shakes it a couple of times and tries again. But the enchantment seems to have faded off. Alone in the prayer room, Dhruv feels frustrated and let down by the senses.

He sits down on the floor and prays sincerely to the senses, imploring them to appear in front of him. Then he tries again with the crown. But it still refuses to take him to the other realm. Dhruv sighs and places the crown on the floor beside himself. He wonders if he had imagined the entire conversation with Dristi. The very idea scares him. Is he losing his mind? Perhaps he needs to socialize a bit with the jerks from his workplace; it can help to prevent his mind from disintegrating. He must go out to buy the beers that Verma was asking for.

Dhruv picks up the crown to place it back in the jewellery box. He brings it close to his face one last time and places his left eye next to the hole. It fits around his left eye instantly and he shifts into the dark world inside. Dhruv smiles happily as the clusters and galaxies of the universe begin to appear everywhere. So, the crown needs him to alternate between his eyes. Dhruv makes a mental note of it.

He wanders around a bit in the nook, waiting for Dristi to appear. Only a little patch of platform is visible under his feet and he has no wish to venture to its edges, lest he falls off. As he cranes his neck trying to figure out where the platform ends, he hears a familiar voice from behind.

"Is it me that you seek?"

It is not the voice that he has been expecting. Dhruv starts a bit and swivels around to face Verma. He figures out almost immediately that it must be another sense who happens to look like his boss.

"Good that you turned," the man says. "We are facing each other now."

"Where's Dristi?" Dhruv asks, his eyes searching around desperately.

"Dristi?"

"Where's she?"

"She's everywhere," the man answers.

"But I can't see," Dhruv says. "Help me to see."

"Can't you see anymore?" the man sounds concerned. "How did you go blind?"

"I can see very well," Dhruv clarifies. "But I can't see Dristi."

"That's because it is my turn," the man says.

"Who are you?" Dhruv asks, his voice revealing his disappointment. "Will it be just you and me tonight?'

"I'm Sparsha," the man answers. "And yes, it'll be just you and me."

Dhruv shakes his head, feeling quite bewildered.

"Why could you not take on the face of someone I like?" he asks resentfully. "Why did you have to look like Verma?"

"Well, that's your fault," Sparsha says. "You should have come in thinking of someone you prefer. I just chose the image I found at the top of your consciousness."

"Damn it," Dhruv swears. "This witchery is terrible. You are the touch sense, I presume?"

"You presume correctly," Sparsha nods.

"What do you actually look like?" Dhruv asks. "You, Dristi, and the other senses?"

"It's not for you to see," he says after a while. "Or grasp."

"I don't quite understand," Dhruv says, looking around for a seat.

Sparsha snaps his fingers and creates a chair for him instantly.

"Thanks," Dhruv says sitting down. "I appreciate your thoughtfulness, but can't help hating your pretentious manners. Explain to me what I don't understand. And please use plain language."

"Think of us as gods," Sparsha begins. "Which god do you believe in?"

"None," Dhruv says. "I'm an atheist."

Sparsha just stares.

"On papers, I'm a Hindu," Dhruv continues. "But you remind me of no god, despite the presence of so many gods in my repository. You and your pretty friend Dristi are more like counterfeit copies."

"We don't want you to worship us," Sparsha clarifies. "But if you imagine your gods to be the ones who design your world and life, then we are the true gods."

"Like how?" Dhruv probes.

"Consider the tool you are sitting on," Sparsha says. "I make your buttocks feel the spongy comfort of a seat while Dristi makes you see a chair. And there, you have a chair for yourself. Whatever you perceive around yourself is through us, the five senses. If we lie to you, you will perceive a world different from the one you are in. Like you are in the prayer room now but you feel like you are in this surreal place, talking to me."

"Are you lying to me all the time?" Dhruv feels very suspicious suddenly.

"No," Sparsha says. "We don't intend to. But the evil group does. That's why we are asking you to help us to find a particular stone. If the evil ones find it first, they can use the holy stone to lie to every living being and change everything."

Dhruv feels a little dizzy on hearing the explanation, so he waits for Sparsha to speak. But he does not add anything else.

"Who is the most powerful sense?" Dhruv asks at last.

"None," Sparsha informs. "We work together."

"Yeah, officially you do," Dhruv says. "But who makes the decisions? Surely, Dristi is more important than you, Sparsha."

"You are trying to incite the base human emotion of envy," Sparsha observes. "But we lack the ability to feel it. While we have a hand in creating the emotions, we lack the ability to feel them."

"So, there has never been a fight about supremacy?" Dhruv wonders. "No kidding?"

"Let me explain," Sparsha says. "If I direct your skin to feel a rose and Dristi directs your eyes to see a lion, do you think it will work?"

"Nope," Dhruv nods his head. "So, the five of you never disagree?"

"Though we don't disagree, sometimes one of us might decide to take away a power from someone," Sparsha says. "And then deaf, mute, blind people are born."

"How rude," Dhruv huffs.

"You have also experienced something of this sort," Sparsha discloses. "When one of us withdraws their blessing from a soul, another sense may take pity and try to compensate for the loss. I did this for you once."

"You helped me?" Dhruv asks, raising his eyebrows. "Or withdrew the blessings?"

"Dristi was the one who took away her blessings," Sparsha clarifies. "So, I had doubled my blessings to help you. You were completely blind in that lifetime."

"Another lifetime?" Dhruv is quite shocked.

"Yes, a rather troubled one," he says. "But don't worry about that. You have already lived through it."

"Shall I get a glimpse through it too?" Dhruv asks.

"Of course," Sparsha confirms. "Why else would I be here talking to you? Take a good look at the times you have lived through. All these memories are necessary for you to figure out your work in your current lifetime."

With these words, Sparsha conjures up a light at the tip of his ring finger and touches Dhruv in between the eyes. Everything in front of Dhruv begins to melt down to give way to idyllic mountains from a faraway place. It is a place that is completely unknown to him, yet Dhruv knows that he has been there. He has lived there in another body, at another time.

Part 3: Story of Mong

Chapter 1: The Situation

A flock of undulating hills and valleys made up the beautiful kingdom of Krai Tang. The capital city was located on a high plateau at the centre, while the rest of the villages surrounded it in concentric circles. Beyond the kingdom, the formidable Niyoshi mountain range stood guard, shielding Krai Tang from the hostile provinces of the south.

Mong was born in a village that lay along the eastern fringes of the kingdom. At eighteen years of age, she was blessed with exquisite beauty, but her own eyes were sightless. The villagers rued about it every other day. They were convinced that blindness was the only thing that stood in Mong's way of finding herself a rich husband from the capital.

On a certain cloudy afternoon, Mong was climbing down the green sloping path that started from her backyard to get to a sweet berry bush. An uproar broke out at some distance away from her.

"Is everything alright?" she wondered aloud as she heard the sound of people labouring up the rocky hillock located to her right. She, too, wanted to find out what was going on, but she would not be able to reach the place by herself. She would need to go further down to even grounds at the market square from where multiple lanes scattered off into different directions. Some paths went up while some went down. It was impossible for Mong to pick the correct path without guidance.

So, she stood there, turning her face towards the clamour, hoping for someone to see her and offer help.

An hour ago, king Fa Ren Sung had come for an excursion in this sleepy village. But just as he was exploring the meadows atop the rocky hillock, a mountain snake had fanged him at the left ankle. The king's men had promptly avenged the crime with their swords, and the errant snake bled to death before it could even attempt to slither away.

King Fa Ren Sung was taken quickly to a clearing away from the tall grass. The king's lean and strong body looked limp as his men helped him to lie down on the ground. His shoulder length black hair fell away from the angular face, making a beautiful frame. A thin moustache on his upper lip helped to offset the touch of femininity in his curved, red lips.

Within minutes, Fa Ren Sung passed out and the experienced ones in his entourage knew that they did not have much time in hand. Commander in chief, Han ordered the team to tie a tourniquet just below the king's knee to prevent the snake venom from spreading upwards. Then he initiated a discussion with officers Wei and Krin Ki. All three men were well-experienced in sorting out knotty situations in the capital, but this odd village fiasco had them at a loss.

A group of children were playing a game of rolling rods nearby when they noticed the distinguished men huddling around someone on the ground. They came running to find out what had happened. The children were young, so young that they forgot to bow in front of the king. They just stared with unabashed curiosity.

"Grave snake bite," Krin Ki informed the children.

Wei nodded his head in agreement. Han, who never talked to commoners, cleared his voice and looked sternly at Wei and Krin Ki. That was not the way for a royal servant to address an issue.

"Master of our holy land, the great king Fa Ren Sung, has been bitten by an abominable serpent," Han whispered into Wei's ears. "We need quick action to prevent his passage to the high skies."

Wei repeated the sentence twice in his mind and then said it out aloud to the group of kids.

The children froze in shock and their eyes doubled in size. They began to clamber down the slope to their respective homes to fetch the adults. Woihong, who was one of the bigger kids, spotted her friend Mong, standing by the sweet berry bush, staring vacantly in her direction. She cupped her hands around her mouth to call out to her.

"Mong, it's Woihong here," the girl cried out. "We might need you at the rocky hillock. Will you be able to come up with me?"

"Oh, how can I ever thank you, Woihong," Mong replied gratefully. "I was just thinking if someone would be kind enough to guide me along."

"Stay there," Woihong shouted back. "I'm coming to get you."

She ran all the way down to the market square and up the green slope to reach Mong. Woihong took her by the hand and together the two friends went down first. Then, they scrambled up to the top of the rocky hillock as fast as they could.

Fa Ren Sung was getting paler fast and by the time the girls reached him, there were some flies buzzing at the bile around his lips. The king's men were working hard to shoo them away. Blue and purple patches were blooming all over the king's fair skin and he was waking up every now and then, only to vomit and pass out from the strain.

"Our beloved king Fa Ren Sung is lying in front of us," Woihong told Mong. "He is in great danger."

"Fa Ren Sung?" Mong asked in disbelief. "His highness has laid his foot in our village?"

"And he'd ascend to the high skies soon," Woihong said earnestly. "Please help him, Mong. Please…"

Krin Ki was trying to squeeze the venom out from Fa Ren Sung's leg while Han and Wei issued various errands to the rest of the king's men. They diligently went looking for the remedial measures suggested by the commander and his officer. But, they could not find much around and whatever little they did manage to find seemed to have no alleviatory effect on the king.

Mong could sense the aura of royal presence in front of her. She took a few steps ahead and deftly broke through the barricade of men to reach the king. She seated herself beside Krin Ki who was mildly annoyed by the sudden intrusion. The burgundy pant of Fa Ren Sung was folded up to his knees, revealing his fair left leg. It looked weak and blotchy with two deep red puncture wounds at the ankle.

Mong could not see any of this. But as she stretched out her hands and laid them on the king's ankle, a hush of whispers rose among the royal entourage.

Woihong cupped her hands together, closed her eyes and murmured a fervent prayer, into the hollow of her palms for the success of her friend.

Will Mong be able to save the king? Will this end the secrecy around Mong's powers?

Chapter 2: The Story of Mong

Mong was born to her parents after seven boys. Her parents had longed for an eighth boy to grace their family and were quite dismayed to get a girl instead. Many curious neighbours bundled into their small hut to take a peek at the new baby. Some consoled Mong's mother, while some said she was being greedy to desire one more boy. But everyone agreed to one thing; Mong was the prettiest thing that they had ever seen. Her parents were so depressed by then that even superlatives failed to bring any solace to their broken hearts.

They sat in silence, side by side, when their boys and the baby had fallen asleep.

"Maybe next year the spirits will be kinder to us," Chow Hee, Mong's father, said.

"We can't have any more children," Sui Hee, the mother, shook her head. "Soothsayer Zing Zin forbade me to give birth after I turn thirty-five."

Chow Hee rubbed his eyes with his small, calloused hands and nodded in agreement. They would have to come to terms with the ignominy of falling short by just one to reach the magic number of eight boys. He lay down on his bed and closed his eyes, trying to sleep. But dark thoughts kept troubling him.

"Do visit Zing Zin tomorrow morning," Sui Hee advised, as she blew out the lantern and crept into her maternity bed.

Their tradition needed her to sleep on a separate bed with her new-born until six months had passed since the baby's birth.

That night Chow Hee dreamt of soothsayer Zing Zin brewing a potion with strange herbs to set things right. As night gave way to morning, he woke up feeling fresh and hopeful.

He started for the bare hillock in the north, where Zing Zin lived in a big brown tent with vibrant motifs painted on. The soothsayer was in a cheerful mood when Chow Hee presented himself at the flap door of the tent. He welcomed Chow Hee inside and offered him a pot of hot tea along with a plate of thin crackers. After listening to the gist of his client's troubles, Zing Zin disappeared into the inner chamber of the tent, leaving Chow Hee alone for a while. Soon, a sharp smell of burnt flowers filled the tent. Zing Zin was incinerating some blossoms to ward off evil spirits before offering any counsel.

The soothsayer came out with a limestone stick and pointed to a yellow cushion placed by a heavy stone slab. Chow Hee instantly shifted to the new seat while Zing Zin sat opposite to him. He began to scratch out numbers and symbols on the stone slab.

"Sui Hee has already stepped into her thirty-fifth year," Zing Zin gave out a mini shriek.

"No, she will complete thirty-five years this autumn," Chow Hee clarified.

"You count the ongoing year, not the completed year," Zing Zin corrected him in a raised voice. "Why did she have the child?"

Zing Zin's face was creased into a severe scowl.

"Will it be alright?" Chow Hee asked in a meek voice.

"Give me the exact birth details of your baby," Zing Zin said.

Chow Hee scratched out the date, and time on the slab as Zing Zin watched.

"I will need to calculate the sky map for her," he informed. "Come back in seven days. Your girl was born in a very crafty period of time. Does not forebode well, not at all well!"

Zing Zin stood up and pulled Chow Hee up to his feet. Then, he pushed him out of the tent so abruptly that Chow Hee had to reinvite himself back in to put the coins into the payment box. After that Zing Zin shoved him out again and zipped up the flap door.

Chow Hee went home and told Sui Hee everything. There was nothing they could do but wait. Seven days passed. On the eighth day, Chow Hee woke up early. He meant to leave without bothering Sui Hee for breakfast, who had been up all night attending to a wailing Mong. Chow Hee grabbed his shawl and pouch of coins. Just as he was about to unbolt the front door, someone knocked hard on it from the other side. As soon as Chow Hee removed the bolt, the door was pushed open and in came the soothsayer, Zing Zin.

"Sheer doom!!!" he announced. "The girl is slated to bring sheer doom upon all of us."

Zing Zin was dressed in a black and green layered dress that flapped about him as he paced up and down the room. Sui Hee sprang up in her bed, hearing his voice.

"Did I not forbid you to give birth this year?" Zing Zin admonished as he took a threatening step towards Sui Hee.

Chow Hee ran to the corner of the room and dragged out the most expensive cushion seat that they had. He spread it respectfully on the floor and waited for Zing Zin to sit down. Meanwhile, Sui Hee hobbled into the kitchen and put her kettle on the firewood-oven to make some tea.

"She is a witch who has dark powers," Zing Zin elucidated as he sat down with a huff. "The Moon god, who protects this world and its dwellers from the gloom of the shadows, is fallen in her sky map. She will never be able to see things as we do."

Sui Hee ran to Mong who was still asleep. She gently caressed the fuzzy patch on her head and examined her face. Her eyes were lined by thick lashes but the gaze always seemed to be vacant. Was it possible that those pretty eyes were not functional?

Zing Zin stayed on and drank two and half cups of tea. He counselled the Hee couple to have Mong locked up in the house or to be given away to a man of high birth who might be able to tame her evil powers.

"Why would a noble man agree to accept a village girl from a lowly family?" Chow Hee wondered aloud.

Zing Zin knew no answer to it, so he sat there, dazed for a moment. And then he got up and walked towards the door. He said that he could not waste all his time on their problems as there were other clients waiting for him to bring relief to their homes. Chow Hee almost ran after him and handed him the coins for his visit as he thanked him profusely for his assistance.

Soon after the incident, the Hee couple took Mong to the revered healers of the west. The journey was arduous, and it cost them more than they could afford. And in the end, the healers confirmed that Mong was indeed blind. They added that blindness apart, she was perfectly healthy. This could not comfort the grieving parents and they went back home wondering if there was a way to undo the inauspicious act they had committed by birthing the doomed girl.

As the months flew on, people in the village grew more appreciative of Mong's beauty. When she took her first steps, it seemed like a real fairy had descended upon earth. However, her parents kept her mostly indoors and did not allow others to interact with her. Initially, Mong's seven brothers were very curious about their baby sister. But their parents were convinced that her proximity might tone down their good luck as well. So, they told the boys that they are not supposed to play with little girls, as that could make them frail and weak. Thus, despite having seven siblings, Mong was not close to any of them.

One day when Mong was around two years old, news came from ten villages away that Sui Hee's mother had passed away. It was the way of their land to celebrate death, so the Hee couple immediately got busy to prepare for a small gathering in their humble home. They prepared soft bread, soup and crunchy vegetable salad for the guests. Mourning the deceased was forbidden in their culture, so when Sui Hee found a few stray tears rebelling down her cheeks she quickly wiped them off and put the blame on the onions she was slicing.

Neighbours came over that evening and everybody said kind things about Sui Hee's late mother. When the guests left, the Hee couple felt worn out. Dishes were cleaned and the children were put to bed somehow. And then they finally turned in for the night.

Sui Hee was unable to sleep. She kept thinking of her mother and found it impossible to be happy about her ascent to the high skies. Suddenly she felt Chow Hee nudging at her.

"Are you awake?" he asked.

"Yes, can't sleep," Sui Hee replied. "Thinking of mother and my childhood."

"I was thinking of her too," Chow Hee said. "She is now happy in the high skies."

"Yes," Sui Hee agreed with a sigh.

"I think Mong too should be made to go to the high skies," Chow Hee whispered and edged closer to his wife.

Sui Hee shuddered and turned to her husband.

"Made to go?" she pressed on the point.

"Yes," Chow Hee repeated. "We, as her parents, should help her to come out of the current curse and find her true happiness in the high skies."

Death of young children was considered to be very special in Krai Tang. They believed that only the holiest of the souls got rid of worldly pains at an early age. The bereaved parents were even worshipped in some clans.

"I cannot do it," Sui Hee replied.

"You think you cannot," Chow Hee asserted. "It scares you. But it is our duty to help our children find their destiny. Will you like to see her suffer all life with her blindness?"

"I don't know," Sui Hee said. "It's very difficult to think about."

Over the next two days Chow Hee pestered Sui Hee about how necessary it was for them to send their daughter off. Her grandmother was now close to the doors of the high skies and would be able to guide little Mong when she arrived. Finally, after about six days of continuous convincing, Sui Hee agreed to work on the plan.

So, a few days later, even before the sun was up, the Hee couple started off with Mong in their arms. They trudged up the green slope to reach the cliff top. Right next to it was a deep abyss into which they had planned to throw Mong.

Just as Sui Hee was about to grip Mong's small body firmly to fling her away, she woke up and began to squirm within the folds of blanket in her mother's arms. Sui Hee felt tears rising to her eyes as she looked down at the yawning girl. She sat down and shoved her daughter into Chow Hee's arms. Mong thought it was a game and squealed in delight.

Chow Hee was not to be moved, though. He put Mong down at the very edge of the cliff and then rolled her over with a firm push.

Mong wailed out in shock as she fell, but she was soon caught in a bush that was jutting out almost horizontally from the side of the cliff. Her parents peered down. She was flailing her tiny hands, trying to grab at the branches that were cradling her. And then, something happened that gave the Hee couple a big fright.

As Mong clutched at the leaves and twigs, her breathing pattern changed. She began to breathe in a fast, rhythmic manner and the plant began to respond to her. The tender shoots twirled themselves around her small body and a stout branch propped her up to the top of the cliff. Then the plant rolled her off into the safety of a patch of moss. Mong laughed aloud in joy after rescuing herself from sure death. But it sounded like the wicked laughter of a witch to her parents. This strange incident made them change their mind, and they took Mong back home. They gave up the plan to kill their daughter and decided to let her be. But with this, they also forsook whatever little feelings of empathy they used to have for her.

Mong grew up with the passing years, in a busy home, but felt no warmth or kindness from anyone. Her childhood was spent mostly in confinement and her only entertainment was an hour in the afternoon when she went out to play with the neighbourhood kids. Her parents did not want her to go out at all, but ever since they got a first-hand taste of her sorcery, they were afraid of restraining her too much.

Soon Mong became aware of the strange power she wielded, the power to fix any kind of ailment or injury that can befall the humans. She just had to shift into an alternate persona by breathing rhythmically. However, her parents had ordered her to never use her evil magic anywhere, as it could bring shame upon them. Her family chose to suffer the maladies that came their way rather than subjecting themselves to Mong's power.

Thus, in the initial years of her life, Mong could apply her power only to cure her own wounds and ailments.

Then came the day when her best friend Woihong discovered her secret. It was a cold, rainy day so most of the kids remained inside their huts. Only Mong and Woihong were running around in the fields, splashing mud on each other. After a while, when both the girls felt that they could not get any dirtier, Mong suggested that Woihong should climb up the Yu-Tallow tree to fetch the ripe, round fruits. Woihong retorted that Mong should climb the tree herself. And then Mong had to remind her friend that she must never make such absurd requests, given that Mong was blind.

Woihong felt a little ashamed of herself and promptly ran to the tree. The first branch shot out from a height low enough to reach from the ground but there were no fruits left on it. So, she was forced to scale the thick, brown trunk until she could find a higher branch. She sat astride on the desired branch, plucking out the fruits and throwing them down for Mong to collect.

When she thought she had gathered enough for the both of them, Woihong started to climb down. But her left foot slipped against a slimy spot and threw her off balance. She panicked and clutched at a fistful of leaves to prevent a fall. It did not help. The wet leaves gave away and Woihong fell on the ground below with a dull thud. The mud softened the impact but she had landed at an unfortunate angle and her right arm snapped instantly.

Woihong screamed in pain and Mong rushed to her. Finding her friend in acute agony, she knew that she would have to break the promise her parents had extracted from her. Mong shifted into her alternate persona by breathing in rhythm and touched Woihong's broken arm. She began to communicate with the broken parts of her body and repaired the damaged tissues. Within minutes, Woihong's right arm was whole again and the pain disappeared completely.

Woihong sat half-immersed in mud, trying to figure out what she had just witnessed. But before she could come up with an explanation of any sort, Mong confided about her powers. All these years, holding on to such an interesting secret had been very difficult for her. Sharing it with her best friend seemed to be very liberating.

"So, you're a fairy," Woihong said, clapping her hands.

Mong blushed.

"My parents think I am a witch," she confessed. "Swear on me that you will never disclose this to anyone. If you do, I'll be thrown out of home."

Woihong nodded her head vehemently to express solidarity. She felt blessed to be the only one to know about the precious secret.

In the following months, Woihong never mentioned the incident to anyone. She did not bring it up even when she and Mong were alone. But five years later, when she saw their king Fa Ren Sung lying pale on the rocky hillock, she thought of Mong's abilities. This was about the king, the master of their land, and she felt that she was duty-bound to do something. So, she promptly fetched Mong to the scene, hoping that she would try to save their king from ascending to the high skies.

Chapter 3: Mong helps the king

"Who are you, young maiden?" Wei asked when he realised that Mong had no intention of introducing herself.

Mong was caressing the hurt leg of the king in a way that only the esteemed healers of the West did before treating anyone. The king's men looked on, a wisp of hope peeping through their derisive thoughts.

"She is Mong," Woihong answered.

She stepped closer to Han, meaning to explain the powers Mong had, but he pushed Wei towards her instead. So Woihong whispered into Wei's ears that her friend was trying to use her powers to revive the king.

Wei fell silent for a moment and then he discussed the matter with Han. The two men promptly started an argument. Han had no wish to let a random village girl try her weird spells on their master. Wei reasoned that the king would die anyway if they were to carry him all the way back to the royal physician. If he passed away after Mong's treatment, then they would at least have a scapegoat to put the blame on. Han liked the reasoning and told Wei that Mong could begin her work.

Mong was not really waiting for an instruction. She put her hands on the bare toes of Fa Ren Sung and slid her fingers down slowly till she reached the two puncture wounds at his ankle through which the snake had emptied its venom into the king's bloodstream. Immediately, she began to breathe in the rhythmic pattern to transcend into her alternate self.

Mong's sense of touch altered and she could now feel the minutest detailing of whatever she touched. She now perceived Fa Ren Sung not as the king, not even as a man but as a community of around thirty-seven trillion small beings who strived together to uphold their world, the body of the king.

The body was a separate world on its own, with different tribes playing out their own roles. Despite the differences that segregated the tribes, they all worked in sync to house the soul safely in the body; because the soul was, in many ways, the sun to their world.

Mong felt the grave agitation of the members of the skin and blood tribe. The sudden invasion of the venom tribe was killing off the small beings in multitudes. The intruders were ruthless and their only purpose seemed to release the soul of Fa Reng Sung from the body for an easy transition to the high skies.

Mong knew that she had to stop the members of the venom tribe from reaching the king's heart. Any harm to the heart would be fatal. She connected with the protector tribe of the body and fired away curative instructions. She soothed the panic-stricken small beings and they imbibed the plan given out by Mong. Earlier, the fighters of the body were charging ahead recklessly towards the incoming venom members. But contact with the invaders was causing an instant death of the fighters. Mong asked them to hold the corpses of the slain warriors as shields and to push the venom tribe members out of the bloodstream as soon as possible.

So, the fighter beings of the king's body held their dead members before themselves and charged again with double ferocity. This angered the venom tribe, and they poked rapid holes into the dead corpses, seeking to make contact. This resulted in a few more deaths, but the new corpses made the shields thicker and almost impenetrable. And gradually, it became much easier for the fighter beings to push the venom tribe members out of the king's body. The body revived after the venom was cleaned from the king's blood and he began to take small gasps of breath. The small beings making up his body rejoiced in their victory. The soul was now safe, and so were they.

Mong hyperventilated for a few long moments to break out of the rhythm and transformed back to her original self. She had saved Fa Ren Sung's life by using her power of touch.

"The body is safe now," she declared happily. "They need a lot of rest now."

"Who are they?" Wei asked her.

"I think she means us," Krin Ki explained. "We had a hard day."

Han knitted his brows and growled at them. Then, he went closer to the king and sat down to prop up his head by his arm.

"Your Majesty," he said as he gently patted Fa Ren Sung's cheeks. "Are you here with us?"

"Han," the king whispered, parting his eyes only very slightly. "I have no strength."

"He needs to sleep," Mong said. "He will feel stronger after he gets some rest."

Han turned to Mong, frowning at her for daring to barge into his conversation with the king. Fa Ren Sung opened his eyes wider to take a good look at Mong.

"Did she ease my pains?" he asked.

The king's men looked at one another and thought for a moment. They had to give Mong her due credit.

"It seems so," Han confirmed.

"We must visit her home," the king said as he smiled in gratitude, looking at Mong.

Mong stared back blankly, not returning the smile. Though the king was not aware of her blindness, the odd gaze did not offend him.

"Come with me," Woihong offered. "I'll take you to her home."

The king's men followed her. They placed the king on a broad, wooden plank and four strong men lifted it upon their shoulders. All marched behind Woihong. Mong followed the strange party sheepishly, wondering how on earth she would explain everything to her parents and brothers.

When the men knocked at her front door, Sui Hee opened it with a good mind to chastise Mong for being out for so long. Instead, she found Han, the royal commander, asking for a comfortable bed for their ailing king. Sui Hee stood there dumbstruck for a moment and then she ran in fast. Nervous and excited, she rearranged a few things here and there, hoping to spruce up her modest quarters for the royal party outside. She called out to her husband and sons and told them to change into their best attire as soon as possible. Then, Sui Hee tried to hand-brush away the wrinkles in her dress, smoothed out her wispy hair as well as she could and rushed back to the men waiting at the threshold.

She greeted them with three long bows and ushered them inside. Han, Wei and Krin Ki walked in to examine the hut. They turned up their lips at the shabbiness of the village home, while Sui Hee stood stiffly in a corner, as if waiting for a sentence to be pronounced upon her.

Han spoke to Wei and Krin Ki in a hushed voice and Sui Hee, despite her best attempts, was not able to make out what transpired between them.

"We observe that the beds are too short," Krin Ki said aloud after clearing his voice. "You must join two of the beds and prepare it with a thick mattress and silk bedsheets for His Majesty."

Chow Hee came out at this juncture, dressed in his blue velvet pants paired with a matching blue shirt. He had also fastened a big yellow belt at his waist, which he usually wore to weddings and holy occasions. He bowed respectfully to his guests and waited for an instruction while his wife went in to look for materials to dress up the beds for the king.

"Make arrangements for us, the king's men, to rest," Wei told Chow Hee, who bowed again in obedience.

Sui Hee asked three of her sons to help her with the house-work. The remaining four went out with their father to spread the news in the neighbourhood. The village now needed to play good hosts to the king and his men.

Soon the sleepy locality bustled with activity. Every house in the area volunteered to take care of a few members of the royal entourage, and the men were soon stationed in different homes.

Meanwhile Sui Hee had the beds joined and decorated with the help of her sons. Fa Ren Sung was fast asleep on the wooden plank and woke up briefly while he was being shifted to the new bed, only to ask for Mong to be present by his bedside.

This very order disappointed Sui Hee very much. She would not be able to confront her daughter in the presence of the sleeping king and his fully awake royal officers. Gossip about Mong having applied her powers on the king had reached Sui Hee's ears. Though it angered her at first, she now could not help feeling a little proud about it.

The royal party was served an early dinner and they went to bed soon afterwards. The day had tested the limits of their mental and physical strength so the worn out men fell asleep as soon as their heads hit the pillows.

Only three men remained awake, at least, in turns, for they had the duty to guard their master. Han, Wei and Krin Ki waited at three corners of the bed on which Fa Ren Sung slept. The other corner was taken up by Mong who crouched on the floor and rested her head against one leg of the bed. Wei and Krin Ki badly wanted to enquire more about her powers but Han did not approve of any such conversation so they kept quiet reluctantly.

Fa Ren Sung woke up very late in the night and called out weakly. Sui Hee immediately set out dinner on a narrow table and Chow Hee pushed it up to the king's bed.

"I'd like some soup from the hands of my saviour," Fa Ren Sung said as Wei propped him up a bit.

Han was a bit hurt that Mong was chosen over him but he decided not to make any comment. Nursing was a woman's job anyway, he consoled himself.

Mong stood up and took a step ahead but her mother interjected.

"Your Majesty, my daughter is blind," Sui Hee said. "May I help you to eat instead?"

Fa Ren Sung turned towards Mong, who appeared stoic and composed. There was no shame, no sorrow on her countenance on account of her blindness.

"In that case, Han will help me to eat," the king said. "It is anyway unfair of me to ask for more favours from someone who has already saved me once."

"It's my duty to help anyone who is willing to take my help," Mong said.

The answer pleased Fa Ren Sung very much and he nodded happily while Han fed him soup with renewed zeal. The king was asleep as soon as he had eaten.

Fa Ren Sung and his men were up at daybreak. The king claimed that he felt fitter than ever and saw no reason to extend their stay in the village. However, he asked the families in the neighbourhood to assemble, as he wanted to thank them for their warmth and hospitality.

The villagers came in twos and threes. They sat down in rows in front of the Hee hut, waiting for the king's address. When Fa Ren Sung appeared, he was fully dressed in his royal attire and everyone cheered spontaneously to see that his health had been fully restored.

Fa Ren Sung acknowledged them with a big smile and raised his hands. Two of his men began to distribute sealed pouches to the villagers.

"Gifts from His Majesty," Han explained. "Each pouch contains a hundred coins."

"It is a mark of my thankfulness to this village," Fa Ren Sung added. "Now, I have something to ask of you."

The villagers were hastily tearing open the pouches, and they stopped as soon as they heard the king's words. They wondered if the taxes were going to be raised.

"My proposal is specifically for the Hee family," Fa Ren Sung said. "I wish to take away their lovely daughter to the capital. She will live there under my protection, using her powers to heal sick people."

Chow Hee almost leapt up on hearing this. Sui Hee looked skyward to thank the Moon god for his kindness. The rest of the villagers were obviously displeased. They reminded Mong's parents that it was not in their custom to let a girl travel to another town unless it was within the bounds of matrimony. This made Sui Hee worried. She whispered into her husband's ears, asking if the king intended to marry Mong. Chow Hee gave her a prompt scolding for harbouring ridiculous aspirations for their blind daughter. He reminded his wife of Zing Zin's advice and said they must make effective use of the opportunity.

"We'd be delighted to put Mong under the king's protection," Chow Hee said with a servile smile plastered on his lips.

Thus, it was decided that Mong will be going away to the capital with the royal party. The king's men had set up the train of carriages on the road. Everyone looked eager for the long journey back home. Fa Ren Sung was about to board the second carriage when Han placed himself in front of the king and bowed.

"Han, you have something to say," Fa Ren Sung stated.

"Yes, Your Majesty, I do," Han smiled. "I see that we are taking a fair, young maiden back to our capital. You are perhaps enamoured by her great beauty and the fact that she saved your life."

Fa Ren Sung looked pleased.

"But you cannot make Mong your consort." Han was terse.

"And why not?" the king asked.

"One of the most revered laws of our monarchy states that the king must never take more than one consort," Han reminded him. "There is a prophecy saying that there will be great danger to our lands if the king marries twice."

"I remember," Fa Ren Sung said, after a while. "Mong is not going with me to be my consort."

The king's face went sullen though.

"Then?" Han persisted. "What will be the role of a blind village girl in the royal palace? Surely, the royal healers will not let her try out witchcraft alongside their work."

"You talk too much these days, Han," Fa Ren Sung rebuked.

"Perhaps I do," Han nodded. "But you gave me ministerial duties, too. I must try and help you assess your decisions."

The king glared at Han and dismissed him with a wave of his hand. He then parted the wine-coloured curtains to step into his carriage. Mong was already seated inside.

Han saw the curtains close after Fa Ren Sung's entry and frowned as he thought of all that could happen inside. He vowed to himself that he would do everything in his power to dissuade the king from taking a second wife. Then he marched off to the first carriage to join Wei and Krin Ki.

After the men of high ranks had boarded the carriage train, the coachman yanked the six leading horses into action and they galloped fast along the broadest road leading away from the market square. The rest of the men followed on horseback. The royal party headed towards the capital located in the central plateau.

Chapter 4: Journey to the Capital

It was in the seclusion of the curtained carriage that Mong spoke about her apprehensions to Fa Ren Sung.

"What will happen to me?" she asked.

The king, who was drinking in her beauty with unabashed eyes, was startled by the abrupt question. He took his face closer to Mong's and noted how her lips quivered slightly as she waited for the king to respond.

"Are you afraid, Mong?" Fa Ren Sung asked. "Will you miss home badly?"

Mong thought of the life she was leaving behind. Nobody in her home had ever loved her. But still, it was impossible to not miss the familiarity of her hometown.

"A little, I'll miss home a little," Mong confessed. "And I'm curious about what lies ahead."

"What do you want?" Fa Ren Sung asked.

"I'd like to be useful, in some way," she replied.

Fa Ren Sung laughed. He tucked away the loose strands of Mong's hair behind her ears. The touch surprised her. But she did not seem offended. Emboldened, the king took her hands in his own and spoke on.

"In my castle, you will be the royal healer," Fe Ren Sung said. "And you will be useful in ending the suffering of my subjects."

Mong was no longer listening to Fa Ren Sung. The warmth of his palms felt wonderful over her fingers, and she gulped nervously. Woihong often told her about things she did with her boyfriend Xiu but, Mong herself had never got the chance to be intimate with a boy. She wondered if it was a sin to suddenly long for the king. Mong fought hard to shake off the thought trail when she felt Fa Ren Sung's lips on hers. For a moment, she knotted up in fear, but then she gave in to the delightful feeling that ran through her nerves. And she kissed the king back.

They withdrew after a minute and sat apart. Mong was too flustered to think coherently, let alone talk. Fa Ren Sung smiled to himself and looked out of the window, watching the dappled sunlight flashing in through the bobbing window panes as the horses galloped on at full speed. He had not felt so happy in a long time.

After a while, Fa Ren Sung took out a sleek chain made of gold from his pocket and put it around Mong's neck. There was a single pendant hooked to it.

"What is it, if I may ask?" Mong asked as she fumbled with the pendant.

"It is my first gift to you," the king whispered tenderly. "I retrieved a precious snake stone two days back, which now adorns this chain. I believe it was the same snake who sought me down and struck me out of vengeance. It's yours; you have earned it by reversing my sure passage to the high skies."

To this Mong could reply nothing. Nobody had ever gifted her anything in life. The surface of the pendant was dotted with fine particles. Mong counted the undulations, there were five. She rotated the pendant between her fingers five times and it seemed to arouse in her a magical sense of confidence. At that moment, she felt sure that she would love her new life in the capital. She knew there was something important and powerful, awaiting her in the future.

The journey continued for two and a half days through the mountains and valleys. They had picnic meals in the woods and halted at two villages on the way to stay the nights. And all throughout the journey, even in the presence of people from other provinces, the king did not make any effort to hide his fascination with Mong. And to the utter dismay of Han, Mong too seemed to be charmed by Fa Ren Sung.

When the carriage-train reached the first gates of the capital on the third day, the king went to the front carriage to sit with Han and sent back Wei and Krin Ki to accompany Mong in the second carriage. Han received him with a broad grin. Perhaps the proximity of his home was bringing the king back to senses. Han took it as a good omen.

Wei and Krin Ki had strict orders to not initiate any kind of dialogue with Mong, so they sat quietly and observed the blind girl. Wei whispered into Krin Ki's ears that their queen, the current wife of Fa Ren Sung was prettier, to which Krin Ki mumbled back that he found Mong to be the more beautiful one. The king had told Mong to ask for anything she needed from these two men, but with Fa Ren Sung gone, she suddenly started to feel homesick and kept to herself during the last leg of the journey.

As Mong leaned her head against the window, she felt a distinct change in the air. The smells of the trees and wildflowers were now replaced by the fragrances of camphor and sandalwood. If her eyes were functional, she would have seen tall granite walls with decorative red crests guarding the capital. There were seven layers of boundary walls that guarded the city. Huge iron gates plated with copper were placed at different points on each successive wall to protect the city from sudden attacks. The coachman driving the carriage-train was an expert in navigating the meandering route that went progressively inward. He led the party deftly while the rest of the king's men followed on horses. Armed men threw open the huge gates at each point to let them pass only after verifying the presence of Fa Ren Sung in the carriage-train.

At the main gate of the royal palace, the second carriage was taken off the train and only one carriage carrying the king and Han remained attached to the horses. The coachman spurred the horses, which galloped away at full speed along the neatly pebbled path leading up to the front entrance of the castle. The men on horseback, having fulfilled their duty of escorting the king to his doorstep, dispersed off in the directions of their respective homes. Mong deboarded at the main gate along with Wei and Krin Ki, and they took entry into the palace boundaries on foot through one of the smaller gates at the side.

The two men guarded Mong from both sides as they walked along the wide green lanes that lined the walls of the palace to lead up to its back entrance. Gardeners were tending to the flowers in the gardens and the scent of freshly cut grass soothed Mong's spirts as she was led into a rest house located right behind the royal mansion. Two middle-aged women and their two daughters maintained the rest house. Wei told them to take care of the new guest, Mong.

Chapter 5: Queen Biyu

At the main entrance of the palace the king was received with much love and fanfare. People performed elaborate dance routines and sang songs to welcome Fa Ren Sung back home, while his queen Biyu stood smiling at slight distance, surrounded by her team of chaperones.

The queen had spent three hours that day with the beauticians who worked on her face and hair. When she was convinced that she looked perfect, she asked to be dressed in a layered peach gown that concealed her baby bump. She had found out only in the morning about the snake bite incident from her attendants. However, they had cleverly omitted the part about a pretty healer accompanying the king back to the capital. So, even though the news made Biyu anxious about her husband's health, she felt completely secure about her place in his life.

The king acknowledged the performance of the dancers and singers with gracious smiles and indulgent claps. As they bowed and separated into two files, the king marched through the space between them to reach his queen. Fa Ren Sung took her in his arms and walked away to their private chambers in the palace. The queen was with his child. The king's heart filled with joy when he thought about becoming a father soon. Many of the subjects cheered openly at this, for most of them had found out about Mong, and were a little apprehensive about the future of the king's current marriage.

In the privacy of their chamber, Biyu broke down into profuse tears as she recounted the days of loneliness when her husband was away on his travels. Fa Ren Sung did not respond. He was busy in peeling off the layers of his heavy formal attire. He felt relieved after slipping into a thin cotton robe and seated himself snugly beside his wife.

Biyu had cast aside her veil and the soft roundness of her breasts was visible as her chest heaved up and down with her sniffles. Fa Ren Sung looked at her closely. She seemed to have grown more beautiful while he was gone. He felt turned on and pulled her closer to himself. Without wasting any time, he began to unbutton her blouse.

The queen withdrew immediately and looked up at her husband in shock. And then she placed her hands on her belly. The king lowered his eyes to observe the bump and raised his face to meet Biyu's eyes.

"Don't you know, it could ruin the health of the unborn prince," Biyu whispered.

Fa Ren Sung's pride was pricked by this and he stood up defiantly.

"It could be a princess as well," he said on purpose to hurt his wife.

"Please don't say that," she pleaded as her hands rose to cover her lips.

"Why not?" Fa Ren Sung asked. "Perhaps then you'd throw yourself at me, hoping to make the next baby."

The sharpness stung and Biyu got hysterical with her tears, which further infuriated the king. He promptly began to change into an evening garment.

"Are you leaving so soon?" Biyu cried. "Will you not even embrace the mother of your baby properly?"

"It could ruin the health of the unborn prince," Fa Ren Sung mocked as he left in a huff.

Biyu clutched her pillow and began to weep into it.

The king went out of his chamber and walked through the huge halls to reach the central corridor of his mansion. This corridor ran through the building, right to the big door at the back. Beyond this door was a narrow passage threading through a garden that led to the rest house where Mong had been put up. It was located in the western side, a direction considered to be unholy for pregnant women and hence currently inaccessible by the queen. That was precisely why Fa Ren Seng had sent Mong there.

As the king strode along fast, the sun-rays filtered through the translucent roof tiles of the corridor, fell on his shoulder, giving him a subtle hint of warmth. He went out through the majestic back door and took to the narrow path. The aroma of flowers greeted him and Fa Ren Sung was much happier by the time he reached the door of the rest house. He went inside without a knock and found Mong surrounded by the lady folks. They were firing away incessant questions, and Mong was struggling to answer fast enough. The king cleared his voice to express his displeasure. He had specifically instructed them to not burden her with questions.

The two women and their daughters stood up, bowed to the king and left the rest house in a single file. Fa Ren Sung felt relieved and turned to take a proper look at Mong. She had bathed and changed into a white gown and seemed happy to sense his presence.

"Are you here?" Mong asked.

She took a few steps and tripped herself on a low wooden stool. Fa Ren Sung rushed ahead and caught her in time. He held her like that for a moment before taking her to a spot by the window and seating her down on the broad sill. The colours of the setting sun fell on Mong's face and she seemed like a magical woman from some enchanted land.

"How are liking your new home, Mong?" Fa Ren Sung asked, leaning his weight against the window.

In the past few hours, Mong had been wondering if she would ever meet the king again and if it was a big mistake for her to come all the way from her small village to the capital. She had even missed her parents and brothers at certain points. But with Fa Ren Sung's visit, all those feelings of doubts vanished.

"I feel very happy here," Mong replied confidently.

Fa Ren Sung forgot all his weariness as he talked to Mong. When the sun went down, there was a knock on the door. The two girls came in to light the oil lamps while their mothers served tea and evening snacks. Then they bowed and left without a word.

With the golden flames gleaming inside the room everything started to look different. Fa Ren Sung held Mong's hand and led her to the dining table. But he changed his mind after taking two steps and flung her down on the large bed instead. He kissed her all over the face. The warm weight of the king's body on herself made Mong feel trapped and she panicked for a second. But as the king caressed her tenderly, her fears dissipated and she breathed deeply. Soon Fa Ren Sung was undressing Mong and himself. Mong found herself pulling the king closer, longing for him to taste her bare body. They blended into each other without the slightest hesitation. Mong's eagerness was vastly different from Biyu's diffidence and it drove the king mad with passion. After long minutes of intense love-making, Fa Ren Sung was spent. Mong and the king hid their faces in each other's necks and stayed like that for a long time.

At length, Mong suggested that they should eat. Fa Ren Sung agreed, but as soon as he started to get up from the bed, he noticed blood-stains on the bedsheet. He wondered what kind of rumours those marks might start.

"Are you not hungry?" Mong asked, sensing the delay.

"I am, I am," Fa Ren Sung laughed and took Mong to the table.

As he ate with Mong, he reminded himself that he was the king of the land and that he should not have to hide anything from his subjects.

When it was time for him to leave, the king saw the full moon in the sky. And he promised Mong to visit her on the nights when the Moon god rose in his finest glory.

As he marched back to the main palace, satiated, he could feel the eyes of some of the servants boring into him. He realised that they had already figured out what their king had been up to. The silent disapproval in their eyes enraged him and made him more defiant. So, he altered his original plan and started to visit Mong every night. And on full moon nights, he spent the whole night in the rest house.

Mong was having the happiest time of her life. She had never known how maddening the joy of being in love could be. The two women and their two daughters brought to her attention, as often as they could, the presence of a king's wife, the true queen of Krai Tang but Mong overlooked their warnings completely. She was convinced that Fa Ren Sung loved her back and nothing else mattered anymore.

The story of the king's affair did not remain confined within the palace walls for long. The whole capital was soon discussing the beautiful witch that His Highness was sleeping with. The ladies taking care of Mong hated her in the beginning, but this started to change the day she cured one girl's permanent limp. From that day, they requested Mong to treat a sudden fever, an upset tummy or menstrual cramps and each time, she obliged them happily. Though the caretakers had never meant to like Mong, gradually they developed a feeling of gratitude towards her. However, to the vast majority of the subjects who never got a chance to interact with Mong, she remained an evil witch who was trying to ensnare the affection of their benevolent king.

Some of the subjects took it upon themselves to stop the wrongdoings and after a lot of careful planning, they decided that the chief chaperone of the queen needed to reveal to her what monstrosity was developing in the rest house at the west.

So, on a fixed day, the chief chaperone narrated to the queen how her place in the king's life was in serious jeopardy. Biyu's first reaction was that of disbelief. The queen had just completed her afternoon prayers to the Moon god when the lady described to her the debauchery that went on behind her back.

The queen got up from her praying stool and placed herself in front of the long, ornamental mirror. Then, as she casually dabbed aromatic oil along her neckline, she began to talk.

"Clean the prayer corner," she commanded. "And keep your mind clean as well."

The chief chaperone was taken aback. Biyu delegated the menial duties to her only when she was deeply offended. She rushed to the prayer corner and quickly put the deities and the stool away. Then she dusted the place and arranged some freshly cut lilies in a big crystal vase.

"Her Majesty," she started. "I request you to authenticate what I reported with any other maid of yours. If I am found to be errant, please order my beheading before sundown."

She made a graceful bow and began to step backwards in nimble footsteps when Biyu stopped her. She asked the chief chaperone to repeat "the facts" that she had amassed about this strange witch who was supposedly hiding in the rest house.

The lady repeated the story of Mong and cautioned the queen about the spells that she was using to influence people. She even cited the example of the care-takers, who once could not stand Mong but were now throwing their weight behind her.

"Her Majesty must act fast," the chief chaperone insisted. "If you don't douse out the flames now, it will soon start a raging fire."

The queen's heart was seeded with a deep hatred that day.

Chapter 6: The King's Decision

Fa Ren Sung was in the open court hearing out his subjects. He handled each grievance with patience and offered fair resolutions. When the court was finally adjourned in the afternoon, the king was happy. His people were content, and so was he.

The king got up, meaning to walk away, when Han placed himself in front of Fa Ren Sung and made an elaborate bow.

"What now, Han?" Fa Ren Sung asked with raised eyebrows and continued to walk.

"Your Highness," Han said, matching his pace with the king. "May I have the pleasure of your company for some time?"

Fa Ren Sung stopped and sighed. It was only the two of them in the passage leading out of the court. Han stood with his head lowered reverentially, but his right hand was pointing to the room of high order. That room was used only for discussing the gravest of the threats and conspiracies. In the past many potential mutinies and internal uprisings had been averted due to meetings held in the room of high order.

Fa Ren Sung opened his mouth in surprise, then clasped Han's extended palm, accepting his invitation. They walked into the room of high order together. It was lit up with ten bright candles and the writing desks were set out. Han seemed to have prepared well for the meeting.

"What problem do we have now?" Fa Ren Sung asked, the minute Han closed the thickly padded door.

"Mong," Han replied curtly.

"Oh, her," Fa Ren Sung's lips bent in sarcasm as he sat down. "Sit down, Han. Let's discuss her. Mong is this blind village girl who happens to save my life. As a mark of gratitude I brought her to the capital to give her a decent life. I believe I told you that I wanted her to be a healer in my capital. Right?"

"Yes," Han nodded.

"Did you try to do anything about it, Han?" Fa Ren Sung asked. "Not a single sufferer was sent to her for healing. Nor did anyone try to acquaint her with our regular healers of the west!"

The king had steered the conversation adeptly to make it about Han's incompetence. Feeling complacent about his own acumen, Fa Ren Rung began to tap a rhythm on the writing desk as he looked at Han for an answer.

"Your Highness," Han began after a long pause. "I did try to set up a system where some of the ailing people could be sent to Mong. However, nobody wished to be treated by her."

"What? Why?" Fa Ren Sung stood up. "Did you not tell them about her powers? How she intervened and prevented my passage to the high skies?"

"I did," Han said. "But there are rumours floating about. Everyone is talking about how she is sharing the bed with you in an attempt to replace the queen. People have come to believe that she is an evil wit---woman."

Fa Ren Sung banged his fist down on the desk and growled in anger.

"Stop the rumours," he yelled. "I command you, Han."

"I will try to do as His Majesty says," Han said. "However, my heart fears what's about to come. If you indeed decide to marry Mong-"

"I will not marry her," Fa Ren Sung cut in. "I remember the prophecy. Only one queen for each monarch. Biyu will remain my wife as well as the queen of this land."

"In that case, sir, we need to stop the rumours right away," Han remarked. "Else, they will cause irreparable damage to Mong. She will be considered as a fallen woman with no hope for a life of grace."

Fa Ren Sung swung his head and stared at Han. The flames of the candles reflected in his small eyes. Han's assessment was not wrong. For the first time, the king realised how selfish he has been in his love for Mong.

"Han, please bring Daik out of the stable," Fe Ren Sung commanded. "I need a quiet stroll in the Wispy Woods to clear my mind."

Han and the king walked out of the room of high order through a hidden door at the side, into the cool twilight air. The king waited while Han went to ask the groom to get Fa Ren Sung's favourite mare ready. Soon he was back, accompanied by the groom and Daik.

Daik let out a neigh of joy as Fa Ren Sung mounted her. Her energy was infectious and Fa Ren Sung laughed aloud.

"By tonight I will have a solution for the concern you raised," Fa Ren Sung promised to Han.

Han felt little relief, though. He uttered a small prayer as he watched Daik trot out of the big gates and then vanish at the first turn of the road that led into the Wispy Woods.

###

The fresh air of the woods helped Fa Ren Sung to calm his nerves. There was no desperate Han trying to influence his decisions. He dismounted and paced around the tree trunks as he reflected on the situation he was stuck in. Mong made him happy in an invigorating way. Also, his feelings for his wife Biyu were on the wane. He wondered if it was ethical to expect the king to live his entire life with one woman. After all, most of the neighbouring kingdoms allowed the king to take as many women as he fancied. Fa Ren Sung cursed his luck. He had to be born into the one kingdom where some kind of stupid prophecy prohibited him from marrying a second time.

He thought of his elaborate coronation ceremony where he had explicitly promised to the Moon god never to disobey the dictums of his title. Everyone in the kingdom of Krai Tang was aware, a king breaking his oath would draw the terrible wrath of fate upon himself and his people.

Daik was now busy munching on some fruits. Fa Ren Sung stroked her mane gently as he made up his mind. There was no point in carrying on an affair with Mong. He was indeed reducing her to a fallen woman under the ruse of love. Soon Biyu would give birth to his baby and he would have to give her the honour she deserves. Maybe it was possible for him to like Biyu again and forget the feelings he had developed for Mong. But he knew it would not be easy, not one bit easy.

Having made the hard decision, the king quickly mounted Daik for a run. As he rode through the woods, Fa Ren Sung thought of Mong and how badly she would be hurt if he left her. And he wondered if she had the ability to heal her own broken heart.

It was getting dark when the king finally made his way in through the palace gates. Wei was training a batch of young soldiers on the courtyard while Han supervised the proceedings. He swung his head as he heard Daik neigh and got up to walk towards Fa Ren Sung. The groom was collecting the reigns of the mare when Han reached them.

"I trust that you have made the right decision," he said and extended his palm towards the main palace entrance, inviting the king for another meeting.

"Yes," Fa Ren Sung said curtly as he ignored the suggested route and walked vigorously towards the rest house, located in the opposite direction.

"What decision did you make, if I may enquire?" Han pressed on, following the king in hurried footsteps.

"You'll find out soon," Fa Ren Sung replied. "I command you to go back to governing the new recruits in our army."

Han stopped immediately and forced a smile out of his lips. He watched the king walk away from him. He shook his head and turned back to join Wei.

Fa Ren Sung felt his steps getting heavier as he got closer to the rest house. Mong must be sitting inside, dressed up and waiting for his arrival. The king wondered if she had left her hair open or if the women had pinned it up on top of her head.

Fa Ren Sung's resolution began to waver and he started to doubt if he would be able to resist himself from spending another magical night with Mong. He tried hard to divert his mind to other constructive actions that he could partake after breaking up. He planned to send ailing subjects to Mong from the very next day. The work would keep her occupied, and slowly, it would give her a purpose to live. When the pain of losing her love be sufficiently dulled out, Fa Ren Sung would pick out a fine young man for Mong to marry. However, this very idea hurt the king too much and he stopped thinking altogether. Thankfully, he had also reached the door of the rest house.

The two women and their daughters were out in the garden cutting some fresh flowers when they saw the king. His appearance seemed to give them quite a shock, for they dropped the flowers and scissors; and all four of them scrambled inside in a tearing hurry.

The king smiled to himself as he imagined them dressing Mong, who, for some reason was still in the bath, unclothed. His smile shrivelled to a frown in the next moment when he remembered his decision of never making love to her again.

Fa Ren Sung took the last few steps absently and knocked lightly on the door. However, when the usual warm reception was not given to him, he pushed it open and went in feeling somewhat miffed.

The scene inside puzzled the king. Mong was huddled on the floor, shaking with furious sobs while her care-takers were crowding near the door at the other end of the rest house which led back to the palace.

Fa Ren Sung strode ahead towards the window and as he looked out, he saw a vanishing train of red satin sashaying away towards the main mansion. The light was low, but the king knew for sure that the disappearing woman he saw was none other than his own wife, Biyu.

While the king was away in the Wispy Woods, Biyu had decided to find out if there was any truth to the rumours of a blind girl bewitching her husband. She marched to the rest house alone and on entering she saw a beautiful young girl tracing her fingers over a stitchwork that decorated one wall of the room. Biyu immediately ordered the care-takers to leave. She wanted to talk to the girl alone. Mong turned towards Biyu following the sound of her voice. She felt a mixture of guilt and anxiety curling up her guts.

"So, you are the witch who is using her spells on my husband," Biyu started, as soon as she heard the door close behind her.

Mong wanted to speak but felt like someone was clamping down her throat. Biyu saw how beautiful she looked and it made her seethe in rage.

"Blind girl," she mocked. "How can you aspire to replace me?"

Mong fell to her knees and joined her palms. She had known all along that Fa Ren Sung was married but the illegitimacy of their relationship had never struck her as odd. But now as she listened to the anguish in the queen's voice, an overwhelming feeling of fear engulfed Mong.

"I… I do not wish to replace Your Majesty," she stuttered. "I am only a mere village girl, sightless and unworthy. My only duty is to offer the king and the queen my humble services."

"Services, you did offer to the king, blind witch," Biyu yelled. "However, your services will soon be unnecessary. The king's baby is in my womb. The boy will be born when the first rays of spring fall upon our land. And, after that the king will dispose of you. What will you do then, fallen woman?"

Each word of the queen rang out loud in Mong's mind. Fa Ren Sung was bedding her because his queen was unavailable. She felt like a complete fool. The king had never mentioned anything about his impending fatherhood.

As Mong broke into copious tears, Biyu began to frame in her mind a final word of warning when the care-takers rushed in and informed about her husband coming that way. The ladies gathered the layers of Biyu's skirt and helped her out through the other door to go back to the castle. The queen managed to exit the rest house at the exact moment when Fa Ren Sung pushed open the opposite door.

Fa Ren Sung tore his eyes away from the window and looked at the two women and their daughters. All four of them were staring at the floor. He felt furious when he realised that Biyu had been spying on him. Not only that, but she had also broken the royal code. A pregnant queen was not supposed to present herself in the inauspicious western section of the castle as it could bring upon bad luck and widespread doom. The king ran to Mong, who was still crying, and took her in the warmth of his arms.

"Please don't cry, Mong," Fa Ren Sung urged. "Biyu must have been very rude to you. Know it for now, and forever, that the love I have for you in my heart is pure and undying."

"The rules of this land allow you to take only one queen," Mong whispered, as she wiped her eyes. "But can I not be the fallen woman, the one whom you can't marry but may visit sometimes?"

"You can never be a fallen woman," Fa Ren Sung said resolutely as he kissed her on the forehead. "You are, in fact, the woman of highest honour to me. You will help my subjects by relieving them of their misery and pain. And I'd find for you a young man who can be a good husband in every way."

"I don't want any of that," Mong protested and extracted herself from the king's arms.

"Neither do I want it," Fa Ren Sung said as he leaned ahead and touched Mong's hair. "It is for the safety of our land that we have to sacrifice our love. No man can love you the way I do. But we have certain duties to our people and we cannot forget that."

To Mong, the fate of being given away to another man through marriage seemed to be more perverse than the label of a fallen woman who belonged to the king. Just as she was about to speak her mind, a shrill cry was heard outside. It came from the direction of the palace. Running footsteps were heard next, and after a few minutes, two of the queen's chaperones barged into the rest house.

"Your Majesty, our queen is about to move on to the high skies," the women said in unison.

For a brief moment, the news of his wife's imminent death gave the king a sense of joy and freedom. But he thought of the young one in her womb and reproached himself for his selfishness.

"Stay here, Mong," the king said as he began to leave. "I promise, I'll be back."

"Take me along, please," Mong pleaded.

"This is not the right time," the king explained.

He paused and thought for a second.

"Maybe, this is the right time. Come along Mong, your healing touch might be required again."

They ran together, following the chaperones to reach Biyu. The queen lay face down, unconscious at the foot of the stone stairs that led up and into the palace. The folds of her skirt were soaked in blood.

Two royal healers were seeking the pulse in her wrists while a third one was rolling her dress up to have a closer look. The team of chaperones stood in a circle around the queen, their hands clenched in tension.

"She's losing her baby," one of the healers said.

It was loud enough for all to hear, and everyone gasped. Mong sat down promptly and touched Biyu's lower belly with all ten fingers. And she began to breathe hard to shift into her alternate self. The official healers watched her in awe, too shocked to voice a protest, while Fa Ren Sung prayed fervently for Mong to perform a second miracle for him.

Mong connected herself to the small beings that made up Biyu's body. The various tribes were in great distress and they now viewed the growing baby as their enemy. They were trying the best to expel it and hold the soul of Biyu within the body. Mong began to communicate with the small beings.

"The new life is not an enemy entity," she told them. "It's a new soul seeking entry from the high skies; please protect this helpless guest within the body."

The tribes listened to her and agreed. The small beings in the body now began to work to protect the little one growing in the queen's womb. They replenished the fluid that guarded the young one and rebuilt the lining that layered the chamber. Soon, the little body was safe and the tribes followed Mong's instructions to repair other injuries on Biyu's body. After a long struggle they got both Biyu and her baby's souls out of danger. Mong thanked the small beings of all the tribes for their cooperation and requested them to go into resting. Then, she breathed herself out of the alternate self.

Mong felt a heavy silence hanging around her. All were kneeling around her, holding their hands in a ball with the fingertips touching, and praying fervently for her success. But Mong could not see any of this, so she waited for someone to speak up. It was Fa Ren Sung who asked her the first question.

"Were you able to save the baby?" he asked in a trembling voice. "And Biyu?"

"Yes, they are both here with us," Mong replied with a smile. "Let them sleep undisturbed to regain their health."

There was loud clapping, followed by long bows made to Mong by the women around. Fa Ren Sung felt his heart warm up as he looked at Mong. He stepped ahead, and holding her by the hands, he raised her to her feet.

Then, turning around to face the ones present, the king declared, "Mong is going to be my official wife. Please consult the men of divination and make arrangements for a royal wedding on a day that they deem auspicious."

The king stood looking more defiant than ever, with Mong by his side. He was ready to face the volley of questions from the chaperones of Biyu. But to his astonishment, the women only took a moment to let the news sink in, and then they accepted it with signs of overt joy.

"Hail our mighty king," they chanted in chorus, clapping their hands.

The women were looking at Mong with gratitude and Fa Ren Sung felt glad that finally they were able to see in her what he had seen, long before. Mong blushed furiously as she felt all the eyes on her. The snake-stone pendant resting in between her collar bones seemed to warm up a bit. Off late, the pendant had started to behave as a part of her body. It felt oddly reassuring. She smiled; all her wishes were finally coming true.

On the next day, when the king presented himself in the open court, he decided to address his subjects and dispel their potential fears regarding his second wedding. He took position on the podium and put his hands behind his back. A murmur of speculations went around as everyone stood up and rested their hands in the same way as the king. This gesture displayed their interest in listening to whatever Fa Ren Sung had to say. Once all the noise had died down, the king raised his head towards the sky and closed his eyes. He uttered a prayer to the Moon god before looking down again. Taking in a deep swig of breath, he began to speak.

"Beloved people of Krai Tang, as you all know, Biyu, the queen chose to break the royal dictum by visiting the western section of the palace while bearing the unborn royal baby. She had put herself and the future royalty in grave danger by her thoughtless action. It was Mong whose divine touch saved the queen and the baby. Therefore, I see no harm in me marrying Mong despite the law forbidding the king from taking a second queen. She has helped me two times over to save my life and the lives of those I care for. In a way, I am duty-bound to honour her as my second wife."

For what seemed like a long, painful moment to Fa Ren Sung, there was pin-drop silence all around him. Then, a lone subject from one corner started to clap. One by one, all of them joined in the clapping until all that could be heard was resounding applause. Fa Ren Sung's grim face broke into the broadest of smiles. The feelings of his subjects were now in sync with his wishes.

In the following days, stories about the upcoming royal wedding spread through the capital. This time people were much more receptive about Mong. Only a few had seen her, and even fewer have had the chance to experience her fabled power. Yet stories of her saving the unborn prince had touched most of them and they now felt that a second queen would not upset the balance in the kingdom. Some people even claimed that it was the responsibility of the king to marry again in order to punish the queen for her disobedience.

There were only two souls in the entire kingdom who could not bring themselves to accept the king's decision to marry again. Queen Biyu went completely silent when she found out. Her chaperones tried to convince her that Mong would be more like a maid in waiting for the real queen but nothing could revive her broken spirits. She noticed that her husband had not visited ever since she had the accident and she wondered if the birth of their baby would at all incite any positive change in him.

The other person was Han. Hearing about the wedding made him so morose that he delegated his duties to Krin Ki for a week citing illness. Wei was busy in supervising the preparations for the wedding ceremony and other than him, it was only Krin Ki whom Han could trust. He kept playing the happenings of the last few days in his mind and each time he grimaced in despair. If Biyu's disobedience was punished so quickly by fate, then it was more the reason for Fa Ren Sung to abstain from breaking another rule. But he knew that the king was beyond listening to him, so he kept quiet.

On a bright sunny day in early spring Fa Ren Sung and Mong were married by the holy priest in a simple ceremony at the temple of the Moon god. The entire kingdom blessed the union while Biyu and Han sulked away in the privacy of their rooms.

The queen gave birth to a healthy boy exactly one week after Fa Ren Sung's wedding. As the queen lay exhausted on her maternity bed, she wondered if the king would care much for his son now that he had Mong as his wife. The healers examined her health while the chaperones gave her a light, comforting massage. Biyu tried to stay awake, waiting for the king's arrival but overwhelmed by fatigue she fell asleep soon. When she woke up, the queen found Fa Ren Sung sitting by her side with the baby prince in his arms. The king tilted his arms to show the baby's angelic face to the new mother. The little prince sensed the movement and briefly tried to open his eyes. But he changed his mind immediately and after yawning as widely as he could, he went back to sleep.

"And the future king of Krai Tang yawns the morning away," Fa Ren Sung joked.

This elicited a round of laughter from the chaperones standing in a file in the same room but about ten feet away from the royals. Biyu breathed in deep. After a long time, she felt a positive vibe from her husband; there was even a hint of smile on her lips.

Fa Ren Sung turned back and summoned one of the chaperones. She stepped ahead and collected the baby from the king. As the king signalled for privacy, the team of chaperones went out along with the baby and his crib in tow.

When the room was quiet again, Fa Ren Sung presented an ornamental box to his queen. Biyu opened it to find an exquisite gold brooch studded with the rarest of pearls. Presenting the new mother with jewellery was an old custom of their land. The queen voiced an awkward word of thanks and avoided meeting the eyes of the king.

"You'll always be the queen of this land," Fa Ren Sung assured her as he touched Biyu's chin to turn her face up towards himself. "And also my wife. Both Mong and you are very special to me."

The king expected his words to have some kind of rapturous effect on his queen. So, when she only managed a strained look in response, it disappointed him deeply.

Chapter 7: Bingwen Bitang comes to Krai Tang

Fa Ren Sung organized a lavish naming ceremony for his son, heir to the throne of Krai Tang. A month before the event, invites were sent out to all the allies and dignitaries of the neighbouring kingdoms. The finest of all invitations was sent to Bingwen Bitang, the father-in-law of the king. Bingwen Bitang was a noble-man who ruled one of the boundary territories. He was a widower and Biyu was his only child. So, he was expected to bring Biyu's cousins, their families and twenty men of high rank along with himself on his visit to the capital.

However, on the evening of the naming ceremony, Bingwen Bitang arrived alone, driven by his long-trusted coachman. This disappointed the people in the capital, who were eagerly waiting to receive the relatives and friends of the queen. Traditionally, it was the duty of the maternal grandfather to name the first-born of every couple in Krai Tang and the occasion held a special place in the heart of every father who had a daughter. Naturally, everyone was shocked to see Bingwen Bitang bring no company to an event of such great importance.

The news of Bingwen Bitang's arrival was sent to Fa Ren Sung, and he promptly came out with Han, Wei and Krin Ki to welcome him. The king's parents were no more, so it was his father-in-law whom he greatly revered.

Bingwen Bitang alighted with the help of his coachman and signalled for him to wait in the carriage. The king's men rushed ahead to request the coachman to join the celebrations, but he politely declined and remained seated while Bingwen marched ahead, his strides stiff and face stoic.

"Dauda Bitang," Fa Ren Sung greeted in a shaky voice. "Where are the others? The family? The esteemed men of ranks?"

"Nobody wishes to visit a king who wilfully puts his kingdom in danger," Bingwen growled.

His eyes were wide and red and Fa Ren Sung felt a sense of panic and helplessness. At this precarious moment, six young women appeared and surrounded Bingwen Bitang in a circle. The women sang a song of greeting and held out silver trays with offerings of tea, nuts, and assorted sweets for Bingwen. He pursed his lips, waiting for the song to end, and then he slipped through a gap in the barricade to continue walking towards the front entrance of the palace.

"I came not to revel alongside, but to chide you for your follies," he clarified as Fa Ren Sung followed him nervously, requesting him to accept a bite.

Han promptly took the tray containing tea while Wei collected the sweets from the women. They sprinted together and placed themselves right in front of Bingwen Bitang. With lowered heads, they urged him to accept the mild refreshment.

Bingwen paused for a second and took pity on them. He took a sip of tea and a bite from a sugar-coated cottage cheese dumpling before moving on. Fa Ren Sung matched steps with him, blabbering anything that came to his mind, hoping for Bingwen's temper to ebb away. Bingwen ignored him and weaved his way in through the corridors to reach the room where his daughter Biyu was. At the door Bingwen raised his chin and folded his arms across his chest. He needed someone at this point to show him in. An anxious chaperone guarding the door murmured a few words to pay her respects and went in to check on the queen. She came back fast to usher Bingwen Bitang into his daughter's room.

Before stepping into Biyu's chamber, Bingwen turned around and signalled at Fa Ren Sung to stop trailing him. Then, he waved his palms at the chaperones, ordering them to leave him alone with his daughter and grandchild. Once he had got rid of all the people, he stepped in and looked around. The baby was asleep in his cradle while Biyu was praying in front of the deity of the Moon god at the corner. Bingwen stood by the crib, staring at the face of his grandson. Then, he sat down behind Biyu, closed his eyes, joined his fingertips to hold his curved hands in a ball and prayed.

After her prayers were over, Biyu turned around meaning to call out to the chaperones but instead she saw her father and squealed in joy.

Bingwen opened his eyes at the sound and smiled at his daughter. Biyu dived into his arms and hugged him like a little girl. Bingwen patted her head as he thought of all the tribulations that his daughter has been through and his eyes grew moist.

"Dauda, I just prayed to the Moon god to see some kind of good sign," Biyu said. "And my wish is granted!"

Biyu sat back and wiped off the two errant tears that had rolled down her cheeks. Her father wondered if a deluge would follow. She held back a great deal of pain.

"Why did you not throw out the blind witch on the very first day?" Bingwen asked her without wasting any time on mellow introductions.

Biyu looked down.

"He kept me from knowing for a long time," she mumbled. "And then, it was too late."

"You could've sent a word to me," her father said after a pause.

"I wanted to, Dauda," she replied. "But so many things happened at the same time that the situation slipped out of my control quickly."

"I wish I had known things sooner," Bingwen said.

Then he looked around to make sure nobody else was listening.

"The time has come for me to disclose a secret," he whispered to Biyu. "You need to know about my past to understand Mong and her abilities."

All of a sudden, the baby began to wail in his crib and, as a consequence, rapid footsteps were heard outside. The chaperones were now waiting to be asked in.

"Dauda, I've to feed my son," Biyu said as she walked towards the crib.

"Alright," Bingwen said. "I'll take a walk in the gardens meanwhile."

He got up, opened the door, and went out. Around fifteen women were standing at the threshold. Some of them went in immediately to assist the queen, while others waited on Bingwen, intending to pamper him with warm hospitality.

"Lord Bitang, allow us to take care of you," the leading woman said while others stood quiet.

Bingwen raised his right hand to block their overtures and went out through one of the heavy wooden doors at the side. It led to a patch of garden adjacent to the queen's room. He started to encircle the flowering shrubs leisurely, staring at the patterns created by moonlight on the bare patches of cool, dark grass. After a while, he parked himself on one of the polished stone-seats under a tree. A light breeze was blowing and Bingwen wrapped his shawl around himself.

Leaning against the trunk of the tree, Bingwen Bitang began to reminisce about the past. There was a time when the Bitang family used to rule over a small province, but a few wasteful generations had squandered away most of the money. The province was annexed to the neighbouring kingdom of Krai Tang. So, when Bingwen came of age, it was only the prestigious family name that he inherited.

In his youth, Bingwen Bitang was an ambitious man who travelled often, trying to forge friendships with men of power. During one of his journeys through a vast wasteland, he lost his way and got separated from his men. For one whole day, he rode through the narrow trails, trying to get back on track. But instead he stumbled upon a valley full of bright flowers and musical streams. The place was called Jiling La and the small community of people who lived there received him with much kindness, offering him food and shelter. They told him about a secret route through the wasteland that would lead back to his home province.

During his time in Jiling La, Bingwen felt that something strange was about to happen. The valley appeared to be steeped in magical vibrations and the place seemed to unlock in him, powers that he had never cared to explore. He met Biyu's mother, Kaya, in this enchanted valley. She was a pretty girl, longing to explore the world beyond the peripheries of Jiling La. He was a brawny young man, with big dreams in his eyes. It was love at first sight.

After seven days, when it was time for Bingwen Bitang to leave Jiling La, he married Kaya in a small ceremony and left for home.

Guided by Kaya, Bingwen rode on horseback through the secret pathways. At midday, when they stopped for lunch, Bingwen noticed a shrivelled, old man curling up against a tree. He seemed to be in great distress and death was probably imminent.

When Bingwen stepped ahead meaning to help the ailing old man, Kaya stopped him.

"Don't touch him," Kaya warned. "He has been cursed by the witches. If you touch him, the curse will pass on to you."

"This is no way to treat a dying man," Bingwen protested and kneeled down beside the old man.

Kaya watched in horror as Bingwen took the man's hands in his own and began to whisper words of comfort. She thought of pulling her husband away from the cursed man when a change came over Bingwen. He began to breathe hard and went into a trance.

"He is passing the curse," Kaya screamed, clutching her hair.

But Bingwen's breathing became normal again and he smiled at the frail, old man. The dying man sat up and returned the smile. Kaya watched in sheer disbelief.

The old man parted his thin lips, trying to speak. At first, no sound came out. But Bingwen urged him and after a while he started to speak in a thin, cracked voice.

"You are gifted," the old man said, taking a ball of rag out of his pocket and placing it in Bingwen's hand. "You're gifted."

"Throw it away," Kaya cried.

Bingwen simply pocketed the rag ball and walked back to his wife. He put his hand around her shoulder, trying to calm her.

"I'll throw it away," he whispered into his wife's ears.

"You must heal others too," the old man shouted as Bingwen and Kaya walked away.

Bingwen turned back and acknowledged the man with a polite nod. After they had gone out of his sight, he pretended to throw away the rag ball deep into the forest, much to Kaya's relief.

They travelled together for three days before arriving at Bingwen's home province. His safe return made everyone so happy that they decided to excuse his sudden marriage to an unknown girl from an unknown place.

After a few months of marital bliss, Kaya announced that she was with child. This made Bingwen's family incredibly happy and everyone looked forward to the birth of a boy, the rightful heir of the Bitangs.

So, after a full-term pregnancy when Kaya gave birth to Biyu, a girl, it came as a shock. The whole family refused to talk to Kaya and even Bingwen felt that his wife had failed him. He declared that he would travel to Jiling La to tell his in-laws about the birth of their grand-daughter. In reality, he needed an excuse to avoid Kaya for some time.

Bingwen Bitang started alone on horseback for Jiling La. It was not a difficult terrain, and he felt that a solitary ride would calm his nerves. He got the shock of his life on reaching the valley where Jiling La used to be. An earthquake had completely destroyed the place. Everywhere he looked, he saw dead bodies buried under rubble. The catastrophe seemed to have happened a few months back, for nature was already reclaiming the valley, with shoots sprouting here and there, thriving on rotting human flesh.

Bingwen kneeled in front of the mass grave and joined his palms to pray for those who had ascended to the high skies. Then he got up and started his ride back home. He had no idea how he would break this terrible news to Kaya.

When night fell, Bingwen lit a fire and sat by it, listening to the sounds of the forest. He had not meant to sleep that night, but as the hours idly rolled on, his eyes felt heavy. Bingwen ate some bread and fruits from his bag. Then, he invigorated the flames by adding some dry leaves, spread a mat next to the fire, and fell fast asleep on it.

Bingwen woke up screaming in the dead of the night. There was a thick, sharp thorn stuck deep into his left eye. His clothes got soaked as blood gushed out and he lost consciousness for a while.

When Bingwen came round, he felt like something was throbbing in his pocket. He dug out the lump immediately and saw that it was the forgotten rag-ball that the old man had once given him. Bingwen hastily peeled of the layers of rag to reveal a small stone of muted glow at the centre. It seemed to bestow him with strange powers.

Bingwen Bitang closed his eyes and began to hyperventilate. He instructed his body to repair the bloodied wound in his left eye socket. The pain was gone within seconds but he felt very weak. Also, his eye was damaged and he had to forsake it. He stood up looking around for some sign of life. There seemed to be no one around. Yet there was a sense of piercing malevolence that seemed to be watching him from somewhere.

Bingwen decided to not wait there any longer. He mounted his horse and started for home right away. When he reached his province, he told everyone that he was attacked by bandits and the fight that followed had cost him his eye. He used the stone that he had got in Jiling La to fashion a false eye and put it in his left eye socket.

When Bingwen entered his own room he saw Kaya sitting with the sleeping baby in her lap. She looked so frail and morose that it moved her husband's heart. He wrapped her in an embrace and told her softly about the disaster that had befallen Jiling La.

Kaya howled into the night, disregarding all rules of not mourning those have passed on to higher skies. Her husband hugged her tighter and comforted her, promising to never shun her again.

Baby Biyu woke up in the commotion and Bingwen scooped her up in his arms. As her curious eyes met her father's, she flashed a huge, impulsive smile. It melted away all the iciness in Bingwen's heart.

From the next day, Bingwen Bitang began to make calls to the homes of the suffering ones. He used his magical touch to heal all kinds of maladies in his province. Within months, he became very popular for his miracles and the Bitang coffer, that had been starving for generations, was once again teeming with wealth.

Chapter 8: Bingwen Bitang Makes Multiple Decisions

Bingwen Bitang was happy to see his fortunes multiply. His bond with his wife improved and little Biyu flooded his heart with love. But there was one nagging concern that gnawed at his heart. He longed for a male heir. When Kaya announced her second pregnancy, Bingwen felt like the Moon god had finally answered his prayers. This time, it would surely be a boy.

But as the months rolled on, he grew restless. What if luck failed him a second time?

One night when his wife came to bed, Bingwen snuggled closer. She smiled and fell asleep in the warmth of his arms. Bingwen immediately shifted into his alternate self and connected with the baby growing in Kaya's womb. To his utter dismay, he found that this one was a girl too.

For an hour, Bingwen tossed and turned in his bed while Kaya slept on peacefully. Finally, he knew what he had to do. He would induce a miscarriage through his magical touch. He decided to do it to all the future babies in his wife's womb until he sensed the presence of a boy.

Bingwen held Kaya's hand and connected to the tribes of her womb. He incited them to expel the growing baby from the body. As the tribes began to follow his instructions. Kaya woke up with severe cramping in her lower belly. When she saw her husband holding her hand and murmuring with his eyes closed, she felt a little braver. He would surely be able to help her.

Kaya endured the pain with the hope that it would diminish any moment. Instead, it escalated fast and suddenly the baby slipped out of her womb. Kaya shrieked and passed out at the horrid sight. The half-formed baby now lay dead between her mother's legs while Kaya kept on losing blood. Bingwen stayed calm. He told himself that he would heal his wife and all will be well. The next day, Bingwen would tell everyone that he had tried to save both his wife and the unborn child, but the baby unfortunately had passed on to the high skies.

Bingwen began to instruct the small beings of Kaya's body to heal the wounds. But there was something wrong. He could not connect to them. He tried a few more times but to no avail. Kaya was losing blood fast and for the first time Bingwen was frightened by the sight of it. He thought maybe he was out of the alternate self. So, he started breathing hard again, hoping to invoke his powers. But nothing worked. Bingwen began to sweat profusely as he held up Kaya's head in his arms. She appeared limp and pale.

And then, the truth struck Bingwen. He had lost his powers! He ran out and woke up the rest of the family. The healer of their province was sent for. It was morning by the time the healer reached the Bitang residence. By then, all was lost. Kaya had left for the high skies along with her baby.

A little later Biyu came running into her parent's room asking for her mother. Bingwen clasped her to his chest and began to cry bitterly. There was no way he could tell his daughter that he had just killed her mother and unborn sister.

Bingwen Bitang never fully recovered from the tragedy. Though everyone told him to find another wife, he did not marry again. He grew quiet and withdrew from most of his engagements. Instead, he spent most of time raising Biyu, the only memory of Kaya.

Sitting in the garden by Biyu's room, Bingwen shed silent tears from his one good eye as he thought of the past. His daughter came out to join him. She had fed her son and sent him with the chaperones for a tour of the castle.

"Dauda," Biyu said as she wiped her father's tears. "Life is so hard."

Bingwen looked at her. It was time to tell Biyu about his powers. He took a deep breath and began the story. He described his childhood, adventures and meeting with Kaya in details. However, when it came to confessing about the murder of his wife and child, he tweaked facts slightly. Bingwen said that Kaya had suffered a natural miscarriage which made Bingwen so nervous that he could not apply his powers properly to heal her. He highlighted the danger of using such powers and reiterated that Mong should be banished from the kingdom for the safety of all.

"Now that you know of the immense powers that your father once wielded," Bingwen stated, "do not feel inferior to Mong in any way. The priceless gem that I wear in my left eye will come to your son's possession once I ascend to the high skies. Stay strong, Biyu, the glory of the future will be yours."

Biyu was both amazed and confused after listening to her father but as always, his words gave her a lot of courage.

"I'd make Fa Ren Sung pay for putting you through so much pain," Bingwen promised as he got up.

Bingwen Bitang blessed his daughter one more time before he walked away towards the open court where his grandchild was taking his fill of royal splendour with his tiny, twinkling eyes. Bingwen took stage and performed all the rituals. He named the prince Reniyu eliciting much applause from all those present. Fa Ren Sung hoped for a reconciliatory talk with his father-in-law after this, but Bingwen kept his lips sealed. He even refused to participate in the royal feast and marched out without looking back. Bingwen's coachman spurred the horses into action as soon as his master seated himself and the carriage left the capital as suddenly as it had arrived.

The hurried departure of Bingwen Bitang hung in the air and everyone remained quiet for some time. But gradually the unpleasantness faded away and the pitch of mirth and merry-making began to pick up. Only the king felt a stinging worry pinch at his heart. He wondered if there will be repercussions.

Chapter 9 : Emperor Ullinki Lays His Claim

Prince Reniyu's childhood started on a happy note. Even though his parents were not on excellent terms, he got his share of love from both. The king was very proud of his son. And as for the queen, her little boy was her only source of joy. Her relationship with her husband grew increasingly formal as time passed on. To her utter dismay, most of her loyal subjects began to revere Mong for her ability to alleviate pain in one and all.

One day when the prince was about eight months old, Fa Ren Sung told Biyu that Mong would present herself to touch and bless the prince at his next public appearance. Though Biyu did not approve of the idea, yet she could not voice a formal protest because if not for Mong, Reniyu would have never seen the light of day.

Thursdays were allocated for public viewing of the prince. The queen sat on the throne with the prince on her lap at the open court. Then the subjects would come up to take a good look at the royal baby. On the next Thursday, Fe Ren Sung led Mong to his son. Biyu hated to see her husband hold his second wife's hand, but there were many subjects present, so she did not let her scorn become obvious.

Mong knelt in front of the queen and touched the fuzzy head of the sleeping prince. He woke up at the touch and, after carefully observing the lady peering down at him, he grabbed her wrist with his fibril fingers. Mong felt a rush of love flooding her heart, and her sightless eyes grew misty with emotions.

"Will you allow me to be his second mother?" she asked the queen without any further thought.

Queen Biyu was about to turn her down when Mong added, "If you share your child with me, I promise to not have children of my own."

This proposition pleased Fa Ren Sung very much. He had been terribly worried all along about the possibility of rivalry between his children from both wives. If Mong agreed to not have children, it would make the future of the kingdom uncomplicated and peaceful. He stared at Biyu, willing her with his eyes to accede to the request.

A hushed silence had fallen at the open court and everyone waited with bated breath for the queen to speak up.

"Yes, you can be his second mother," the queen whispered at last, buckling under pressure.

After this event, things fell into a steady routine at Krai Tang. For almost three years, nobody had to deal with any real problem or threat. And then one day, when the kingdom was getting ready to celebrate the third birthday of the prince, trouble presented itself right at the gates of the capital.

Hordes of armed soldiers laid seize to the city in the dead of night. The security people at the gates could hold them off only for a short while. Then they had to choose between letting them in with dignity or getting trampled under broken gates and rushing men. Not wanting to seal the room for negotiation they chose the first option and soon, the intruders were swarming all over the capital. The next morning people in the capital woke up to a rude shock.

Han assessed the situation and ran to fetch Fa Ren Sung from his chamber to the open court at the wee hours of dawn. There was an emergency, he explained to the king who dawdled by him. Stepping on to the court the king was stunned. There was someone seated on his throne whose broad silhouette was visible against the first rays of the morning sun. The man's thick brown mane blew slightly in the gentle wind as he inspected the blooming buds quivering in the garden. The view gave Fa Ren Sung a visceral sense of fear. He gulped and cleared his voice.

"Who is that, in my place?" the king whispered to Han.

"That man in your place is Ullinki, the emperor of the South," Han answered, hiding half of himself behind a pillar.

Emperor Ullinki ruled over his ever-expanding kingdom that lay on the other side of the Niyoshi mountain range. People of Krai Tang had heard tales of his horrific cruelty and they had always hoped that they would never come face to face with the emperor or his barbarians who lived in the southern terrains. The towering mountains that separated the northern territories from the empire of Ullinki had acted as a safety shield for long. But that day, their luck seemed to have just run out.

"Why did he come without a word?" Fa Ren Sung whispered to Han.

"That I am not aware of," Han mumbled. "Perhaps you should speak to him."

Fa Ren Sung held his head straight and walked up to the stranger occupying his throne.

"Whoever you are, you are in my rightful seat, without my permission," the king boomed in his loudest voice.

Emperor Ullinki stood up without haste and turned around to face Fa

Ren Sung. He towered above the king in length and in breadth. His muscles bulged out obscenely and though there was a smile gracing his thin lips, there was nothing reassuring about his demeanour.

"Fa Ren Sung," Ullinki began. "I'm Emperor Ullinki from down south."

At this, Han stepped ahead and introduced the King of Krai Tang with a bunch of flowery epithets. Then, he asked Ullinki the purpose of his visit. Ullinki stroked his beard as he listened and when Han was done, he laughed aloud.

"Can your king not speak that another man has to take the trouble?" he mocked.

His gruff voice rang out loud and those around him felt terrified.

"I came because I wanted to. My men have accompanied me as well. Make provisions for them. None of my people should be inconvenienced."

Ullinki was now commanding the king's men in his presence. They hung their heads and waited for his direction. This offended Ullinki and he shrugged his shoulders.

"Is this how you greet guests?" he asked, raising his voice by another notch.

"No word was sent, and we weren't ready to receive you," Han clarified. "Please pardon us if our ways seem unfriendly."

"Bring the queen out," Ullinki ordered. "The king clearly is incapable of talking."

"Don't you know, you uncouth emperor from down south, that it is wrong to ask to meet a king's wife without the king's consent?" Fa Ren Sung tried to roar back, but his voice shook, giving him away.

"I heard you have a spare wife," Ullinki sneered. "Why do you then refuse to share the first one with me?"

Fa Ren Sung hissed angrily. But his legs seemed to be made of concrete, and he could not make himself step towards Ullinki.

"Bring her out or I shall go in," Ullinki boomed.

Han requested for some time and rushed in to fetch Biyu. He briefly described the situation to the queen and stuffed a shrivelled root extract into her right palm. If the evil stranger made any attempt to defile her, Biyu was to ingest it and seek escape to the high skies.

A trembling Biyu walked out to the open court. She had hastily wrapped an embroidered shawl around herself. But her hair was wiry, face undecorated and the extravagant royal jewellery was missing. Ullinki took a long, hard look at her and turned to the king.

"Is this the way to treat your queen?" he yelled at Fa Ren Sung.

Ullinki took off the clunky gold chain from around his own neck and walked up to Biyu. He double-folded it before gently placing it around her slender neck. Then, he made a small bow. Biyu flinched at his proximity.

"I almost forgot how great your beauty was," Ullinki said.

All eyes in the court turned to Biyu, who stood there rock solid, too shocked and too afraid to speak.

"I'm Emperor Ullinki now," Ullinki said. "But don't you remember me back from the good old days, as a boy named Ju-Long?"

And, in a flash, it all came back to her. Ju-Long was the eldest son of the slaves who worked for the Bitangs. The boy sometimes played with Biyu and made up enchanting stories for her. He used to daydream about building his own kingdom. And then one day Ju-Long ran away from home. That was the last that anyone had seen the boy. After conducting minimal searches, people gave up on him. Nobody cared much about a missing son of the slaves. Biyu missed her friend badly at first, but as she grew up, her memories of Ju-Long sank under piles of newer experiences.

"Ju-Long!" Biyu uttered as she stared at the huge form of Emperor Ullinki.

Ullinki stepped ahead to enfold Biyu in a hug. Everyone present in and around the court cringed at this. Biyu felt herself blush within the strong arms of Ullinki; the boy she had known as the lanky Ju-Long had grown into one of the mightiest rulers. All her fears faded away at his touch. When Ullinki released Biyu from his grasp, there was nothing but joy in her eyes.

"Please make arrangements for Emperor Ullinki," she firmly ordered her subjects. "For his relation with me goes back to the times when we were both much younger. He is a very dear person to me and hence, an esteemed guest in this land."

"How about letting me stay with you?" Ullinki said cheekily, as he winked at Biyu.

It made Fa Ren Sung's blood boil with disgust. To his complete shock, he saw Biyu giggle like it was some kind of joke.

"I believe it is ok for you to stay with me," the queen said after a pause.

"The king, these days, is busy elsewhere anyway."

A hushed wave of despair passed through the court as soon as people heard Biyu's words. Fa Ren Sung stood by the side of Han, hoping that everything happening around him was just a wild nightmare that would end any moment. He hoped and then he prayed, but nothing could prevent his queen from taking Ullinki inside the palace, into her private chamber.

Over the next few days, the intruders from the southern empire began to forcefully occupy the homes in the capital. The legitimate owners were driven out, and those who dared to protest were killed by Ullinki's people. Soon, most of the subjects in the capital were living in servitude, acting according to the whims of the barbarians. And all throughout, Queen Biyu's closeness with Emperor Ullinki grew with an unabashed overtness. Han took a desperate message from Fa Ren Sung to his queen, requesting one meeting of the king with Biyu. But she only smirked at the idea and turned it down.

"Now that I have found a real man," Biyu told Han. "I don't want that eunuch of a king anymore."

Han diligently passed on the reply message to Fe Ren Sung. The next day, Biyu asked Han to choose between her and the king, and he immediately opted to serve the queen. When given similar options, Wei and Krin Ki refused to leave the king's side, so they were promptly put into prison by Ullinki's men. In fact, most of Fa Ren Sung's trusted men were jailed in succession. The positions of power were handed over to Ullinki's aides, and there were six prominent men who now helped their emperor to run the capital of Krai Tang.

The ousted king, Fa Ren Sung spent most of his days in the room of high order, alone. Han's betrayal had hit him the hardest. Without him, he felt incapable of making any firm decision. He longed to see Mong as well, but Ullinki had special orders issued to not let the king meet her. Fa Ren Sung knew that it would not be long before Ullinki put him behind bars too and that he needed to plan a resurgence fast. But he had neither manpower nor ideas at his disposal. And he grew desperate with each passing day.

Biyu and Ullinki, on the other hand, were profoundly happy in their untamed lust for each other. They would spend a lot of time in their private chamber, getting intimate on the huge bed. As Ullinki traced the soft curves on her body with his lips, Biyu moaned in pleasure. She had felt unwanted for a long time, and the attention that Ullinki showered on her seemed to take away all the hurt. He would undress the queen gently and place strawberry slices on her bare skin. He would ask her to stay still as he nibbled on the fruits. By the time he had eaten the last of the strawberries, Biyu would beg him to take her. And then Ullinki would enter her with all his hardness and bear down on her in a delicious, ancient rhythm. Finally, something would explode within Biyu making her go blank in the mind. She would pant in Ullinki's strong arms, unable to speak. It had never been like that with her husband. With Fa Ren Sung, she had not known that it was possible to fall apart like that in bed and find herself in euphoric bliss.

One evening, as the queen lay beside him, Ullinki pulled her closer and said casually that Fa Ren Sung has to move on to the high skies. Biyu sat up at the suggestion.

"High skies? Surely, he will, when his time comes-" Biyu began.

"The time has come," Ullinki sat up too and placed his arm around her belly from the back.

He planted a kiss on her neck and tickled her at the waist. Biyu breathed in deeply.

"I need you to be my wife," Ullinki said. "Fa Ren Sung is no good for you."

Biyu thought of the insults she had to endure from the king and then she thought of the son she shared with him.

"What about Reniyu?" she asked, even as she twitched, responding to the gentle caresses of Ullinki's fingers.

"He'll have me as a father," Ullinki assured. "A stronger father who loves his mother."

"And will you raise him with enough care to make him into a worthy king?" she turned around and succumbed into Ullinki's arms.

"I will," Ullinki promised before starting to suck on Biyu's lips.

They made the most intense love that night. Sealing Fa Ren Sung's fate turned them on like never before.

On the following day, Ullinki spent several hours planning the king's end with his six trusted men. When the meeting ended, they felt they had come up with the perfect plan.

At night, Fa Ren Sung's long trusted man servant served him his dinner of dumplings, soup and steak. No one knew that one of Ullinki's six men had emptied a vial of poison in the soup.

Fa Ren Sung prayed to the Moon god and began to eat. He dunked half a dumpling into the soup and placed it in his mouth. It tasted funny. The king sniffed the food and took a closer look but there was no odd smell, no suspicious colour. He drank some more soup. Again, he got that overpowering taste. Perhaps Ullinki's men had cooked his meal, thought Fa Ren Sung. The barbarians must have put in the spices in the wrong order.

The king continued to drink the soup. He failed to note that his tongue was becoming heavier with each spoonful that he washed down. A drowsiness came over him and started to cripple his senses. He felt for a split second that he needed to see Mong and ask her to revive him. But then, his thoughts got locked into a stupor. His heart pumped erratically a few more times before giving up and going quiet.

In the morning, when the man servant came to serve Fa Ren Sung his morning tea, he found the king's lifeless body lying by the unfinished food. He pushed the body a couple of times, called him aloud, hoping that Fa Ren Sung would respond. When he got nothing, the servant ran out to bring the royal healers, but the six men of Ullinki were waiting outside.

"Mourn him not," said one of them, grabbing the man servant by his shoulder.

"You lost one king," said another man. "But you will get another."

"In no time," whispered a third man, articulating each syllable clearly.

Then all six of them broke into cruel laughter.

By midday the news of Fa Ren Sung's passage to the high skies was released to the people of Krai Tang. Though Ullinki and his men claimed that a sudden spasm of the heart had taken away the king, everyone understood that he had been murdered. No one cried for the king in the open. But they knew that the days of peace were over in Krai Tang and dark days of anarchy lay ahead of them.

Chapter 10: The Dark Times

When Biyu learned about the death of her husband, she found that she was unable to feel any joy. Memories from the past, of their happy times together, came rushing to her, making her feel empty. Ullinki was busy that day, so Biyu spent her time with her son. She sat with him in front of the deity of the Moon god, praying for the wellbeing of Fa Ren Sung in the high skies. Reniyu asked her constant questions about his father, which further depressed Biyu. She was relieved when fatigue wore out the boy and he fell asleep on his mother's lap.

But no matter how hard Biyu herself tried to sleep, she could not. At last, Ullinki entered the room when he felt sufficiently assured that the day's business had been taken care of. He made an elaborate sign of victory and hugged Biyu tight.

"We belong to each other now," he gloated. "But one more task remains; tomorrow I will kill off the witch your husband was bedding."

For a second, Biyu was jealous as she imagined Mong reuniting with Fa Ren Sung in the high skies. But then she brushed the feeling aside and agreed with Ullinki that it would indeed be the best thing to do.

So, on the very next day, after the sun had set, Ullinki stormed into the rest house unannounced. He saw Mong seated by the window, seemingly gazing out at the full moon. She was dressed in a simple white dress and the moon shone down on her face. For a moment, Ullinki was stunned by her beauty and thought he was staring at an ancient goddess. He took quiet steps to take a closer look.

Mong's eyes were red from crying and her countenance soaked in grief. She seemed to sense the presence of Ullinki because she turned towards the spot where he was and asked, "Is anyone here?"

There was no reply but Mong could feel a strange kind of charge emanate from someone around her. Ullinki remembered that she was blind. He began to retrace his steps silently. The charge weakened before Mong could be sure of its presence. She let out a long sigh and turned her face towards the open window again.

Ullinki went straight to the room of high order, which he used for his meetings now, and closed the door. He had never seen anyone so drenched in sorrow as Mong. He thought of the beautiful women he owned in his empire down south and wondered if anyone would miss him if he ascended to the high skies. And he felt envious of the dead Fa Ren

Sung for the first time. Surely, it must be her blindness that made Mong love him so dearly. Ullinki knew he had vowed to behead Mong with his own hands but he now felt an urge to spare her life.

Queen Biyu, on the other hand, was busy recruiting a new staff of chaperones. She replaced all those women who had rejoiced over the second marriage of the king. She was briefing the new team about the preferences of prince Reniyu when Han presented himself and bowed.

"Some subjects have come hoping to see Her Highness," Han said. "Would you be able to come out for a short while?"

Biyu ordered the new chaperones to mind her son and walked out with Han. There were scores of women and girls waiting for her at the open court. Dressed in torn, soiled clothes, they looked pale and devoid of any hope. They complained that Ullinki's men were mercilessly killing off the men of Krai Tang. Their widows and daughters were then reduced to slaves. They requested the queen's intervention to end their misery.

Biyu took one hard look at the assembled group and broke into wild laughter. The lady folks were shocked by her reaction and the change in their expressions seemed to incite more bouts of joy in the queen. She finally stopped her jeering after a long while and took a moment to catch her breath. Then, in a voice that sounded colder than ice, the queen reminded them of the times when she had sought their support and how they had chosen to offer their allegiance to Mong instead. Biyu told them that she would not move a finger to help them out and perhaps they should run to their favourite witch for alternative solutions.

"Where is Ullinki?" Biyu asked Han, suddenly swivelling around to face him.

"He was slated to execute Mong today," Han answered.

"Oh right," Biyu nodded. "Tell him to come to me once the witch is done away with. And then, you must personally go around checking on our subjects. Find the ones who had opposed the king's marriage. The time has come for me to reward them for their loyalty. Bring them over, for they will now enjoy the queen's protection."

"I will get things done," Han promised and started to walk across the court.

He went down the stairs and took the pebbled pathway running between the gardens. At a little distance, he saw the women and the girls leaving. Their droopy shoulders and sluggish pace reflected their despair; there was no one left to fend for them anymore. Han sighed and looked back at the court. The queen had disappeared into the palace. For a second, he felt like giving up. But Han took a deep breath and refocussed. Then, he changed his course to walk all the way to the rest house on the western side of the palace.

When Han arrived, he found Mong's attendants packing at a corner. They too had been dismissed from their jobs. The two women and their daughters walked out after whispering sombre goodbyes to Mong and Han. Mong sat alone in the middle of the floor with Han in front of her.

"If you have come to ask for my head," Mong said to Han. "I bid you to take it right away."

"I am not who you think I am," Han clarified as he sat down in front of Mong. "I am Han, not Ullinki."

"It doesn't matter," Mong vented. "If you could help Ullinki to take my husband's life… your master's life, then you can very well behead me."

"I've always looked down on you," Han admitted. "Yet today I ask you for your forgiveness."

Mong kept quiet.

"I didn't help anyone to kill Fa Ren Sung," Han continued. "Ullinki does not share all his plans with me. I had no idea about what was going on in his mind."

Mong still made no comment, so after a short pause Han carried on.

"I was trying to gain Ullinki's trust and plan a coup meanwhile," Han explained. "But things happened all too fast. Queen Biyu might have faith in me, but Ullinki is shrewd enough to not trust me fully."

"I do not understand why you are telling me all this," Mong said. "What I desire now is my passage to the high skies. It is a sin for me to end my life, but if you can end it for me, I shall be highly obliged."

"This is not the time to give up," Han urged. "Our people need you."

"I'm only a blind girl," Mong retorted. "Are you trying to ridicule me?"

Han dipped his hands into his pockets and dug out two chains.

He handed them to Mong and said, "Can you smell the scent of your family in it?"

Mong fingered the chains gently and recognized the metallic touch. The chains belonged to her parents Chow Hee and Sui Hee.

"Have my parents come to see me?" she asked.

"They'll always watch you now," Han replied. "Ullinki's men have killed your family. And the small hut which you once used to think of as home is now occupied by his people."

Mong's grip on the chains loosened and they fell in a sorry huddle close to her feet. All these years she had tried to think as little as she could about her family. But when her thoughts did veer towards them, she imagined her parents to be happy with her seven brothers. She always thought she would get to visit them again in the future, when her brothers would marry one by one. And now all of them were gone, dousing out her hopes of a reunion. Mong started to cry uncontrollably.

Han placed his palm over her head and said, "You need to be steady now. We must not mourn the ones who have found happiness above."

Mong howled for long and Han sat by her quietly, waiting for her grief to subside. Finally, when her cries had given way to sniffles, he spoke again.

"Ullinki is not going to kill you so fast," he said. "He came to me in the early hours asking if he can take you for his own."

Mong creased her face in disgust and pleaded to be killed immediately.

"Please Mong," Han begged. "You have to pretend to be his love. And try to buy us time. We need you to do this. For Krai Tang, for Reniyu, for everyone! Ullinki's men have spread out beyond the capital. They are already capturing one village after the other. We need to do something."

"I can't believe you'd ask me to do this," Mong said. "I just cannot-"

At that very moment, an approaching commotion was sounded outside. Han peeped through the window to see Ullinki drag a protesting Biyu towards the rest house. Han described the scene briefly to Mong and swiftly went out through the door on the opposite wall.

Ullinki did not bother to knock or ask for the door to be opened. He kicked it hard and the latch holding the door closed fell apart, throwing it open. Ullinki shoved Biyu in first, and then he walked in.

"You are not in your right mind, Ullinki," Biyu warned as she rubbed the redness on her upper arm where Ullinki had grabbed her. "Don't forget that you can be the King of Krai Tang only if the queen says so."

"No, no, you will be the Queen of Krai Tang for as long as I want you to be," Ullinki corrected her.

He stepped closer to Mong and placed his hands on her shoulders. And at that instant, Mong could again feel the same charge that she had sensed earlier. She recoiled in fright, but Ullinki had moved back towards Biyu.

"Mong," he spoke to Mong while looking at Biyu. "After meeting you, I realised why Fa Ren Sung chose you over Biyu. But I will offer you what Fa Ren Sung hadn't. I'll make you the queen and Biyu will serve you as your maid."

"Stop this nonsense," Biyu screamed.

"Stop shouting," Ullinki said firmly. "You're just like your arrogant father."

"Don't you utter a word against Dauda," Biyu threatened, her voice sounding feral.

Ullinki laughed.

"I've so many things to say about your father," he said. "Listen carefully, Biyu, for I will tell you the truth now. Bingwen Bitang had been in touch with me for decades. He thought himself to be important enough to earn my respect. I never paid much attention to his overtures until recently, when he invited me to his home, promising to help me to invade Krai Tang. This time my interest was piqued, and I did go to see your father."

"Don't forget that you worked for the Bitangs once," Biyu said. "And this is how you are repaying the debt to Dauda! You have the blood of slaves in your veins, Ju-Long… you are not fit to be a king!"

Ullinki laughed again and brought his face closer to Biyu.

"Who's Ju-Long?" Ullinki hissed. "Do you even know that Ju-Long did not actually leave home on his own? He was sent away by Bingwen Bitang to my kingdom as an informer. He was the link through which your father and I kept in touch for decades. And your Ju-Long passed away last month trying to defend your old father. I'm no sweetheart from your childhood. I just used his name to gain your favour. I'm Ullinki, Emperor of the South and you dare not speak to me with such disdain, you filthy woman."

Biyu covered her ears with her hands and fell to the floor. She felt dizzy. Ullinki clutched a fistful of her hair and pulled her up roughly.

"Look at the belt I wear, Biyu," he said, placing his arms at his hips and puffing out his chest to hold the belt in full display. "Look closely at the single stone that shines at the buckle."

Biyu stared at the broad belt adorning Ullinki's waist. The stone at the centre glowed in the light and it seemed to remind Biyu of something very precious. And then it struck upon her. The stone was the false left eye of her father.

If Biyu could gather even a little bit of strength, she would have killed Ullinki then and there. But grief seemed to have paralyzed her. She stood still, stiff from shock. Despite her best efforts to not do so, her mind pictured the horrible ways in which her father might have died in the hands of Ullinki.

"I stabbed your father in the heart," Ullinki ended her doubts, after a while. "Then I scooped out his false eye for my belt."

Ullinki marched to Mong again and ran a finger along her cheek. Mong felt the same sensation that she had felt earlier. Then she understood what was creating the charge.

The magic stone of Bingwen Bitang was interacting with the pendant in Mong's neck. She knew she had to protect the snake stone pendant that Fa Ren Sung had given her from evil hands. If Ullinki found out what she had in her possession, he would most certainly put it to unholy use.

Mong breathed hard and fought to stay in control of herself. The charge was getting stronger and she felt afraid that it might overpower her any second. So, she tore herself away from Ullinki and rushed to the window.

"Emperor Ullinki," Mong began abruptly. "Forgive me for shunning your proximity. But I will let you have me as your own, only after you become my husband. Let us be wedded tonight, let no Biyu stand between us."

Mong's words stung Biyu and she hurled a slew of expletives at her. Her jealousy delighted Ullinki very much.

"I'd send for the men of divination, pretty one," Ullinki said. "We will marry tonight as per your wish. And never mind the words of Biyu. The ugly one can only have ugly words."

Biyu clamped her teeth down on Ullinki's wrist, who grimaced for a moment before jerking his hand away. He pinned Biyu's arms behind her back and grabbed her hair to hold her still.

"A couple of women will come to get you ready to be my bride," Ullinki told Mong. "Let me throw this one into prison first. She is wrestling like a rabid bitch now."

Ullinki left with Biyu as hurriedly as he had arrived. But his steps sounded jauntier. He had not hoped to win over Mong so fast.

As soon as they were gone, Mong bolted the door and took off the snake stone pendant from her neck. She put it in the jewellery box and sat down to think. Whatever she decided had to be done fast; time was running out.

A little before midnight a team of women came and helped Mong to change into bridal attire. They dressed her in a pink and magenta gown and placed jewels on her neck and hair. Then they guided her to the temple of the Moon god where Ullinki was already waiting to marry her. The night was starry and a dainty breeze was blowing when Ullinki and Mong joined hands in front of the men of divination. The men prayed to the Moon god first and then they began the chants to solemnize the bond of marriage between Ullinki and Mong.

But Mong was not listening to any of it. She prayed for courage and then she began to breathe heavily. It took her a few seconds to transform into her alternate self. Ullinki was about to ask Mong if she felt alright but he could not bring himself to speak. Mong had established connection with the small beings of his body. She cajoled them into rebelling against the body that housed Ullinki's soul.

Ullinki felt a sudden surge of pain in his chest as blood stopped flowing to his heart. He could have saved himself by freeing himself of Mong's touch. But in his confusion, he clutched her hands tighter. And Mong went on firing rapid instructions to the small beings that constituted his body. Ullinki fell to his knees as the pain worsened.

The men of divination paused their chanting and observed everything with open mouths. They neither helped Mong nor protested as her touch squeezed the soul out of Ullinki's body and set it free after twenty minutes of struggle.

Only after the men were sure of Ullinki's death, did they run and get help. Han was one of the first ones to arrive. He felt a surge of relief when he saw the lifeless body of Ullinki lying at Mong's feet. He whispered a word of thanks into her ears and then he asked the men of divination to arrange for Ulllinki's body to be put into an ornamental coffin as a mark of respect. He gave out a few more instructions to those present regarding their course of action. Then Han steadied himself for the long night ahead. He needed to be at his diplomatic best if he was to turn Ullinki's death into an advantage for Krai Tang.

The first thing that Han did was to get the queen released from prison. He met her in the room of high order.

"Ullinki has been slain by Mong," Han informed Biyu as soon as he had closed the door.

Biyu looked puzzled for some time, and then she nodded knowingly.

"We need to release the news of Ullinki's passage to the high skies with utmost caution," Han advised. "His barbarians would seek vengeance if they suspect our involvement, and my hunch is that they will."

Biyu massaged her temples gently and thought for long.

"Make arrangements for my morning address at the open court," she commanded. "I know how to handle the masses."

"Very well," Han agreed. "Tomorrow we would give Ullinki an ostentatious burial. Now, I'll go and try to pacify the six loyal men of Ullinki."

"No," Biyu said with a raised hand. "Send them here. I'll talk to them. You can oversee the rest of the proceedings."

"But they are dangerous," Han reasoned. "And are likely to attack any time."

"And that's why I need to talk to them," Biyu replied calmly.

The six men were roused from their sleep and brought to talk to the queen. Han wanted to stand guard at the door, but he knew that he had many more things to take care of. He placed ten soldiers outside and instructed them to break the door and go in at the slightest hint of struggle or violence. But they sensed no such disturbance, and it was nearly morning when the door to the room of high order opened again. Biyu walked out first, followed by the six men of Ullinki. They looked more like ferocious tigers with fire in their eyes. The sight alarmed Han. The only saving grace was that the queen was unharmed.

That day, the open court was crowded beyond capacity. There were rumours in the air about Ullinki's sudden demise, and everyone demanded to know the truth. People of Krai Tang looked very worried as the discontent among Ullinki's men grew with every passing minute.

The stage had been prepared for the queen's address. Mong was already seated in the middle of the podium as per Biyu's instructions. Han stood just by the dais, holding firmly onto little Reniyu's hands. His job was to protect the prince's life in case trouble broke out. Queen Biyu had the good judgement to not keep people waiting for long. She stepped on to the stage, her face completely devoid of emotions. Ullinki's people got so restless on seeing her that it seemed like a riot could break out any moment. At this juncture, the six loyal men of Ullinki stepped up and stood behind Biyu. Seeing them Ullinki's people calmed down a bit, deciding to listen to the queen before taking any action.

"Today is a dark day for all of us," Biyu began. "We will keep Ullinki, the Emperor of the South in our hearts forever, though his holy soul has departed his body and ascended to the high skies."

This announcement was followed by ten heavy gongs. Eight uniformed men marched in, carrying the ornamental coffin containing Ullinki's body. They placed it in front of the podium for all to pay their last respects. Through the corner of her eyes, Biyu checked out Mong. The queen's men had not given Mong much time before she was almost dragged to the podium. But she had managed to put Fa Ren Sung's chain with the snake stone pendant around her neck. As Mong felt the chunky pendant against her skin, she felt brave. To Biyu, she appeared proud and defiant. The queen liked it very much.

"We need to find ways to get on with our lives," Biyu spoke again as soon as the reverberation of the last gong faded away. "So, I have entered a royal treaty with these great men who will now go on to rule the six major provinces of Ullinki's empire. As the Queen of Krai Tang I promise to these six new kingdoms that we will always stand by them and never start any internal war. From today, we are seven friendly kingdoms, ready to uphold each other."

This announcement got some support from the crowds. The six men stepped ahead and raised their hands to lap up the attention showered on them. They felt grateful to Biyu for elevating them in status. But she did not allow them to get carried away in celebratory joy.

"Now, I ask the people of Ullinki," she continued, "who have come all the way to Krai Tang, with hopes and dreams in their hearts, would you not want to know what ended the stay of your emperor amongst you?"

In response, the crowd yelled for a full minute in affirmative. The six men of Ullinki had to gesture frantically to calm them down.

"And I ask my own subjects of Krai Tang," Biyu spoke again. "Would you not like to know why our very dear king, Fa Ren Sung had to leave us so suddenly for the high skies?"

The people of Krai Tang tried their best to match the tempo of the barbarians and though they could not sound just as fierce, it was not too bad a show either.

"The two great men were ruined by the same witch," Biyu said, wagging an accusatory finger at Mong. "Some of you have witnessed her sorcery. It is not only the power to heal that she wields, but she also wields the power to kill. She made her way into the capital by putting an evil spell on Fa Ren Sung. And then, when she found him ousted from power, she sent him off to the high skies, decimating his strength through her manipulative touch. Her plan was to be the Queen of Krai Tang. So, she put a spell on Emperor Ullinki next. Mong tried to marry him by using her witchcraft. Alas, so impatient she was to be the queen, that she didn't even let the men of divination finish their duties. She held Ullinki's hands tight and squeezed his soul out using her treacherous skills."

Mong sat in shock as she heard Biyu's words. But the men of divination were walked in next, followed by the women who had dressed Mong on the previous night. One by one they all agreed with what Biyu had claimed. They had all seen Mong use magic to make Ullinki ascend to the high skies. Once this part was established, everyone felt that she was responsible for Fa Ren Sung's death too.

With a single speech, the queen had her subjects of Krai Tang and the people of Ullinki, united in hatred. They were all livid with anger and thumped their chests demanding justice for all the wrongdoings.

"What are you waiting for?" Biyu incited them further. "Do you wish to invite more doom and disaster upon yourselves? Or would you do something about the wicked witch who has slain two great men?"

People rushed towards Mong but before they could reach her, four of the six men on the podium caught hold of her frail frame and lifted her off the ground. The other two men signalled at the crowds to keep their patience. Leaving her new allies to deal with Mong, Biyu stepped off the dais and walked over to Han. She found him shouting at the top of his voice. But there was too much noise around and Biyu had to strain her ears to hear him.

"You know she didn't kill Fa Ren Sung… She isn't a witch… Ullinki needed to go to the high skies… She isn't a witch…" Han blabbered.

Biyu rolled her eyes and looked around. Everybody else was baying for Mong's blood.

"Death to the cruel witch," they screamed.

"Would you like to shoulder the blame, instead?" Biyu whispered into Han's ears, taking Reniyu's free hand.

Han looked at the queen, his eyes wide and brows raised, but she only twisted her lips.

"Come into the safety of the palace," she offered. "You are strong, clever and loyal. Protect the future king of Krai Tang and his mother. Forget about Mong, Han. Do your duty, as you always have. Your future will be bright."

Han looked back at the podium liked a crazed man and cried out Mong's name one last time but Biyu pulled him away firmly. She took him and Reniyu inside the palace.

At the open court, the four men held Mong up for the crowd to judge.

"Take a good look at the witch," the two other men boomed. "It is time to send her away to the high skies where the Moon god can punish her suitably."

All through the morning while Mong had been sitting on the podium, listening to Biyu's allegations, she had felt surprised but not frightened. She was glad that she had done the right thing and felt that she was ready to face the consequences. But now, as everyone cursed her and revelled at the thought of her imminent death, raw fear grabbed her senses. Mong started to hyperventilate in an attempt to shift to her alternate persona. But no matter how much she tried to summon her powers, she could not do it.

Meanwhile, the four men set her down and made her stand straight while the two other men prepared to plunge spears into her chest from both sides. Mong was still breathing heavily in desperation, but to no effect. She did not know that the wilful killing of a mortal had robbed her of all the healing powers. Mong kept trying hard until she felt the sharp iron rods piercing into her from both sides, scarring the various tribes of small beings that made up her body. She smiled one last time, feeling immense pity at her inability to guide her own body out of the predicament. And then all her pain and anguish began to melt away as her soul started to depart the ravaged body.

There were loud cheers from all around as everyone witnessed Mong's dying moments. The girl who was born amidst tears died amidst hooting and laughter.

Part 1: Dhruv's story continues

Chapter 6: Sparsha explains the Task

Dhruv is back in the dark void facing Sparsha, who is looking at him rather intently.

"What happens after that?" Dhruv asks, but his throat is too dry and he breaks into a coughing fit. He realises that he has been holding his breath for the last few tense minutes. Sparsha holds out a glass of water to help him get control. Dhruv sips, breathes in a large swig of air and calms down in a while.

"Thanks," he says to Sparsha. "I could see only to the point where Mong was murdered."

"And that tells you what?" Sparsha prompts.

"Nothing," Dhruv replies. "It tells me nothing about what happens after she dies. Why do you stop the stories so suddenly? Trying to emulate the Arabian Tales or what?"

"We've no control over it," Sparsha says, shaking his head. "You can only see until the point you were alive in the particular lifetime. You do realise that you were Mong, don't you?"

Dhruv widens his eyes as he ponders over it. For a while he feels sorry for himself and his past blindness. Then he jerks himself back to current times.

"How come I have always been born as women in the past?" he prods.

"Oh no, you have been born as men too," Sparsha clarifies. "We decided to start with the lifetimes you have lived as women, hoping that it might help you to understand women better."

"So, I have a problem in understanding women in this lifetime?" Dhruv asks.

"You didn't even know?" Sparsha wonders.

Dhruv does not like his tone and changes the topic.

"I had horrible deaths in both the previous lifetimes I saw," Dhruv says. "Will I meet another horrible end, in this life too?"

"That isn't decided yet," Sparsha shakes his head. "You need to play well this time. We are counting on you."

"Alright, you need to stop doing that," Dhruv says, throwing up his hands in air. "You cannot confuse me so much and then expect me to do whatever you are hoping I'll do for you."

"But we don't intend to confuse you." Sparsha protests. "We just wish to help you out. That's why we're showing you the past."

"I don't even know what happens after I die as Mong," Dhruv reminds him. "Tell me at least."

"Yeah, that's not a problem," Sparsha says. "Nothing much to say there. Ullinki's men took her body and threw it into the Kinera river. The people of Krai Tang watched the river turn scarlet as it flushed away the ruptured body, but all they could feel was a sense of relief. They took her to be the cause of all ruins. The waters of the Kinera carried the lacerated lump downstream for miles until it disintegrated into indistinguishable bits. Finally, they mixed with the regular debris of the sea. The snake-stone pendant that once adored the slender neck of Mong found itself floating down to rest in the ocean bed. It remained there for a long time until the opportune hour came for it to slip into the hands of the next owner.

"On the other hand, with Ullinki and Mong gone, queen Biyu found it easy to regain her position of command. Han, though heartbroken, chose to help the queen to restore order in the kingdom. The queen declared Reniyu as her lawful successor and even honoured the six men of Ullinki as his royal uncles. They were pleased with Biyu and remained lifelong friends of her kingdom. Ten days after Ullinki's death, all the people that had crowded into Krai Tang from down south began to leave, led by their respective kings.

"It was a sign of immense peace for the original inhabitants to see them go back, finally leaving their lands and homes to them. Wei, Krin Ki and other brave men were freed too. Thereafter, Queen Biyu ruled Krai Tang with Han's help for many years, until Reniyu was old enough to assume power. At his coronation, his mother handed over to him the stone-studded belt of Ullinki that contained Bingwen Bitang's magic stone.

"Over the course of time, the kingdom of Krai Tang grew in power and the belt came to be revered as the most important symbol of royalty. It was passed down from one ruler to the next."

"Hmmm, at least this race did not get obliterated due to my actions," Dhruv observes. "My sacrifice was useful."

"Your sacrifice wasn't quite useful," Sparsha informs. "You could not put the snake-stone to correct use. We need you to do that in this lifetime. It may be our last chance."

"So, the snake-stone gifted by Fa Ren Sung was the holy stone?" Dhruv asks.

"Yes, it was," Sparsha agrees. "It came into your hands so easily and yet you made a mess of the whole thing and died before doing the real task."

His tone irritates Dhruv. As if Mong had nothing better to do than to guess ways to use a stupid stone. But he does not say that aloud.

"What if I fail again?" Dhruv asks instead.

"Then everything will be doomed," Sparsha replies. "This world, this universe, as you know it through your five senses will end. An era of chaos will begin because the evil ones will rise with our downfall."

"You make it sound like something very important," Dhruv wonders.

"It is," Sparsha claims.

"Would you mind telling me the whole story?" Dhruv asks.

"Hmmm, I guess now is the right time to tell you about the beginning of the universe," Sparsha begins. "There is an awful lot of theories about how the universe was born. None of these are true, unfortunately. The universe you perceive is limited by your five senses. So that is what happened at the beginning of everything."

"The creation of the five senses?" Dhruv prompts.

"Exactly," Sparsha nods. "The holy stone was the origin of the five senses. Initially the stone wanted to create ten senses. But just after the birth of the five senses, something happened that halted the process."

"The holy stone was stolen?" Dhruv offers.

"No," Sparsha says. "Along with the creation of the five benevolent senses, five malevolent senses had been born too."

"Ah, but that is so obvious," exclaims Dhruv. "One can't create anything out of nothing. If you try to pull that off, you must balance positive things by negative counterparts."

"Well, the holy stone had not bargained for that," Sparsha accepts. "It was during the creation of the sixth sense that we all got a whiff of what was happening. With every new sense, not just new hope but new dangers were being born too. And the strain of balancing the good and the evil was gradually ripping apart the holy stone, the origin of our life force.

"When the first part of the holy stone got chipped off, it became an evil stone, the source of power for the evil senses. That was the first damage done to the integrity of the universe. We, the five senses, lost a fragment of our power to the five evil ones."

"Then? Did the disintegration stop?" Dhruv asks. "Or is the holy stone becoming smaller with each passing day? And losing power?"

"That would have been an uncontrollable disaster," Sparsha says. "But thankfully, the disintegration was stopped. The sixth sense was never fully formed. It sacrificed its own life to prevent the birth of another evil sense. And this sacrifice generated enough power to stop the disintegration of the holy stone."

"So, that is why we don't really have a proper manifestation of the sixth sense," Dhruv exclaims.

"Exactly," Sparsha agrees. "But it did not die completely. The sixth sense exists in a rudimentary form. And in some ways, it is the most important sense of all. The sixth sense enabled the fine balance necessary for the universe to exist."

"All's well, then," Dhruv sighs.

"Unfortunately not," says Sparsha. "Since the holy stone is lost, it means that the evil ones can acquire it any time and manipulate its powers. We need to find it before they do."

"And by 'we' you actually mean me?" Dhruv asks.

Sparsha nods in agreement.

"Let me get this straight," Dhruv says. "You have bestowed me with magical powers in many of my earlier births, hoping that I'd find the holy stone and put it to proper use. And me, with all my super powers, have never succeeded in fulfilling the task. So, in this birth you decided to give me no power and you still think there is a chance of me achieving the feat? I'm sorry, Sparsha, your reasoning makes me want to laugh at you. You should forget about your ambition of being accepted as gods!"

"We don't have such an ambition," Sparsha says simply.

"So, you accept the rest of it?" Dhruv probes. "That I am incapable of doing the task?"

"In this life, you are blessed by the sixth sense," Sparsha discloses. "We believe that you are capable of locating the holy stone."

"Why can't you use your powers to locate the holy stone?" Dhruv asks.

"Because the holy stone does not come into just anyone's possession," Sparsha explains. "It came to you because it believes you can protect it from misuse."

Dhruv listens, but he is deeply puzzled.

"Now I'll tell you something that will prove that you are the right man for this job," Sparsha continues. "You remember how you came here, don't you?"

Dhruv nods.

"The crown that you found in your mother's trunk has a gaping hole in place of the central stone and that's the portal through which you come here to interact with us, right?"

"Correct," Dhruv agrees.

"Well, the gaping hole was not always empty," Sparsha discloses. "It once held a precious stone as its central piece, the same one that we are looking for now."

"What??" Dhruv exclaims, jumping up. "The holy stone?"

"Yes, you see how closely you are connected to all this?" Sparsha highlights. "If you investigate some more, you may discover where the missing stone is."

"I'll try hard," Dhruv promises, meaning his words.

"Very good," Sparsha says. "It is now time for us to part ways. Goodbye and good luck."

With this, Sparsha disintegrates suddenly and blends into the blackness of the cosmos. Dhruv has many more questions running through his mind, but no one to direct them to. He can now feel the cold metallic touch of the crown pressed around his left eye and has an awareness of his right eye being closed. Sighing, he takes the crown off his face and runs his fingers over the antique piece of jewellery. It had once held an all-powerful jewel. The thought gives him a mixture of pride, joy, and hopelessness. He puts it back in the trunk. He has no idea about how to trace the missing stone. Had his parents been alive, he would have asked them and maybe they could have helped, but alas, they are both gone.

Dhruv locks the prayer room and comes downstairs. The more he thinks about the task ahead, the more worried he feels. So, he goes out to catch some fresh air and eats a small dinner from a roadside shack. Getting back into the house, he decides to wake up early and buy booze for Verma. Then, he would head off to the picnic spot.

Dhruv climbs into the big bed and a snuggly feeling of comfort seems to reach out to him. He flicks the bed switch turning out the lights. In less than a minute he falls asleep. He dreams in an erratic pattern for a while, sometimes of the past and sometimes of the present, finally settling down on a dream about his office. Dhruv finds himself trying hard to debug an essential code snippet while Verma stands in the opposite cubicle, with his arms crossed and eyes watchful. Verma reminds him every five minutes that the code interacts with live data and they cannot afford to mess things further. Dhruv tries hard to focus on his work but the only thing that he can think of is how it is almost impossible to tell Sparsha apart from Verma unless they start to talk.

Then suddenly the code vanishes from his screen and in its place he sees a scene from the past. Juthika and Dhruv are sitting at their teak wood dining table with Suprava, who is talking continuously to her daughter-in-law, sharing advice and ideas. And Juthika is nodding obediently.

"I bet she isn't listening to a thing," Dhruv remarks in disgust as he observes the bored countenance of his ex-wife on the screen. He is about to shut down the laptop when Suprava takes out a small red velvet box and opens it. She displaces a beautiful ring and puts it on the middle finger of Juthika's left hand.

"Never lose sight of this ring," Suprava cautions as Juthika admires the ring from close quarters. "It's rather precious."

Dhruv sits up in bed, fully awake. Though the room is cooled to a comfy 22 degrees by the AC, cold beads of sweat are forming on his forehead. It is no ordinary dream. Dhruv gets up and pours himself a glass of water as he recounts the last bit of what he has seen. Indeed, his mother had gifted such a ring to Juthika back when they were married. In his dream, he had recognized the ring. It was holding the holy stone. His mother must have got it made into a ring, and then she unwittingly went on to present it to her daughter-in-law. Dhruv clutches at his hair and bends his head backwards. He knows it is not going to be easy. But he will have to go to Juthika and ask her to give the ring back.

Chapter 7: Juthika's Side of the Story

Juthika is putting a second layer of tinted balm over her lips when Rudolf cries out from the next room. Her mother Smita rushes to the baby.

"Jui, come quickly," she calls out in a minute.

Juthika makes a face and moves on to brushing her hair. She is supposed to see Roshan for lunch. Soon Smita walks in cuddling the pacified baby in her arms.

"Why didn't you come?" she asks, her voice accusatory.

"Where's Nalini?" Juthika replies with a question.

Nalini is the woman appointed to take care of Rudolf.

"Nalini is there," Smita says. "Does it mean that your son no longer needs his mother?"

"Stop lecturing me, mamma," Juthika snaps. "You have tried to be a good mother. See what a wreck you've raised."

Juthika points to herself, using both her hands. Her eyes look wild and Smita wonders if her daughter is losing her mind. She muffles the rising sob with the end of her sari and leaves the room, hugging her grandchild tighter.

Juthika walks to the window and fumes. This is not how she had wanted her life to turn out. Overwhelmed by bitterness she mentally blames her parents for the failure of her marriage. It was an arranged marriage, after all.

To be very fair, Juthika's parents could not be absolved of all blame. Juthika had passed out of college after pocketing job offers from three reputed companies. She had started to work with Sun Super Systems and for two years, she was happy. She worked well, earned praises, enjoyed popularity with teammates and life was good. It made her parents very worried. Smita felt that her daughter needed to be married off. She did not like her wasting away her youth doing "nothing". Juthika's father, Pramod agreed that she was, indeed, wasting her time. He told his daughter to either study for MBA entrance exams or to consider getting married because her current carefree state was clearly unacceptable.

Juthika had no intention to be a B-school graduate. She had enjoyed a reasonably successful student life and somehow everyone close to her assumed that she should try to veer her career towards business management. The thought of returning to "slog-exam-slog" mode seemed pointless to Juthika. She weighed her options and decided that marriage was the easiest route to take. After all, she loved getting pampered. Getting a nice man's dedicated attention for the rest of her life seemed to be quite an exciting idea. Alas, no one had told her back then, that marriage was anything but a way to secure that.

Smita and Pramod began the search for a suitable groom and they were quite elated when they found Dhruv's profile on a matrimonial site. Dhruv's parents seemed equally enthusiastic about the proposition so the baton was passed on to Juthika and Dhruv. They started to interact with each other, trying to gauge if they could fall in love and be married. They were both young and attractive so every time they met to discuss important things about their future, they ended up imagining what it would be like to get into bed instead. The idea of nakedness pleased them both and they consented to marriage quickly. Juthika left her job in Pune and moved to Kolkata after marriage. She had not thought twice about it. Dhruv assured her that she would find a suitable position in Kolkata soon and she had no reason to disbelieve him. At that point, both were looking forward to living a happily married life.

Juthika felt the first hint of problems after her marriage, the minute she entered her in-law's place at Raukipur. She placed her mehendi-adorned left foot into a tray of rose-pink *aalta* and stepped carefully on a piece of white cloth laid out to welcome Dhruv's bride. The ritual highlights the importance of the new member as Lakshmi, the goddess of wealth in the household. Juthika felt real goosebumps rising while taking her first step. The whole house was bustling with excitement and she felt a strange mixture of fear and joy to see so many new faces.

"Our Lakshmi sure has huge feet," a lady bellowed, before breaking into loud laughter.

Juthika's eyes shot up to see the person. It was her mother-in-law's sister who had made the comment. A chorus of laughter rose from the rest of the ladies, throwing their weight behind the joke. Suprava laughed the hardest. All eyes were on Juthika. She was the only one not smiling. She wanted badly to check Dhruv's expression but he was posited behind her and it seemed like an impertinent thing to seek validation from her new husband in front of the in-laws. So, she forced a brief and awkward smile instead.

Juthika tried to let go of the comment but more reminders came her way in the coming days. The broadness of her forehead, the lack of volume in her hair, the presence of too many lines on her palms which allegedly showed a complicated mind, and many more. In those seven days, Juthika found out more flaws in herself than she had in the previous 26 years. Some of them were quite true, and they hurt her the most. She consoled herself that she would soon be moving into Dhruv's flat at Newtown and certainly, life with him will be full of maddening passion and true happiness.

Then, this illusion broke too when she was in bed with Dhruv.

"You need to put on some weight," he said before making love to her for the first time.

The rest of the night was a blur to her. His words kept echoing in her ears, and she could not feel anything.

When Dhruv was done, she felt a wave of grief rising within and trying to burst out through her eyes. She had to find a way to push back the tears. So, she laughed instead. She thought of how careful she had been in not mentioning Dhruv's extra weight and how he had absolutely no qualms in judging her thinness, and she laughed heartily.

Henceforth, laughter became her easiest defence. Whenever any criticism came her way, she tried to laugh it off. It would make life easier. Or at least that is what she thought.

Juthika and Dhruv lived together, but just like the parallel lines of a railway track; their hearts remained apart. They both knew after a while that the marriage was not working, but they were afraid to talk about it. The longer they avoided the problem, the harder it weighed down on them. And then came the day when Dhruv went away to the US, without offering to take his wife along. Juthika had often longed for her life in Pune, and with Dhruv gone, she knew she had to get it back. So she went back to her parents, trying to heal her heart, that seemed to have shattered into pieces from the lack of love.

###

As hot tears fall on Juthika's hands, she comes out of the bitter recollections of her past. She wipes her eyes and wonders if she should call Roshan to cancel the date. But her phone rings in the next instant. It is Roshan.

"Hello?" she says in a hoarse voice.

"Hello? Is anything wrong?" Roshan asks, his voice ever so calm, so healing.

"Nothing. Nothing new at least," Juthika says, sniffing hard to stifle the sobs.

"Let me pick you up," Roshan offers. "Splash some water on your face and pull yourself together. I'll be around soon."

Juthika obeys him and freshens up. Then, she climbs down the stairs to meet him in front of their house. She feels so much better to leave everything behind and get into his car.

Roshan greets her with a smile and hands her a Hajmola packet. Then, he pulls her cheek lightly and gives a firm squeeze on her right hand.

"Look ahead," he urges as he starts to drive.

Juthika smiles despite her troubles. It is so much easier to smile when Roshan is around. She looks at him, observing every little detail about him. Roshan is of medium height and pale complexion. His face is very appealing, though. He has a pair of striking eyes, thickset eyebrows and a strong, masculine jawline to go with. If he took a little more care to sculpt his body, he could have qualified as handsome or at least dashing. But that is the thing about Roshan. He does not care about his appearance, not even the least bit. At first, Juthika had found it hard to understand Roshan. After all, it is not under ordinary circumstances that they had met.

###

When Juthika went back to Pune from Kolkata, she had expected to feel happy in the safe haven of her parental home. But it was not that simple. Her mother cried all day, worrying about Juthika's failing marriage while her father told her to try to get back into the race. Her friends and colleagues had all moved on in life, and she could not find a single person who could relate with her anguish. One day, Pramod sat Juthika down and talked to her for a while.

"I've been watching you," he began as he sipped his morning coffee. "Your shoulders are drooping, your eyes look dull. What is this? You can't let one wrong decision ruin your life."

Juthika looked up at her father. So, he had seen through her quiet façade.

"I think you should either start to look for jobs again or apply to good universities for a master's degree," Pramod continued. "As for your marriage, end it."

"I don't have any ground to come out of my marriage," Juthika confided. "I'm not happy, but I won't be able to point out any instance of domestic violence or infidelity. I am very confused."

"Hmm," Pramod said and thought for a while. "Perhaps you should wait till your husband comes back to India before you make a decision on that. But there's no reason why you shouldn't work on your career now."

"Shall I start over, papa?" Juthika asked in so earnest a voice that it almost broke Pramod's heart. But he restrained himself from showing anything on the outside.

"Yes, take my car and go to the JJT campus," he said. "Collect the forms for MBA entrance preparation. Look at the energy of college going kids, it'd give you hope."

Juthika sat there, unsure.

"Shall I come with you?" Pramod offered.

"No, I'll go alone," Juthika said, getting up. "You're right, papa. I need to pick myself up again."

From that day, she began to drive to the campus regularly. Sometimes she withdrew money from the ATM inside and sometimes she collected registration forms for random courses but on most days she sat under the shade of a huge Peepal tree and reflected on life.

Juthika thought of all the students who lived in the campus. Only the best ones in the country got admission in that college. They were all so much better than her. Looking up at the dense foliage of the Peepal tree that quivered only so slightly in the autumn wind, she felt like it was looking down on her reproachfully. Perhaps it hated to provide shade to an unsuccessful person. It seemed to be calling out to her at times, inviting her to suspend herself from a stout branch and offer her frail body to the tree. In return, the tree would liberate her from all pains.

Juthika kept going back to the Peepal tree, and every day the message of the tree seemed to get clearer. She had no idea that someone was watching her from the fourth floor window of the hostel building in the front. It was Roshan. He hated seeing her come every day and sit down, lost in thoughts under the Peepal tree that used to be his spot for contemplation.

One day Roshan had enough. He marched out of his room, ran down the stained staircase of the hostel building, and went up to face Juthika.

"Who are you?" he questioned, panting a little.

Roshan's tone was aggressive and his thick brows were creased with ferocity. Juthika felt scared.

"Why do you sit here every day?" he asked.

Juthika felt uneasy. She could not tell him her reasons. She did what she always did when she was uncomfortable. She smiled.

"I knew it," Roshan continued. "You are one of those narcissists who gets everything. Beautiful, successful, never had to deal with a real problem in life. So, you sit alone and try to explore depression like it was some kind of luxury."

Roshan noticed the smear of vermillion on Juthika's hair parting as he ranted.

"Married too!" he exclaimed. "All sorted in life and now you spend your time in idle musings."

He narrowed his eyes and brought his face closer to Juthika. A gentle breeze blew in and Juthika realised that he smelled of Cinthol soap. She inhaled spontaneously.

"I know exactly what's on your mind," Roshan said. "You are thinking about the failed students from the campus who go on to hang themselves from this tree. And you are pitying them!"

"They do that?" Juthika asked, suddenly finding her voice.

"You didn't know?" Roshan asked, straightening himself up again. "Well, how would you? People with perfect lives don't have time to look beyond their boundaries."

"Were *you* thinking of committing suicide?" Juthika blurted out, feeling courageous. "Did I ruin your plans by sitting here all day?"

"What? No," Roshan replied.

His tone was softer now. He looked around and crumbled a dry leaf on his palm.

"Yes, you were," Juthika insisted.

"Go away," Roshan ordered. "You don't belong here."

"Of course not," Juthika accepted. "I wasn't bright enough to get into this college. So, I studied at another institution. Sorry to step into the hallowed boundaries of JJT. I'll leave now."

She got up and began to leave.

"Wait," Roshan called out. "Don't tell anyone about the suicide thing."

"Ok, I won't," Juthika said and kept walking.

"And I'm sorry about being so rude," Roshan admitted. "Please sit. I'll go elsewhere."

"To hang yourself?"

Roshan stared oddly for a few seconds and then he flashed an awkward smile. It looked like the purest thing that Juthika had seen in a while. She sat down under the tree again.

"Tell me why you wish to end your life," Juthika asked simply.

Roshan fidgeted for a while and then he sat down beside Juthika.

"I wasn't really," he mumbled.

"We both know you were," Juthika stated. "But why? You are obviously talented, all set for a great future. What could possibly make you so depressed? Parents not approving of your girlfriend? Or she left you?"

"Will you stop?" Roshan raised his voice. "You won't understand my case. You are just too used to getting what you want. It is hard for some of us."

Juthika went quiet and looked down. Soon Roshan began to talk again.

"I have been, always been, the first boy in my village," he started. "My parents gave me everything they could afford and sometimes even those things that they couldn't. They believed in me, they always thought that I am gifted and that one day I'd make not just them but the entire country proud. My teachers said that I should try to get into the JJTs because no other college will be able to do justice to my talent. As you can see, I did get into a premier JJT."

Roshan paused and breathed hard. He was twisting his lips while a careless wind tousled his hair.

"Then?"

"Then what?" Roshan continued. "I found out that I am no match for my batchmates. Everybody else is ten times brighter than me. I wish I could say that I was too poor to afford a better primary education, but in reality there are boys poorer than me, doing way better. It is hard for me to accept, but the truth is that I am the dullest boy in the JJT. From being the cream of my school, I have been reduced to the scum of JJT. You wouldn't know how it feels if all your worth got wiped out one fine day without a warning. You wouldn't understand the pain of being devalued overnight."

"I understand perfectly," Juthika interjected firmly.

She did not say why, but the intensity with which she spoke made Roshan believe her. That is how their friendship had started. That is how the two of them, after falling out of favour with life, began to grow closer.

The more they talked, the better they liked each other, and Juthika realised that she had to end her marriage with Dhruv. She had given up the hope of being understood altogether. But now that she had found Roshan, she badly wanted to give life another chance.

Juthika got a job within a few days of meeting Roshan. It was a typical software job, much akin to the one she had left when she got married to Dhruv. But it made Juthika very happy and she celebrated her success with Roshan.

At that point, Juthika was thinking of divorcing Dhruv as soon as he got back in the country. But it did not turn out to be that easy. Dhruv seemed to make an effort initially, and Juthika's parents also felt that their daughter should not give up on her marriage. It was only after an excruciating year of going back and forth in her relationship with Dhruv that she could finally extricate herself from the marriage.

Juthika now looks at Roshan and thanks her luck. He drives to their favourite restaurant for brunch and then they catch a movie together. Roshan has passed out of college and is currently working. He has landed a cushy job despite being the last boy at JJT. And he is madly in love with Juthika.

It is almost evening when Roshan begins to drive her home. When they are close to Juthika's place, she pulls out her phone, intending to lift its sound ban.

"Can you believe it?" Juthika says, holding up her phone for Roshan to see.

17 missed calls from mamma.

"Well, good that we are back," Roshan says. "Wasn't your phone on vibration? Why do you try to screen her calls?"

"You don't know?" Juthika asks back with a raised eyebrow. "Because she doesn't like the concept of "us"! Because she thinks it is inappropriate for a single mother to go out and enjoy herself!"

"I'm with you," Roshan reminds her as he pulls into their driveway. "Ignore such expectations. I was just worried that she could have called regarding an emergency, too."

"I am pretty sure there wasn't any good reason for her to get paranoid," Juthika says.

As soon as the words leave her mouth, she realises that her assumption was wrong, for Dhruv is seen waiting in front of her home. He has his hands in his pockets while Pramod is standing beside him, keeping a close watch on his ex son-in-law.

"What does he want now?" Juthika mutters under her breath.

"Is that…" Roshan begins, peering hard at Dhruv.

Dhruv stares back unabashed and checks Roshan out.

Juthika is dating someone. Dhruv makes a mental note. Damn it. He had been so sure that she would not find anyone so soon.

"It's my ex," Juthika explains to Roshan.

"Shall I come with you?" Roshan asks, squeezing her hands.

"No, I can handle this," Juthika asserts. "Drive safe, I'll call you at night."

Roshan looks at her for long before finally breaking off eye contact and driving away. Dhruv follows him with his eyes for as long as he can. When the car disappears, he turns his head to find Juthika standing in front of him.

"What do you want?" she asks.

Dhruv smiles. The directness makes things easier for him because he, too, has a rather straightforward demand to make.

"Do you remember a ring that my mother had gifted to you?" Dhruv begins.

Juthika creases her eyebrows and waits for him to go on.

"It had a single white… yellowish-white stone set in gold," Dhruv describes as he gestures in air.

Juthika's expression does not change.

"Well, I want it back," Dhruv finishes firmly.

"What ring?" Juthika says. "I don't remember any such ring."

Her voice trembles and it is easy for anyone to get that she is lying. It offends Pramod who has been standing right next to Dhruv, this entire time, observing everything with keen interest.

"Jui, give him his ring back, if you have it," he bellows, even before Dhruv can say a word.

"I… I've lost it," Juthika claims.

"I'll pay for it," Pramod offers immediately, though he continues to glare at his daughter. "Dhruv, tell me how much it was worth?"

"It is quite priceless to me, sir," Dhruv clarifies. "My mother had given it to her, hoping that we'd remain married forever. Now I want it back because as it has her love and blessings. You can't compensate that with money. And if you watch your daughter carefully, you'll see that she is lying, though I don't understand why she is withholding the ring. She never liked my mother in the first place!"

"I'm not lying," Juthika insists, her voice a little louder. "I will pay for it myself, papa."

"You embarrass me," Pramod bawled at his daughter. "Dhruv is quite right here. You can't equate sentiments with money. And what good would that ring do to you? Give it back now; it is obvious from your face that you have it in your possession."

"My mother-in-law wanted me to keep it with myself," Juthika states in a last-ditch attempt.

"Are you her daughter-in-law anymore?" Dhruv asks with a smirk. "By what stupid right are you keeping it?"

Juthika stands quiet for a while and Dhruv gets impatient.

"Is Rudolf my son?" he probes. "Is that why you want to keep the ring?"

"No, he isn't," Juthika says. She hesitates for a moment and then adds, "Wait here, I'll fetch the ring for you."

As Juthika goes in, Pramod and Dhruv let out a sigh at the same time.

"Come in for a cup of tea," Pramod says after a moment of silence.

"Don't bother with the civilities, sir," Dhruv tells him. "But I appreciate you forcing Juthika to return the ring."

Pramod opens his mouth twice but eventually restrains himself from saying anything. He hates to see his daughter as a single mother. But there is no way he can ask Dhruv to reconcile with his ex-wife and play father to a child that is not his.

Juthika reappears and thrusts the little red box into Dhruv's hands, who immediately checks the content. His mother's ring is inside, unharmed and unaltered.

"Thank you," Dhruv says, meaning it. "I wish you and your son well."

Then, nodding politely at Pramod, Dhruv walks away. His return flight is scheduled in less than an hour, but he is not worried about that. He has probably got hold of the holy stone and it fills his mind with too much excitement to allow space for any other feeling. On his way to the airport, Dhruv indulges himself with visions of being felicitated by the senses on account of his success.

Meanwhile, Juthika dials Roshan's number the minute Dhruv leaves.

"Are you alright?" Roshan asks. "I was so worried."

"I'm ok. I guess I feel a little shaken," she says. "Dhruv took away the ring that his mother had presented to me. She had wanted me to pass on the ring to my child. But he just kept pressing for it and papa took his side too. I wish you were there."

"Did you give it back?" Roshan asks.

"I had to," Juthika sobs. "The only way to keep it was to tell Dhruv that Rudolf is his son."

"Let go of it, dear," Roshan says. "No point in making yourself sad over it."

"I know," Juthika sniffles as she dabs her handkerchief at her eyes.

"Listen, do you have your purse close by?" Roshan asks. "The one that you were carrying today?"

"Yes, it's right in front of me," Juthika says. "Why?"

"Open the main chamber," Roshan instructs. "I slipped in a small gift for you."

"Oh, you didn't have to do such a thing," Juthika says as she pulls her purse closer and unzips it to reveal a dainty little present.

She pulls it out and tears off the flower-printed wrapper. There is a jewellery box and inside it an elegant ring studded with a single diamond.

"Will you marry me?" Roshan whispers into the phone, the second he hears Juthika gasp.

"What? Did I hear you right?" she asks.

"Yes, you did," Roshan laughs. "I know I don't have much in the world. But I think we make a wonderful pair and we should live together as a married couple."

Juthika pinches herself.

"Are you there?" Roshan begins to feel a little tense.

"Yes, very much," Juthika assures. "I will marry you. I just couldn't bring myself to believe it all!"

"That makes me so happy," Roshan exults. "Next, we will share our

plans with our parents, but no matter what they say, we *are* getting married. Don't change your decision based on what others say. Ok?"

"Ok!" Juthika giggles.

She is about to add something when Smita calls out for her. Rudolf is crying again.

"Run along," Roshan urges. "Very soon you, Rudolf and I will live in the same house."

Juthika blows a kiss into the phone before disconnecting the call. She realises that it is the first time that she has done something so cheesy and it makes her blush. Her mother calls again and this time Juthika rushes. She feels very happy as she enfolds her child in her arms. Soon there will be many roles for her to juggle with, but with Roshan in her life, she is confident to do just about anything.

Chapter 8: The Last Lap

By the time, Dhruv is back to Kolkata, it is twilight already. He books a cab to Raukipur and settles into the seat, wondering what the senses would have to say about the recovered ring. Outside, the sky looks a combination of pallor and colour. The large bill-boards are coming to life one by one. A particular glowing sign catches Dhruv's eye because it is promoting the virtues of the company he works for. He makes a face at it and reclines on the seat, only to spring back at the next instant. The forgotten office picnic has resurfaced in his mind. It is almost over now.

Dhruv plucks out his phone from the pocket and keys in Verma's number. The phone rings for long, giving Dhruv a chance to invent an excuse.

"Heylo, Dooby boy," Verma answers in a fruity voice. "You never showed up!"

"I'm really sorry, sir," Dhruv apologizes in his sincerest voice. "I… I had to deal with a personal emergency. In fact, I'm just getting back from Pune."

"Oh, is that so?" Verma's voice seems to drift off.

"Yes, sir," Dhruv says. "I'll mail you my tickets too, as a proof."

"What sort of emergency was it?" Verma asks, his voice slurry.

There is a lot of noise in the background.

Dhruv surmises that the picnic is drawing to a close and everyone is pretty drunk by now. He can visualise the scene very well. Most of the women employees have left and the men, emboldened by their disappearance, are fooling around, singing in off-key notes and drinking just about anything that they can set their eyes on. Dhruv feels a little better; Verma is a lot more forgiving when he has some alcohol in his tummy.

"It's a little embarrassing," Dhruv begins. "You know, sir, about my messy marriage and subsequent divorce. Well, there was a piece of jewellery that I had to recover from my ex-wife."

"My, my, she stole your jewellery?" Verma prompts.

The tone annoys Dhruv.

"No, my mother had gifted it to her," he clarifies. "But it was a family heirloom, so I went to take it back. I'd like to preserve my mother's memories and the ring might not mean a thing to my ex-wife."

"Obviously," Verma agrees. "She has no right to retain the ring. What else did she take from you? Tell me something Dooby-boy, between you and me, is she still exploiting you financially?"

Dhruv gulps uncomfortably.

"No, sir, it was just the ring," he says after a pause.

Verma chuckles in response.

"We missed you, bro," a colleague cries from the background. It creeps Dhruv out.

"Bye-bye, Dooby-boy," Verma says and disconnects the call abruptly.

Dhruv puts back the phone in his pocket and purses his lips. He tells himself that he needs to switch to a new job. Placing his head on the backrest, he stares outside lazily for a few minutes, until he snoozes off.

Dhruv is very close to his parental home when his phone rings again. It is Meher. He smiles as he receives the call. Seeing Juthika with Roshan has reinforced his feelings for Meher.

"Hello," Dhruv says.

He notices that his voice comes out all nice and pleasant when Meher happens to be the recipient.

"Dhruv, I called you to tell you something." Meher sounds anxious.

"Is something wrong? Are you ok?" Dhruv is now fully awake.

"I'm fine, it's not about me. It's about you," Meher says. "Your boss did an awful thing today. He put you on speaker at the picnic."

"Oh really?" Dhruv says as he sits up.

"I'm in my car now," Meher continues. "There weren't many people around, but everyone was making lousy jokes about your ex-wife and you after that call."

"Hmm, forget it," Dhruv opines, biting his lips. "I have never had any respect for them to begin with. Don't feel bad, Meher. I'm looking forward to our date tomorrow."

"About that," Meher says, her voice sounding a little apologetic. "Can we postpone it a bit?"

"Don't want to be seen with Mr. Unpopular?" Dhruv asks.

"Come on, I don't care about what others have to say," Meher clarifies quickly. "I had to make an appointment with my doctor. My carpal tunnel is acting up again."

"Oh, that's bad," Dhruv says. "Shall I take you to the doctor?"

"You're very chivalrous," Meher laughs. "But I can manage this on my own. Maybe we can see each other next weekend? Or, on an evening during the week?"

"That sounds good," Dhruv says. "I'll call you tomorrow. Good luck with your hand. Let me know how things go at the clinic."

"Thanks, take care," Meher says before hanging up.

A little while later, Dhruv reaches his ancestral home and gets out of the cab. A frenzied excitement grabs hold of him as he rushes to his childhood home and gets in. His hands shake uncontrollably as he runs up the stairs to the prayer room in the mezzanine floor. Standing in front of the locked door, he takes a moment to calm his racing heart and digs into his pocket for the key, only to realise after a minute of mad fumbling that he has forgotten it at his apartment.

Dhruv flops down on the floor and scrunches his hair with both his hands trying to rip out some of frustration that is raging inside him. Exhausted from his travels he feels like crashing in one of the bedrooms downstairs and falling asleep right away. But he knows that he has to go back to his apartment at Cinnamon Residency. That way, he can come back in the morning with the key. He pulls himself up reluctantly, locks the house and takes a cab to Newtown.

As the cab runs back towards his apartment through the near-empty streets, Dhruv stares out. Silvery moonlight has splashed all over, softening the harsh visage of the city. Everything looks enchanted and for a moment, Dhruv feels that there is nothing extraordinary about his interaction with the senses. In fact, it would have been strange, if he were to live and die without having the senses walk into his life. He feels satiated with this sudden epiphany and smiles. Dhruv notices that only a few other vehicles are about and realises how late it is. Some of the vehicles are snazzy, high-end cars and he ogles at them for a few minutes. He owns a red Honda City which has been cooling its wheels in the garage off late. Juthika and he used to go to fancy places in it, together. Dhruv silently admits to himself that they did have fun socializing. But with Juthika out of his life, he does not have the heart to ride in that car.

Basically, the social engagements seem to have vanished from Dhruv's life, along with his wife. The mandatory office parties are the only kind of occasions that he attends these days. And there he gets so high on booze that he is barred from driving anyway. Dhruv wonders if he should sell the car while he can. In the middle of such profound musings, he sees that his cab is at the gates of Cinnamon Residency. He yawns happily. The thought of hitting his bed makes him feel wholesome. Whoever said it is sad to return to an empty home probably had never been sleepy enough.

Dhruv just cares enough to lock the doors of his flat and then heads straight into the master bedroom. He checks his phone once and sees a notification about an incoming WhatsApp snippet from Meher. It makes him happy. But he knows he lacks the energy to type out an answer and he does not wish Meher to think that she is not important enough to get an instant reply. So, he sets aside the phone without reading the message and drifts off into a heavy, dreamless sleep.

It is the sharp ringing of his phone that wakes Dhruv up in the morning. He opens one eye and reaches out to silence the noise, and then he goes back to sleep. The phone rings in silence for a minute before dying out. But within a few seconds, it resumes its shrill screaming.

Dhruv grabs his phone and raises his head from the pillow. He wonders who can be so persistent at this hour. A look at the screen gives him a small shock. Ramala mashi, the housekeeper of his parental home, is calling.

"Hello," Dhruv grunts into the phone.

"Babu, the house has been burgled," Ramala mashi says between sobs. "I came in the morning and found the locks broken."

"What?" Dhruv is now fully awake. "What have they taken?"

"I don't know exactly," Ramala mashi answers. "The rooms have been ransacked. Maybe they took money and jewellery and important papers. You need to come and check, babu."

Dhruv rubs his eyes. Burglaries are not that common at Raukipur. Why did they suddenly choose his parental house as a target? A faint answer tries to peep out from his subconscious, but Dhruv is not ready to accept it. He promises Ramala mashi that he would be home soon and gets out of bed immediately.

Dhruv rushes through his morning routine and within fifteen minutes, he is inside a cab, riding back to Raukipur. A frazzled Ramala mashi welcomes Dhruv into the house. She takes a few minutes to recount the terror she felt earlier that morning before retiring into the kitchen to make breakfast for Dhruv.

Meanwhile, Dhruv goes about the house, trying to assess the extent of loss he has suffered. By the time he sits down at the dining table to eat, he has found out what the burglars were after. The crown from the prayer room is the only thing that is missing.

As Dhruv savours his luchi and potato curry breakfast, he wonders how powerful the evil ones are. This time they had come for the crown. If they found out that he had the holy stone in his possession, they might attack him in person. Suddenly, Dhruv feels very nervous and helpless.

"Are you feeling ill, babu?" Ramala mashi asks. She is sitting on the floor watching him eat.

And those words, wrapped in unsullied concern, are enough to put Dhruv back on track.

"No mashi," he replies. "I'm ok. And you mustn't worry too. I'll leave now and head off to the police station. See if you can clean the place up. Take your time and don't feel scared at all, I'll take care of everything."

Ramala mashi gives him a bright smile full of hope as Dhruv leaves. But he is not going to the police station. Instead, he will be going to see a jeweller. He has many strange ideas swarming in his head and he knows that he needs to put some of them to execution, if he has to remain sane.

In her heydays, Dhruv's mother frequented a local jewellery store named Shri Durga Jewellers to buy sundry ornaments. The owner valued loyal customers, and he always agreed to knock off the tax amount from the final bill. It was not that hefty an amount, but Suprava got a kick out of tricking the government. From nose-pin to earrings, whatever she bought from them got blessed by the touch of illegality. Dhruv's mother felt that it added some spice to her otherwise vanilla existence.

Dhruv reaches Shri Durga Jewellers after a short walk of about fifteen minutes. The store is obviously not open. Nobody likes to run on time in Kolkata. Even though the sun is up at five in the morning, the people will not be until it is ten. They open their shops at some-time around eleven o'clock, only after they have successfully whiled away the gentler morning hours. Dhruv decides to wait outside the locked gate.

At quarter to eleven, the manager of Shri Durga Jewellers is seen, arriving in a rickshaw. He flashes a broad grin at Dhruv even before he has deboarded. Handing the rickshaw-puller his fare, the manager introduces himself as Baniram. Dhruv smiles back. Baniram is of middle height and has small mouse-like eyes that cannot stay still. The corners of his lips are perpetually bent upwards, giving him quite a smug look overall.

As they walk into the store together, Dhruv shows Baniram the ring he has taken back from Juthika. He asks if it is possible to remove the stone from the socket. Baniram extends his palm, meaning to take the ring but Dhruv holds on to it tightly.

"Why do you want it removed?" Baniram asks, scratching his head to compensate for the awkwardness.

The question perplexes Dhruv, but he realises quick enough that he can tell the truth. The partial truth, at least.

"I want this stone to be made into a ring of my size," Dhruv explains holding up the ring. "This one's too small."

"I see," Baniram nods.

A few more members of the staff walk into the store and move over to the changing rooms to put on their uniforms. Baniram eyes them for a few moments and then turns to Dhruv.

"The craftsmen are here," Baniram says. "Leave your measurements and they will get it done within 7-10 days."

"7-10 days!" Dhruv pockets the ring and turns to leave. "I'll have to go to some other jeweller then. Goodbye."

"Wait, wait," Baniram urges. "I didn't know that you were in a hurry. When do you need it? I can expedite the process in case of emergencies. Give us five days."

"I need it now," Dhruv says. "Also, I'll will be watching your men work while they take the stone out and put it into another ring. You can't take this ring out of my sight."

"Now, now, don't be unreasonable," Baniram pleads. "Which goldsmith will craft your ring in front of you? Leave it with us. Enjoy your Sunday and come back to collect the new ring in the evening."

"Bye," Dhruv says tersely as he begins to walk away.

"Wait!" Baniram grabs hold of Dhruv's arm to stall his exit. "I will try to arrange things for you, exactly the way you want. But it will cost you more."

"How much more?" Dhruv asks raising an eyebrow.

"Five thousand bucks on top of the original bill," Baniram answers.

Dhruv grunts audibly to make a show of displeasure, but agrees to pay the amount. Baniram grins and leads Dhruv out of the store to take him to a building located a few blocks away.

"This is where some of our craftsmen put finishing touches on jewelleries," he explains as he leads Dhruv into a brightly lit room.

Baniram walks up to a particular work desk and introduces the man seated at it as Pal-babu to Dhruv. Pal-babu has wrinkled skin, and dirt seems to have gathered in each crease, accentuating the lines. He stares at Dhruv through his rather thick glasses with a stoned expression.

"Pal-babu, meet our respected customer Dhruv," Baniram starts. "He has brought a ring that you need to fix, meaning that you will need to pull out the stone and put it into another ring."

"Let me see the ring," Pal babu wheezes, craning his neck up.

Dhruv reluctantly hands him the ring. Somehow, he is unable to say no to this man. Pal-babu is harmless, though. He examines the ring and says it will be fairly easy to extract the stone.

"Thank you," Dhruv says as he seats himself in front of Pal-babu's desk. To his utmost annoyance, Baniram also sits down beside him.

"What is the big deal about the ring?" Baniram asks.

Dhruv glares at him sharply and Baniram immediately adds, "if you don't mind me asking!"

"It belonged to my mother," Dhruv says with a small sigh. "But the ring does not fit me. I wish to wear the stone to feel her presence."

Dhruv feels that Baniram will easily lap up such sentimental garbage. He hopes his mother's soul, if anywhere in the great universe, will forgive him for the lie.

"Ah, so it belonged to Suprava Devi?" Baniram says, looking very pleased. "She made many purchases from our store. But I don't recollect selling anything like that ring to her."

"You get many customers," Dhruv interjects quickly. "It is not possible to remember everything that you sold in the past."

"But this ring isn't from our store," Pal-babu comments. "That we are sure of."

He holds out his hands for Dhruv to see. On his right palm is the empty ring, while on his left palm is the dislocated stone.

"Great," Dhruv exclaims, taking the empty ring back. "Now fix this stone to a ring of my size."

"This part will be a little complex," Pal babu says. "I will bring some basic gold rings for you to choose the correct size and then I can fix the stone to it. However, the finishing will not be tidy enough. This kind of work requires a lot of time and proper attention. If I do it in haste, the quality will be compromised."

"That's alright," Dhruv assures. "Make it as well as you can."

He turns to Baniram only to find him staring acutely. It makes Dhruv very uncomfortable.

"That ring was very precious to your mother, wasn't it?" Baniram asks.

Dhruv's heart leaps up in fright and begins to bob up and down in his chest. Has Baniram seen through his ruse?

"Maybe, maybe not," Dhruv tries to keep his answer ambiguous and breaks eye contact.

"I know what sort of ring that is," Baniram continues, undeterred. "It offers special powers."

The colour drains from Dhruv's face. He wonders if Baniram is the agent hired by the evil ones and if he has unwittingly walked into the lion's den.

"That stone is supposed to restore harmony in domestic life," Baniram whispers bringing his face closer. "Your parents must have had a troubled marriage."

"What?" Dhruv sounds confused.

"And you now want the same ring to help with your marriage, isn't it?" Baniram cannot suppress his joy. The seeming unravelling of family gossip makes him very happy.

"You think that is an astrology-prescribed stone?" Dhruv asks.

"Think? I know it," Baniram claims shrugging his shoulders. "But the stone is a fake one. Your mother probably bought it from a shady store to keep family matters private. And they pushed a fake product onto her. Listen to me and buy a real gemstone from us. This one will not help to salvage your marriage."

Dhruv stares at Baniram and wonders if he should be angry or disappointed with Baniram.

"Keep it a secret, please," Dhruv requests after a long pause, deciding to make use of his presumptions. "It's rather embarrassing."

"I know, I know," Baniram smirks. "Don't worry, your secret is safe with me."

Dhruv knows that it is not exactly the kind of safety anyone would care for, but he does not mind. Baniram has not unravelled the true importance of the stone. If he had then Dhruv would have been in a difficult spot. What would he have done, he wonders. And then he spends a few delightful moments considering different ways to murder Baniram without leaving a trace.

Dhruv's reverie is cut short as Pal-babu hands over the finished ring to Baniram who polishes it once before packing the ring into a neat velvet-lined box. Baniram is saying something about how no other jeweller would have done what they did for Dhruv but he is only half-listening. Dhruv grabs hold of the box containing his new ring and settles the bill while nodding vaguely at Baniram. Then, he leaves the store in a huff, forgetting even to say thank-you for the prompt service. Baniram does not like his attitude one bit and makes a silent vow to spread the story of Dhruv's dysfunctional marriage to as many willing ears as he can manage to find.

This time Dhruv does not go to his Raukipur home. He informs Ramala mashi that he is returning to his flat. Then Dhruv puts the new ring on his finger, pockets the empty ring and heads straight to his flat in Cinnamon Residency. It is while wolfing down a lunch of rice and fish curry that Dhruv finally forms a vague idea of what he would do with the two rings.

He rushes to his bedroom and closes all the curtains. Then he holds the empty ring against his eye. And though it does not exactly fit around his eyes, the trick works and he finds himself drifting into the known nook of the Universe.

Dhruv loiters around for a while, smiling a self-congratulatory smile for his absolute brilliance in finding the way back in. Then suddenly, he spots Baniram looking at him. It startles Dhruv for a second, but then he connects the dots and grunts.

"Alright, tell me your name," Dhruv prompts. "You must be another sense."

"Quite so, I'm Ghraan," says the man who looks like Baniram. "The sense of smell."

Dhruv is disgusted by the idea of having to confide his theories to a Baniram-lookalike, and he scowls in exasperation.

"Is anything wrong?" Ghraan asks. "Your face seems so twisted and ugly!"

Dhruv wants to tell Ghraan that between the two of them, the right to call the other one ugly lies completely with Dhruv but he restrains himself.

"I had a rather hard time in the last twenty-four hours," Dhruv says instead. "I wish to share my views with the senses and get some pointers."

"Share," Ghraan says, almost like a command.

"I don't trust you," Dhruv declares. "Please let me talk to Dristi or Sparsha."

"We are all the same," Ghraan echoes what others had claimed. "They aren't any better than me, I am not any better than them. Tell me about your woes and worries."

Ghraan looks straight at Dhruv and crosses his arms. His sole attention seems to be focused on hearing out Dhruv's troubles. And despite the similarity, he now looks like nothing like Baniram. It relaxes Dhruv.

"I went to recover a ring from my ex-wife," Dhruv begins. "I had this intuition that the ring is of some importance; it's hard to explain. I kind of saw it in a dream."

"Ah, the sixth sense," Ghraan remarks, sounding pleased. "Were you able to recover the ring?"

"Yes, I could," Dhruv confirms.

He hesitates for a moment before taking the ring off his finger. If Ghraan said that it was not the correct stone, it would break his heart. He hands the ring over to Ghraan, who examines the central stone carefully. It makes Dhruv very anxious. He feels like he is twelve and waiting for the annual results to be shared at his school. His torment grows with each passing second. Why is Ghraan taking so long? Why is there no sign of jubilation on his face? Is the stone a fake? Will Dhruv have to embark upon another journey trying to locate the holy stone, with practically no help and no hint to lead him on? The pessimism of his thoughts weighs Dhruv down and he feels very dizzy.

Ghraan snaps his finger without looking up and a chair appears for Dhruv. He sits down gratefully with a small nod of acknowledgment even though Ghraan's attention is still held by the stone.

"Great work in finding the holy stone," Ghraan declares after what seems like an eternity.

Dhruv cannot believe his ears.

"You did it," Ghraan beams, looking at Dhruv.

"Are you saying that I have been successful in this lifetime?" Dhruv asks, his eyes sparkling with joy.

"It is certainly a great start," Ghraan nods.

"Start?" Dhruv is surprised. "How is this only a start?"

"You'd also need to locate the evil stone," Ghraan says casually. "The missing part of the holy stone."

"But that belongs to the evil senses," Dhruv protests.

"It passed into their control, but it's not theirs," Ghraan enlightens him. "Remember there was a magic stone with Jhluk and a similar one with Bingwen Bitang? That is the evil stone."

Dhruv nods his head briefly. His dizziness is back with full force.

"You need to retrieve the evil stone from their possession," Ghraan explains. "Then the holy stone can be made whole again, taking away the powers of the evil ones."

Dhruv can only stare at Ghraan, not wanting to believe what he has just heard.

"Maybe it is not so bad that the evil ones are holding the evil stone," Dhruv says. "They have some power, but with the holy stone being back in your possession, you do have maximum control over the universe."

"See, the holy stone is like a lock to the evil ones," Ghraan says. "And they have the key to it, the evil stone. Thus, the huge risk still remains. Of them accessing the holy stone somehow and taking full control."

"Let's assume the evil senses are rising to power," Dhruv says with a degree of resignation in his voice. "How bad could it get?"

"How do you differentiate between life and death?" Ghraan questions. "When someone dies, what do they lose? They lose the body and with it, all five senses. So, the five senses are essential for life to thrive."

"Yes, I suppose so," Dhruv agrees.

"If the evil senses annihilate all the five senses, that'd mean immediate death for all," Ghraan continues. "The end of humanity, or rather of all life forms."

Dhruv thinks for a while and retorts, "Is death so bad after all? In the end, we all die. It's inevitable."

"But everybody does not die at the same time," Ghraan shakes his head. "Death is indeed the ultimate resting phase. But life is important too. When some souls die and enter the resting phase, others take birth and keep an eye on the world. The dead can rest because the living are keeping watch."

"Oh, not keeping a very good watch, I'm afraid," Dhruv mocks. "Everywhere I look, this world is riddled with problems."

"Which brings us to the second thing that the evil senses can do or rather, are doing," Ghraan quips in.

"And that'd be?" Dhruv asks.

"The evil senses can corrupt all five senses for the human beings," Ghraan explains. "If someone sees evil, feels evils, and so on, they are very likely to do evil. Don't you see the human beings harming fellow human beings? These people have lost their ability to perceive the universe in a positive way."

"But that has been going on for ages," Dhruv counters.

"Because the evil senses have been around for ages, too," Ghraan answers. "Just imagine, if with their partial power they can corrupt such a huge chunk of humanity, how much severe their effect would be if they could fully control the senses."

"The world would become a living hell," Dhruv says in a grave tone. "Even death would be better than that."

"Now, do you see why it is so urgent to save the holy stone?" Ghraan prompts.

"Hmmm, I do," Dhruv agrees. "Still don't believe that I'd succeed this time when I've failed in the past lifetimes."

"You got our help in the previous lifetimes," Ghraan says. "We thought our blessings would help you better, since we are fully formed senses. But that's not how it works. Those were trial runs that proved that the holy stone does tend to come to your possession. It feels one with you, responds to your thoughts and actions. And this time you have with yourself, the blessing of the sixth sense. The sense that sacrificed itself to save the holy stone. The sense that is trusted most by the holy stone."

Dhruv takes in a large breath and nods his head thoughtfully.

"Now, hold on to this carefully as you go looking for the other part," Ghraan advises, as he holds out the ring. "The last thing we want is for you to lose this one as you go hunting for the rest of it."

"You keep it with yourself," Dhruv says. "Protect it while I look for the evil stone."

"There could be attempts of theft now," Ghraan steps ahead and slides the ring into Dhruv's finger.

"Do you think the evils ones are sitting idle? No, they will also work hard through their agents. You're not getting it."

"I'm getting it very well," Dhruv asserts, getting up. "My home at Raukipur was burgled last night and the crown through which I used to meet the senses was stolen. Nothing else is missing. This was clearly the work of your rivals. I was so worried that I shall never be able to connect with your lot again."

"Is that so?" Ghraan is listening intently now.

"Why do I have to tell you this?" Dhruv is miffed. "I thought you would know."

"Tell me one thing," Ghraan prods, completely ignoring Dhruv's question. "Was your ex-wife happy to part with the ring?"

"No, she wasn't," Dhruv says. "She is not greedy or anything, but she can be quite a pain at times. I guess she was reluctant to give it back to me because it enrages her to see me get anything that I like or want."

"That's probably not the real reason," Ghraan comments. "I'm wondering if Juthika is from your past life or a new person."

"What do you mean?" Dhruv asks.

"See, Bhmana and Fa Ren Sung are the same," Ghraan elucidates. "They were your partners in the lifetimes you saw. So, there is a chance that Juthika too is the same soul."

Dhruv ponders for a minute and then jumps up in excitement.

"Of course, she is," Dhruv says, flaying his arms wildly in air. "She has always brought doom to me. In every life I have been true to her and she has used my feelings to bring damnation upon me. It's all clear to me now, Juthika *is* Bhmana and Fa Ren Sung."

Ghraan furrows his forehead and waits for Dhruv to calm down.

"There is also the chance that Juthika is the one hired by the evil forces," Ghraan discloses, after Dhruv stops yelling.

"Of course! Of course! She is the one who sent burglars to retrieve the ring," Dhruv concludes with a snap of his fingers. "They took the crown as they couldn't find me or my ring. Can you track her movements?"

"We can't," Ghraan confesses regretfully. "We can access such details only after a life is over. For a person like you, who is very close to us, we might retrieve some details while they are alive. But Juthika isn't close to us."

"That doesn't please me at all," Dhruv shakes his head. "I feel no joy in being close to a bunch of loonies like you."

"But you are winning this time," Ghraan assures him. "You are on your way to save us all."

For a minute, Dhruv is awed. No one, absolutely no one, has ever expected to be saved by him.

Ghraan observes him intently. He has not told him the complete truth. Dhruv is not exactly blessed by the sixth sense. Dhruv is the sixth sense, the only sense capable of acquiring mortal lives. But he needs to remember his true powers himself, only then he will be able to unlock the energy required to repair the holy stone. The other five senses can only guard and help him in his journey. They are not capable of doing it for Dhruv.

"It is time for me to depart," Ghraan says, coming out of his thoughts. "I will be back with the story of another lifetime when I can. And you must take good care of yourself and the ring as you launch your search for the evil stone."

With this Ghraan begins to disappear from the nook and Dhruv too finds himself back in his bedroom. He goes out onto the balcony and lets the afternoon sunshine down on the holy stone sitting in his ring. It emits a surreal glow and Dhruv playfully reflects the bright dot of light on a shadowed portion of the parapet.

Dhruv thinks of all the people who have messed with him across lifetimes and for the first time, he feels the desire to avenge all wrongs. He vows to not let Juthika keep him from happiness this time. He will go on to have a fulfilling love life, perhaps with Meher. But first, he will snatch the magic stone from the clutches of the evil ones and their accomplices. He now has a purpose in life, to save himself and the world he lives in. Dhruv clutches his fist and breathes in hard.

About the author

Tanima Das Mitra is an author from India. She works as a software developer while giving her hand to fiction. Her stories have won major contests including the prestigious Write India contest hosted by the Times of India. Her stories have also been published in various reputed magazines and anthologies all over the world.

Tanima lives with her husband and son in Kolkata. The Sorcery of the Senses is her first novel.